WHO KILLED THE SORCERESS?

Charlene tossed a few ideas out. "Someone familiar with the play. Someone with a grudge against Madison. Hunter said he was told to drop the musket at the word *yield*. Maybe we should be thinking of who had the most to gain from her death. Her family? Danielle, jealous, or Neville, to appease his wife, or a disgruntled fellow actor?"

Jack swiveled toward her. "This was a one-time-only performance, according to the announcer. Did you get a playbill?"

"Yeah. I might still have it." Charlene searched through the pockets of her purse, tugging free a much-folded list of the play's actors, the plot, and other points of interest. She smoothed it flat next to her computer on the table. "Here you go. What's on your mind?"

"If we're searching for who would be familiar with the play, we could be looking at our list of suspects."

She rubbed her arms and studied the smiling faces on the full-color playbill that she'd used as a paper fan during the summer heat. Madison Boswell, Hunter Elliott, Amy Fadar, and Neville Hampton. "I like my lists, Jack, but this might be a bit too on the nose . . ."

Books by Traci Wilton

MRS. MORRIS AND THE GHOST

MRS. MORRIS AND THE WITCH

MRS. MORRIS AND THE
GHOST OF CHRISTMAS PAST

MRS. MORRIS AND THE SORCERESS

Published by Kensington Publishing Corp.

Mrs. Morris and the Sorceress

TRACI WILTON

KENSINGTON
PUBLISHING CORP.

www.kensingtonbooks.com

KENSINGTON BOOKS are published by

Kensington Publishing Corp.
119 West 40th Street
New York, NY 10018

All Kensington titles, imprints, and distributed lines are available at special quantity discounts for bulk purchases for sales promotion, premiums, fund-raising, educational, or institutional use.

Special book excerpts or customized printings can also be created to fit specific needs. For details, write or phone the office of the Kensington Sales Manager: Attn.: Sales Department. Kensington Publishing Corp., 119 West 40th Street, New York, NY 10018. Phone: 1-800-221-2647.

The Kensington logo is a trademark of Kensington Publishing Corp..

First Printing: April 2021
ISBN-13: 978-1-4967-3303-0
ISBN-10: 1-4967-3303-7

ISBN-13: 978-1-4967-3306-1 (ebook)
ISBN-10: 1-4967-3306-1 (ebook)

10 9 8 7 6 5 4 3 2 1

Printed in the United States of America

CHAPTER ONE

Salem Common

Charlene Morris caught her floppy red, white, and blue sun hat before it was whisked off on a summer breeze toward the historic bandstand to her right. Yellow caution tape was the odd non-patriotic color this July Fourth as the structure was in the process of refurbishment.

The annual reading of the Declaration of Independence had just finished, so Charlene gathered her bed and breakfast guests before the wooden stage that had been erected earlier on Salem Common. Metal benches fanned backward in a semicircle toward the food vendors.

"Only ten minutes until the play starts!" Charlene glanced back at the frozen lemonade kiosk, tempted by the tart refreshment on such a hot day, but it would need to wait until intermission.

Her friend Kevin strode down the aisle and hugged her hello. "Good seats, Charlene."

"Second row. We saved you one—everybody, this is Kevin Hughes. If you're interested in any of the paranormal tours, he's a fantastic guide. His girlfriend, Amy Fadar, will be in the play." Charlene introduced her guests. "This is the O'Reilly family from Dublin. Martin, Judith, Aaron, and their precocious daughter, Shannon."

Kevin shook hands but kissed the back of Shannon's, which made the little girl giggle.

"Tim Barker is a horse buyer from Kentucky; Angela Sanford and Jackie Shephard are from Connecticut." Charlene gestured to the plump brunette snapping pictures with a Nikon camera. "That's Michelle Fendi, a traveling nurse taking the scenic route to a job in Long Island."

Michelle smiled brightly as she clicked a picture of Kevin and Charlene. "Hi!"

"At breakfast this morning I told you a little about Kevin . . . born and raised here in Salem, he knows the history much better than I. He'd suggested you might like the play, *Salem's Rebels*, performed by our own theater troupe." Charlene tucked her hands into the pockets of her sundress. "I asked him to join us so he could give detailed information about the actual events the play is based on and answer any questions."

Kevin rubbed his chin and grinned. "I'm also the manager of Brews and Broomsticks, a popular bar here in town. Come by for a drink—half price on all beers for Charlene's guests."

Angela, a museum curator with the cutest dimples Charlene had ever seen, immediately engaged Kevin in conversation about Salem's witchy past. Jackie, tall and slim in jean shorts and a T-shirt embroidered with the American flag, sat down—her sparkly cap twinkled in the sun, and her long blond ponytail flowed down her back.

A palpable excitement grew as the actors and stage crew completed the last-minute preparations before the play began. A woman in coverall shorts and a red tank top darted around with a clipboard, tweaking details, ensuring the red swooped cloths hiding the framework of the stage were just right.

Michelle dropped her camera bag to the bench and uncapped a bottle of water. "What's *Salem's Rebels* about, Kevin?"

Kevin placed one foot on the bench in front of him and started his spiel. "Okay, folks! You're about to hear it live and direct from Salem, Massachusetts." He lowered his voice in a theatrical manner to draw them all near. "Salem might be best known for the witch trials, but our citizens have always been very patriotic. This grass we're standing on has been a training ground for the militia since 1637."

The O'Reilly children fidgeted on the bench. Kevin winked at Shannon, which won him a smile. "In this play, the War of Independence hasn't started yet. That happens in April, and this was February. The colonists—that's us—were up in arms, chafing against British rule."

"Seventeen seventy-six?" Angela asked. Charlene wasn't surprised the curator knew her history.

"Yeah . . . we think the war *almost* started right here"— he pointed to the ground—"in Salem."

"I thought Boston was where all the action happened," Tim said.

"No, sir," Kevin answered confidently. "The British mistakenly thought they could control the Province of

Massachusetts Bay, as the colony was called then. The Brits planned to guard the ports and stomp out the rebellion."

Aaron thumped his feet against the lawn.

"Exactly. But they hadn't counted on the people from the rural areas banding together against royal oppression." Kevin dramatically clenched his fist and shook it at the sky. His jaw was set, and he made a magnificent figure.

Shannon blinked up at him, smitten.

"Then what happened?" Michelle's camera rested at her hip.

"Well," Kevin continued in low tones, "the new governor, General Thomas Gage, tried to stop the colonists from meeting, which didn't fly, and as things heated up before the war, the colonists started to collect weapons, like guns, gunpowder, and cannons."

"Is *collecting* another way of saying stealing?" Charlene joked.

"Better they have it than the enemy, right?" Kevin shielded his eyes from the sun with his palm as he gazed at all their rapt faces.

"*Enemy* is subjective." Tim wiped perspiration from his forehead with a paper napkin. "My ancestors are English."

"You're right—the term depends on which side you're on." Kevin leaned forward conspiratorially. "There was *no doubt* that we in the colony wanted to be free men. British General Gage had four brass cannons kept under guard against the rebellious colonists, but somehow"—he winked—"the weapons he needed were stolen right from underneath his nose."

"Was it a ghost?" Shannon touched her thumb to her

lower lip.

"Not a ghost," Kevin assured her, "just very determined militiamen who had to have those cannons in order to fight the royal army and win their freedom."

"Did the British find the cannon?" Aaron asked, perched on the edge of the bench. "Did the rebels get caught?"

Kevin's proud grin was as if he'd been alive hundreds of years ago to be part of the colonists' coup.

"Nope. When the three hundred British soldiers marched across Salem to search where they suspected the cannon might be, our colonists dismantled the bridge—took it apart—so the army couldn't cross! Not a single shot was fired during the standoff, and that's what this play is about."

"Amazing!" Jackie sipped from an iced tea bottle. "The first peaceful protest."

Kevin chuckled. "The rebels were stalling for time to hide the cannon in a different town . . . after a while the colonists put the bridge back together. The army crossed and searched all of Salem—but no brass cannons were ever found."

"I'll need to write that down later," Angela said with excitement. "I collect historical folklore, and I've never heard this version before."

To the left, the busy young woman in denim coveralls climbed the metal stairs at the side of the stage and crossed to the center. The curtains behind her remained closed. She spoke so low it was hard to hear.

Kevin whistled for the throng to quiet, and they all planted themselves on the benches facing the stage.

"Five minutes!" The woman ran off as if chasing her words, cheeks as red as her tank top. Actors in militia costumes roamed the aisles and offered programs for the play to the spectators.

Charlene set her phone on the tripod before her and hit the record button just as a beautiful woman with long brown hair appeared from between the curtains, holding a British officer's hat. "Thank you for joining us! I'm Madison Boswell. This play, *Salem's Rebels*, was written and produced by the talented Neville Hampton, who also manages our motley crew at Salem Stage Right, for a one-time-only performance."

Lukewarm applause sounded as folks found their seats.

Charlene glanced down at her pamphlet. Madison Boswell played the lead British officer, Colonel Alexander Leslie. The attractive woman reached out a slim arm to point to the man on the grass at the left of the stage, talking heatedly with the lady in coveralls. "Neville?"

Neville Hampton lifted his hand in acknowledgment. He wore the clothes of an eighteenth-century militiaman, complete with musket at his shoulder and a tricorn hat over shaggy brown hair. His half smile smoldered sensually.

"He's a hottie," Jackie observed, removing her glittery cap to fan herself.

"My hopes for the play have just improved." Angela ruffled the damp curls at the back of her neck. It was in the eighties with no breeze.

Madison's voice was melodious, her golden-brown eyes hypnotic. She was not just beautiful, but captivating, making it difficult, even for Charlene, to look away.

Amy Fadar was playing a male rebel colonist named Nathaniel Biggs. Charlene shook the program. "Kevin, why are there more female actors than male?"

Kevin clasped his hands over his bare knee. "I don't know. We can ask Amy later."

Madison waved to the crowd of a hundred squeezed together on the benches, and a large emerald set in thick gold flashed from her left hand. Married? Engaged? Her charismatic gaze dazzled, and Charlene wondered why the actress wasn't in the movies. Or at least a higher-class venue than this hokey local production.

"Enjoy the show," the actress breathily instructed. "We'll sign autographs after the performance in the main tent behind the stage."

The curtains drew back with a creaking noise. Act one of *Salem's Rebels*—1776 began with the power and might of a British Army being held at bay by the brave colonists. It had all the drama that Kevin had laid out for them, a thrilling tale of the rebellion. The first act ended with a bang of musket fire, followed by hearty applause and the peppery smell of fake gunpowder.

Charlene quickly turned off her phone to stop recording while the actors on stage broke for intermission. "Filming for posterity?" Kevin asked.

"To show Mom and Dad." Charlene was really videoing for her ghostly roommate Dr. Jack Strathmore, who missed the festivities he'd once been a vital part of in Salem. Trapped by the boundaries of their home, he couldn't leave, so she'd promised to bring some of the fun to Jack.

Kevin stood and scratched the blond scruff at his jaw, his biceps flexing. Michelle watched him with appreciation, and Charlene bit back a smile. Couldn't blame her—Kevin was a cutie. "I'll be back," he said. "I want to see how Amy's doing. The costumes are hot."

"Tell her hello!" Charlene checked her watch. "I want

to get a frozen lemonade. Can I get something for anybody else?"

The O'Reillys had already gone for ice cream, and the rest of her guests said no, so Charlene followed the grass path to the vendors near the old bandstand. This area was quaint America at its finest. Lemonade stands, kids playing tag, folks on picnic blankets with friends and family.

When her husband, Jared, had been alive, they'd watched the fireworks on Navy Pier in Chicago. Ten months had passed since she'd fled the memories to make a new home for herself in Salem.

She got in line at the kiosk that sold frozen lemonade as well as frozen Frappuccino, directly behind a man who could've been Leonardo DiCaprio's twin when he'd played the lead role in *Titanic*. Same face shape, same piercing blue eyes. He wore white linen pants and a billowy navy-blue shirt untucked, his leather sandals designer. His Ray-Bans were nestled in his longish blond hair on the top of his head. His Rolex glinted in the sunshine.

He reached the counter, and the young girl selling drinks blushed when she saw him, he was that beautiful. "What can I get for you?"

He didn't notice her flustered admiration. "I'd like a Frappuccino, made with almond milk, and add an extra shot of coffee."

"We don't have almond milk," the girl stammered. "I can—"

"Whatever you have then." He pocketed his phone and waited for her, impatience evident in his posture and the tap, tap, tap of his sandal against the grass.

Charlene found the man abrupt, but held her tongue.

"Sorry." The girl's bottom lip wobbled. She filled the cup as quickly as she could, adding the extra espresso.

He pulled a five-dollar bill from his wallet and dropped it on the counter. Without waiting for change, he swung around, cup in hand. Charlene attempted to get out of his way, but in doing so he collided with her, and cool, sticky liquid spilled on her bare arm.

"Oh!"

"Damn—I didn't see you." He handed her the paper napkin from around his cup, his expression annoyed.

"It's fine." It wasn't fine, but his entitled attitude bothered her more than the spill. Definitely a tourist. She stepped toward the clerk and ignored the man's partially open mouth as he apologized.

The girl behind the counter flashed a sympathetic smile. "Need another napkin?"

"No, it's okay. Thanks though."

"What can I get you?"

"Frozen lemonade, please."

The stranger dropped another five on the counter for Charlene's drink, and before she could say anything about it, he slipped out of sight.

The clerk shrugged and put the change in the tip jar as she and Charlene exchanged a grin. *People.*

Charlene turned and sipped, surveying the crowd. The citrusy-tart drink eased her parched throat, and her body temperature cooled in relief. She recognized a few people she'd befriended since her move, and hoped to catch up with them after the play. Salem had a tight-knit community at the heart of the tourist town.

Silver gleamed from the last empty bench in her row, the seats saved with a beach bag. She maneuvered down the center line between the rows of benches, passing a family with all orange-red hair, faces slathered in sunscreen. A young couple held hands; a woman joked with her kids. Charlene reached her row and her phone on the tripod. Kevin stood to let her pass.

The shy woman in coveralls ascended the stage steps from the left, this time with a handheld gong instead of a clipboard. She swung a mallet, and it chimed loudly. "Five minutes," she told anyone who was listening as she remained rooted to the platform.

Charlene sipped from her plastic cup, then put it on the ground and turned her phone on to record.

"Jane!" A statuesque woman with a voice as sharp as her cheekbones called to the timid announcer from the lawn on Charlene's left. "You need to speak louder."

Jane cleared her throat. "Act two, North Bridge," she shouted to the tops of her sneakers, accidentally clanging the gong.

The bossy woman shook her head and rolled her eyes in frustration. Charlene hid her amusement at the drama offstage and shot one last video of the whole grounds, in a complete circle, to show Jack, before balancing the phone on her tripod.

"How's Amy?" Charlene shifted on the bench to face Kevin.

"Good—the actors all spent their break in an air-conditioned tent to save their makeup from melting."

She laughed and fanned her throat with the program. "The Stars and Stripes Forever" by John Philip Sousa played from speakers on each side of the stage.

Amy peeked around the side and blew Kevin a kiss. Her long light-brown hair was tucked out of sight beneath a tri-corn hat, her musket strapped across her shoulder, brown leather boots to her knees. The costume designers had transformed the slender woman into a man in breeches.

"Who's that guy?" Shannon asked Kevin.

"My girlfriend, Amy," he said with a smile.

"A girl?" Shannon made a funny face. "That's weird."

Before Kevin could explain, the canvas curtains slid aside to reveal a bridge—cardboard painted to look like wood—lying in sections on the stage. There were eight British soldiers on one side and five militiamen on the other. Blue fabric between them was meant to be the North River. Outnumbered, the rebels in brown homespun clothes refused to back down.

Madison, as Colonel Alexander Leslie, threatened and coaxed, citing royal orders as his soldiers waved their bayonets in the faces of the rebel colonists.

Neville, the militia's leader, defied the colonel, stalling with witty jokes. Madison seemed to physically grow taller as she tugged on the lapels of her jacket, strong with the might of the royal army at her back.

Amy (Nathaniel Biggs) paced behind Neville, as did a few other militiamen. A twitchy fellow (unnamed rebel colonist played by Hunter Elliott, Charlene read) tripped over the river, causing giggles from more than one spectator. Amy kept in character—a fierce colonist ready to fight to the death for freedom.

Neville raised his rifle at Madison, shouting that he would rather die than give in to the king's tyranny. He wanted freedom, and it was worth dying for, by God!

Madison raised her bayonet. "Yield!" she shouted. The colonist with the attack of nerves yelled, dropped his weapon, and his musket fired.

Smoke billowed.

Madison screamed and clutched her heart. She stood at the edge of the stage, surveying the crowd of faces all watching her. She pointed to someone, shouting, "Logan!" Then her mesmerizing eyes slid back in her head.

Pale, she slipped off the stage to the green grass less than ten feet from where Charlene and her guests sat, riveted.

Red stained the white on her uniform.

Amy, on stage, stared over the four-foot edge, then flung off her hat and jumped down to cradle Madison's head in her lap.

"Madison?" Amy lifted her face and glared at the man on stage who'd dropped the musket. "Hunter—no shots were supposed to be fired!"

Charlene couldn't move from her place on the bench. Was this all part of the show? But no, Kevin had just told the story of how the colonists had kept the royal army busy for hours *without* a shot fired.

Where had it come from? The stage? A man behind her stood and yelled, "I think she's really been shot! I'm calling an ambulance." Charlene turned to see the red-haired family and other spectators all on their feet, the beach bag knocked to the path in the crush.

Kevin leaped over the people in front of him to reach Amy. Jane, the lady in coveralls, wadded up a cape to place beneath Madison's head. Charlene's guests clustered around her. Michelle put her camera in the camera bag and handed it to Jackie. "I'm going to see if I can help." The nurse darted around the benches.

"She's been shot," Charlene murmured in disbelief. She turned off the video function of her phone and dialed Detective Sam Holden.

CHAPTER TWO

The Salem Police Station wasn't far from where Charlene huddled with her guests on the benches. The actors on stage had all gathered in groups—some horrified, some disbelieving, all confused. Neville leaned on his musket as he stared from the stage to the actress below.

Sam finally answered his phone. "Detective Holden."

"Sam—it's Charlene. I'm at the bandstand. There's been a shooting!" Her voice hitched.

"Charlene." Sam Holden's deep tones normally calmed her, but not now as she struggled to make sense of the chaos before her—what was real and what was part of the production. "Are you hurt?"

At first she didn't recognize Officer Bernard kneeling by Madison, as the man was out of uniform and wearing shorts and a red, white, and blue T-shirt. "I'm fine, my guests are fine."

"I just heard a call for assistance over the scanner. Tell me what happened, Charlene."

"We were watching the play, *Salem's Rebels*—a reenactment of the scene at North Bridge."

"I'm familiar with the story."

"Well, a musket fired, and at first we thought it was part of the show, but it wasn't. One of the actresses has been shot, for real. Michelle's a nurse and is helping Officer Bernard—she's a guest."

Shannon buried her face in her dad's neck, while Aaron climbed on the bench next to Charlene to get a better view.

"I'm on my way."

"You might want to walk rather than drive—there's a bunch of people here." The off-duty cop had taken the cape Jane had put under Madison's head to press against the actress's chest. Michelle was on her knees in the grass, her fingers on the fallen woman's wrist.

"Good idea! See you in a few."

Sam ended the call. Charlene, phone in hand, stood on the bench with Aaron and searched for Kevin. She spotted him with his arm around Amy as he led her away from Madison, behind the stage. Neville had hopped down from the edge to hover at Madison's head. Hunter was behind him, as were Jane and the haughty woman. Charlene discreetly took a few photos to show Jack later, noticing that she wasn't the only one to do so.

"Where are the cops? Or security?" Tim groused with agitation.

Charlene put her phone back on the tripod to record the scene, this time thinking of Sam, who might find something of value for an investigation—especially if the actress, heaven forbid, died. Officer Bernard stood and scooted folks back. Michelle kept the homespun cape against Madison's chest.

Charlene rubbed her damp palms together and tried to rein in her own fear as she comforted her guests. "This is tragic, but help is on the way."

The O'Reillys exchanged concerned looks over the top of Shannon's bowed head.

"Martin, Judith, I have to stay here and give my report to the police. Why don't you take your children to the B and B?" She thanked her lucky stars that she'd paid extra for her housekeeper to prepare lots of snacks before the fireworks. "Minnie's there, and I'll follow shortly."

"That's a great idea," Judith said.

Angela and Jackie whispered together, Jackie patting Angela on the shoulder. Charlene squeezed Angela's hand. "Do you two want to join the O'Reillys and go back to the house?"

"Yeah. Won't you come with us, Charlene?" Jackie pushed back the brim of her sparkly cap. "It could be dangerous until they catch who did this to that poor actress."

"I know Detective Sam Holden and want to tell him what we saw." Charlene leaned toward the artist and her friend. "Do you mind helping keep things calm until I get there? Will you be okay to hike back?" The crush of people would've made driving difficult, so she and her guests had all walked to the park.

"Of course." Angela settled Michelle's camera bag over her arm.

"I'll go too." Tim adjusted his hat. He'd be all right. Though nearing sixty, he'd told her earlier that he stayed fit with horseback riding.

"I'll call Minnie to let her know to expect you." Charlene watched her guests depart—Martin had tearful Shannon at his hip, and Aaron held hands with his mother. Angela and Jackie beelined out of the park as Tim trailed them. Michelle remained with Madison and Officer Bernard.

Charlene called Minnie and left a message on the house phone, then released a long, shuddering breath. Her battery flashed red. *Darn it.* The video she'd recorded had drained the power. She hoped the film would save automatically once her phone died.

The crowd thinned as the wail of police cars and the ambulance approached. Others stayed behind to watch the drama unfold. Charlene made her way through the lingering people to Kevin and Amy, near Madison.

"You all right?" Kevin asked. They'd gone through similar drills before, but it never got easier. At Halloween, they'd been on a haunted bus tour with her guests when they'd stumbled upon a witch who'd been murdered. Kevin had been at the opening of "Charlene's," her mansion that she'd turned into a bed and breakfast. During the party, she'd discovered Jack's killer.

"As well as I can be." She put a hand out to Amy. "I'm sorry about your friend," she said gently. "It all happened so quickly that I'm still reeling."

"You were recording, right?" Kevin asked.

"Yes, but my phone just crashed—no battery left. I'm hoping the video automatically saved."

"It should," he assured her.

Amy had lost her musket as well as her tricorn hat, and her long, light brown hair was loose. "How could Madison have gotten shot? Who would do such a thing? It can't have been an accident."

Charlene happened to agree but asked the actress, "Why not?"

"For one thing, even though we were using real muskets, the gunpowder was fake."

Her stomach clenched at the anguish in Amy's eyes. "Charlene?"

Charlene pivoted toward Sam behind her. At six and a half feet tall with wide shoulders, the detective exuded strength. Intelligence shone from his brown eyes, kindness too as he smiled at her beneath a thick brown mustache. Relief made her knees go weak. "Sam! Thank heavens you're here."

Sam clapped Kevin on the shoulder and nodded at Amy and Charlene. "Thanks for the reminder about the traffic, Charlene. It's a nightmare because of the parade later, so I cut across the park." He tucked a loose section of his navy-blue polo into his jeans, the only sign of his exertion. "Where are your guests?"

"I sent them home; they were pretty shaken up."

"Good idea. There're too many people hanging around here, contaminating the crime scene, as it is." Sam greeted Officer Bernard, who'd stood up and joined them. "Thought you were going to have the day off, huh?"

The officer shrugged. "Never a dull moment."

"Is she . . ." Sam asked Michelle, who remained at Madison's side.

Michelle gave a shake of her head and mouthed, *dead.*

Sam's jaw tightened. He ordered the actors to all stand back as the EMTs unloaded a stretcher.

The detective dropped to one knee by Madison's supine body and lifted the cape that had been used to stop the blood. Pointing at a hole above the brass center button on the British officer's uniform, he murmured, "Dead center. That took skill." He ran his fingers down his mustache. "You thought it was part of the show?" He looked at Charlene and Kevin. "You were watching the play—did you see anything suspicious?"

"The actors on stage were shouting at each other about the bridge and the stolen cannon. It seemed very real and highly dramatic." Charlene glanced at Kevin. "Then we heard the shot, and Madison fell off the stage to the grass here."

"It wasn't until Amy jumped down to the lawn and yelled at the other dude that I realized it wasn't part of the performance." Kevin raked a shaky hand through his short blond hair, then wrapped his arm around Amy's waist. "Could've been Amy lying here. She was standing right across from Madison."

Amy sniffed.

The first EMT reached them, and they all shuffled out of the way to let the paramedics do their job. As they worked, Charlene's gaze dropped to Madison's pale hands, her body limp and lifeless. Within moments, Madison was strapped to a stretcher and rolled to the ambulance.

Michelle had tears in her eyes as she joined them. "Such a tragedy to have her life cut so short."

"Shot by a musket." Amy shook her head.

"That wasn't a musket shot," Michelle clarified. "That precise of a wound came from a nine millimeter hand-gun."

Sam lasered his attention on the nurse. "And how do you know that?"

Michelle reached into her cross-body purse for hand sanitizer. "I do a lot of my shifts in the ER."

"I'll need your name and number. How long are you in town?"

"Tomorrow afternoon."

Charlene bristled at the way Sam was questioning one of her guests. "Michelle helped, Sam."

Officer Bernard agreed. "Thanks for stepping up, ma'am. Not everybody does. Boss, can I go to the station and shower?" He showed his bloody palms.

"Yeah. Thanks." They watched the officer jog off across the lawn, then Sam pulled his notepad from his back denim pocket. "Michelle?"

"Fendi." The nurse rattled off her number to Sam. "Where did the others go, Charlene?"

"Home—you can too. Angela has your camera bag."

"I think I'll take a walk by the water and clear my head." The nurse ambled off without her previous smile.

Officer Jimenez combed the crowd of actors and spectators, asking questions. Another officer blocked off the scene with crime tape. Sam surveyed the area. "Where were you at? Where did the shot come from?"

Charlene, Kevin, and Amy had their backs to the stage. Amy pointed to the food vendors and the drink stand. "That way."

"Did you see anything strange, or odd?"

Amy shrugged. "I was into the part."

Charlene nibbled on her bottom lip. "What about the actor who dropped the musket? He seemed nervous about something."

"You got a name?" Sam asked.

"Hunter," Amy said, her face turning the color of sour milk. "Elliott. But he couldn't have—"

"Where is he?" Sam lowered his pen and notepad.

"I haven't seen him since right after the shooting. He was with Neville." Amy scanned the stage and empty benches. "Maybe he's in the back tent to change?"

"He was right here," Charlene seconded.

"Can't be that easy, right?" Sam's eyes flashed as he studied Charlene. "Not with you around, that's for sure."

She slipped her hands into the pockets of her sundress and tilted her head. "And what's that supposed to mean?"

Kevin snorted and winked at Charlene. "I think I'll let you two argue this out. C'mon, Amy, let's go find Hunter."

"Have him talk to one of the officers," Sam said as the pair walked off. "We'll need to speak with all the actors before they leave. Spread the word." He faced Charlene and his mustache twitched. "Why does trouble seem to follow you?"

A trickle of perspiration slid down her spine, and she fanned her face. "It doesn't! Got any more questions for me, Detective? If not, I'll get back to my guests." She pursed her mouth. "I better go quickly so trouble can't follow me home."

He chuckled, and the deep rich timbre made her warmer than the sun. If she didn't have the most charming, devilishly handsome ghost haunting her home, she might be interested in more than friendship. But as things stood, that's all there could ever be.

"Get going, Ms. Morris." Sam folded his arms over his chest. "I've got a crime to solve, and you're a distraction."

He wasn't the only one distracted, she thought as she yanked her gaze from his muscled biceps. "This one should be easy for you," she said ever so sweetly. "You know she was shot with a nine millimeter. You're searching for someone with a handgun."

"If things are good, I've got the shooter on security cameras."

"In the park?" She looked around but didn't see anything.

"All over the city, including here." Sam subtly gestured to three different directions in the Common.

"Piece of cake, Sam. You should have the culprit caught and in jail before the parade starts." Giving him a saucy smirk, she headed to the tent where the actors would hang out. They'd planned to sign autographs after the performance, but that wouldn't happen now. She wanted to see if Kevin and Amy had found Hunter. Why had the guy been so nervous?

The door of a large luxury tent was partially open, and the actors' voices were raised as they all talked over one another. Charlene could imagine the topic—dead Madison.

A smaller tent was to the right, and Charlene heard arguing. She stopped to listen, wondering if this would be about Hunter or Madison. A woman shouted, "This is just too much! Your lover gets shot on stage, and you blame *me*? Are you nuts? I'm not that stupid. If I was going to shoot anyone, it would have been you."

Charlene inched closer. Who was that talking? She lifted the canvas a fraction and saw Neville seated in a chair, his head buried in his hands. It was the statuesque woman from earlier—her white fitted blouse unbuttoned at the top to display her generous cleavage. Her bleached hair framed her oval face, and her pale blue eyes were artfully accented. This close, Charlene guessed her to be in her forties. She wore hot-pink lipstick and sported an even hotter temper.

When the woman caught sight of Charlene hovering near the door, she snapped, "Who are you, and what are you looking at? My husband, the famous Neville Hampton? Cheating husband, lousy father? Take a number, my dear; you just moved up a notch in his list of available and tempting lady friends."

"I don't know your husband, nor am I interested." Charlene spoke in a civil manner, hanging on to her dignity by a thread. She *had* been snooping. "The detective asked that the actors all speak to an officer before packing up."

The woman arched a brow. "Do I know you?"

"No. I'm Charlene Morris. I run a bed and breakfast in town. I'm a friend of Kevin Hughes and Amy Fadar. Are they still here, do you know?" She decided not to ask the volatile couple about Hunter.

Neville stood. His dark brown eyes smoldered, and he scraped his short beard with strong fingers. "Excuse my wife," he told her with a hint of amusement. "She's a real harlot at times. Jealousy does not become her."

His wife heaved an angry breath.

Neville continued. "I haven't seen Amy or Kevin, but she might be at the big tent, getting out of her costume to give to Jane."

"Thank you." Charlene eagerly avoided more conversation with the furious Mrs. Hampton, or her husband, and hustled toward the large tent.

She ducked in. A lot of the actors were already changed into their street clothes. The inside was not very sophisticated, just a series of small sections draped for privacy. Several standing mirrors had been set up for the actors to check out their wardrobe, and there was a folding table in the middle with eight plastic chairs, empty at the moment.

Kevin and Amy chatted with Jane, the shy girl in the

coveralls. Her cell phone peeked from a side pocket, as did a pencil. Papers poked from another, and she wore a pincushion attached to her wrist. Her pockets overflowed.

"Thanks, Jane. I hope you can get the stain out." Amy sniffed and blinked her eyes. "The blood has to have been when I kneeled down by Madison. Why did this happen?"

Jane pulled Amy into a hug and patted her back. "I'll take care of it, Amy. I'm a wizard with the stain pen."

"You're a wizard, period."

"Hi," Charlene said, interrupting the scene. Blood? Madison's? Amy had been the first to go to her friend, then Jane. "Any luck finding Hunter?"

"No." Amy stepped toward her and the tent door. "Nobody's seen him since the ambulance arrived." Charlene followed Kevin and Amy out.

"I know you well enough to understand you aren't going to leave this alone. So, what's on your mind?" Kevin put a hand on Amy's back, including her in the conversation. "Charlene's like a bloodhound," he told his girlfriend.

"Ha—that's me, a regular Angela Lansbury." Growing up, she'd watched the mystery series with her parents.

"You realize that she was famous for far more than that role of an amateur sleuth in *Murder, She Wrote*?" At Kevin's confused look, Amy teased, "Don't worry. It was before your time. She's still alive, you know."

"You're kidding!" Kevin walked between the two women.

"Nope—she's ninety-four. I hope I'm still acting when I'm ninety."

"Her and Betty White," Kevin mused. "I wonder who else is over ninety and still acting."

Charlene steered the conversation back to the shooting. "Amy, you worked with Madison closely at the theater. Do you know who might not have liked her?" Would Amy know about Madison's affair with Neville?

Amy averted her gaze and shrugged her slender shoulders. "Not really."

Charlene didn't believe her and wondered at the evasion. "I'm sure you're in shock right now, and I don't blame you a bit. But you know the actors, so I just thought . . . you might know if anyone held a grudge."

Amy glanced at Kevin, then shook her head no.

"I heard him and his wife arguing in their tent. About an affair?" Sometimes you just couldn't be subtle. "Madison and Neville?"

Amy halted abruptly and whirled to face Charlene. "Danielle is Neville's wife. She wanted Madison fired; that was no secret. Can't blame her." Amy's demeanor turned defensive. "What would *you* do if some big-eyed starlet slept with your man?"

Kevin whistled low.

"I'm not trying to badger you, Amy, I promise," Charlene said, taking a slow step toward the vendors. Maybe Sam would be able to find out where Hunter had gone when he viewed the camera footage around the Common. "Can you think of any reason why Hunter would have been so nervous today?"

"Madison could be . . . *cutting* in her remarks to other actors." Moisture beaded along Amy's collarbone. "But just because she wasn't the nicest person to work with, doesn't mean she deserved to die."

"I agree—listen, thanks for answering my questions . . . I suppose I should leave the detective work to Detective Sam," she said with a self-mocking smile. It was obvious that Amy was unsettled, so Charlene backed off. "Do you think the parade and fireworks will still go on later?"

Kevin nodded as they reached the bandstand, the caution tape the same bright yellow as the crime tape that blocked the area by the stage as police officers combed the lawn for clues. "It's a huge deal around here, almost as big as Halloween."

"I'll see if my guests are interested in coming back then, after a rest and some snacks. I'm sure Minnie has spoiled them all with her tasty treats. See you later! If you hear anything about Hunter, give me a shout, okay?"

"You do the same," Kevin said. He and Amy walked toward the shops away from Salem Common, the stage, and the police.

Charlene had hiked into town with her guests, pointing out places of interest, but couldn't summon the energy to race home. Since her phone was dead, she flagged down a cab and told the driver her address on Crown Point Road.

"That big ole mansion? The one with the widow's walk on the roof? Blimey, you're staying there? Used to be the grandest house around. Lots of big parties too. Not that I was ever invited, of course, but I dropped off plenty of ladies and gentlemen, I did."

Charlene pulled some cards from her handbag. "I recently bought the place and turned it into a B and B. I have some business cards if you'd like a few."

"Why sure. No harm done. Many times I've made a recommendation." He eyed her from the rearview mirror.

"Pretty fancy place you got there. Daddy must be rich, right?" He smiled, and she couldn't help but notice his teeth were yellowed with age.

"No rich daddy. I don't own it, per se, the bank does." Charlene turned to the window, effectively ending the conversation. From her back seat, as they rounded the corner, she caught a glimpse of the eight-thousand-square-foot mansion, the brick-red roof, and the widow's walk, and felt a moment of pride. It really was a magnificent structure, and she had made it her home.

Well, hers and Jack Strathmore's. He was the previous owner. The idea of coexisting with a ghost had once shocked her Midwestern mentality, but not so anymore. She quite enjoyed the arrangement.

The cabbie drove down the flagstone driveway and stopped next to the beautiful old-fashioned porch. Her engraved CHARLENE'S sign brought a smile to her face.

The vast property had mature oak trees and a sweeping lawn with lovely flower beds nestled in white stones. Minnie's husband, Will, was her sole gardener. He insisted that he didn't need any extra help, but maintaining the yard was strenuous work.

When she'd mentioned this to Minnie, her housekeeper said it kept her husband fit and trim and to leave him happily alone.

"Madam has arrived," the cabbie drawled. He didn't get out of the car, but Charlene paid him in cash with a healthy tip, then slid out the rear door.

"Thanks for the lift." She ran up the stairs of the porch, past the four Adirondack chairs, to the gleaming wooden double doors.

The door was unlocked, and she rushed in, nearly knocking over the elegant oval vase that she'd bought from Vintage Treasures, an antique shop in town that she frequented often.

"Hello, everyone," she called from the large foyer, heading for the kitchen. The O'Reilly children sat on bar stools at the kitchen counter, eating freshly baked chocolate chip cookies still warm from the oven.

Martin and Judith were enjoying a platter of finger sandwiches and iced tea at the kitchen table, chatting with Jackie and Angela, who drank white wine and shared a plate of crackers and cheese. A bowl of fresh fruit, filled with apples, pears, and peaches, was centered on the table.

Jack was nowhere in sight. She didn't know why, but she was the only person who could see her ghost.

Minnie washed her hands, dried them on her apron, and then turned around, smiling broadly. "My, my, got another incident on your hands, I see. I've heard all about it, my dear. Detective Holden called and said he'll be popping over soon. He wants a word with your guests, but I have my suspicions it's actually you he's coming to see!"

Charlene hoped he had news on Hunter and the shooter—and she wanted to share with him the video she'd taken.

"Thanks, Minnie. I'm sorry for keeping you late. Enjoy the afternoon with Will, and happy Fourth of July to you. Are you doing anything special?"

"Well, we're barbecuing this afternoon with the family." Minnie had four adult children; three had stayed in Salem, while another had moved to Maine. "My eldest son and his brood will arrive tomorrow to spend the weekend with us. Haven't seen them since Christmas."

"Family is always the best." She thought of her mother

and dad, and how they'd visited her for two weeks during the Christmas season. It had not gone without quarrels, but it had brought them closer. They were due back at the end of the month.

Shannon squealed and giggled as Aaron tickled her and pretended to steal a cookie.

One of her regrets in life was the fact that she and Jared had been unable to have children. Now, her guests and their children filled her home with laughter and happiness—something she needed to hold on to when she was touched by death.

CHAPTER THREE

Charlene poured herself a glass of iced tea and headed to her private suite of rooms on the back of the kitchen, careful to shut and lock the door behind her.

She turned on the television and whispered for Jack. Silva, her silver Persian cat, meowed a greeting from her place on the armchair by the window, luxuriating in the sunshine.

"Hey, sweetie." Charlene, not a cat person before Silva's arrival, gave her silky ears a scratch. The beautiful feline had permanently paw-printed Charlene's heart. Where was Jack? He came and went like a magic trick, and she never knew where he was when he was gone. She still worried that one day he might never return.

She pulled her black-screened phone from her purse and plugged it into her charger on the desk. A few tense moments later it was up to twenty percent battery, and

Charlene was able to open the video she'd recorded—saved!—and sent it to her email to show Jack.

In the past few months, they'd been experimenting with his ghostly energy and discovered that he gained strength from the television and internet—electromagnetic fields gave him fuel, allowing him to stay present with her for longer periods.

Goose bumps dotted her neck, and cool air preceded his deep voice. "You called, Charlene?"

"Jack!" She whirled around and there he was, standing before the television. Turquoise eyes, dark hair, clean-shaven—he took her breath away. She knew he manifested his appearance for her, and today he'd donned a red Salem T-shirt depicting Pickering Wharf. His image was so powerful that she couldn't see the TV through him—as sometimes happened.

"I did, I have so much to tell you!"

"I can't wait to hear." He moved away from the television toward her. "I'm glad you're home—how was the play? Did you enjoy the reading of the Declaration of Independence? They've done it every year, for as long as folks can remember—over a hundred years at least."

"It was very patriotic, but Jack"—she lowered her voice so that no one could hear her—"there was a murder."

"What?" His question was heavy with worry. "Tell me everything."

She brought her hand to her chest. "During the second half of the *Salem's Rebels* play."

"Charlene, are you all right?" His image wavered as he studied her from head to toe.

"It was frightening, Jack, but I'm fine. Upsetting for

my guests, as you can imagine." She opened the laptop on her narrow desk along the wall, going to her email to open the recording. "One of the actresses was shot . . . I might have it on film. Sam's on his way over to ask questions, but I was wondering if you could watch this and see if you notice anything odd?"

"Of course I will. Glad to help."

A knock reverberated on the door. "Charlene?" Minnie called. "The O'Reillys are wondering about the fireworks later."

"I'll be right out!" Charlene fast-forwarded, then gestured for Jack to see the video. "Here. All you have to do is hit play. I've skipped through the beginning—it was good, but this is more important."

Jack sat in her chair before the laptop. "Got it."

Charlene left her suite with the television volume low—Minnie no longer questioned her leaving it on for background noise.

Entering the kitchen, she noticed Minnie hovering over the tray of cooling cookies, stacking the ones she deemed ready to the side.

"Sorry to bother you, Charlene," Martin said from the kitchen table. "But do you know whether the fireworks will still take place tonight?"

"It could be dangerous." Judith glanced at her husband and put a hand on her daughter's shoulder. "If the shooter isn't caught."

"We'll check with Sam when he comes by, but from what Kevin said, things will stay on schedule. Salem is very big on the Fourth of July." Charlene noticed two empty chairs at the table. "Where are Jackie and Angela? Have they gone to their rooms?"

"No. You'll find them on the porch in the Adirondack chairs, sipping wine." Minnie headed for Charlene's suite with a pitcher of tea. "Can I refill your glass?"

She'd left it by her computer. "That's okay!" Charlene intercepted her housekeeper—not that Minnie ever saw Jack, but still. "Shannon and Aaron, did you get a chance to see the wooden swing in the back? I set up a bean-bag-toss game in the grass; we also have croquet. Silva likes to chase the squirrels and birds, but I think she's napping."

"Can we go play, Mom?" Aaron asked.

"I'll go with you," Martin said, rising to his feet. "Where do you keep the croquet? I wouldn't mind clacking the balls around."

"In the wooden storage box near the back stairs. Might find a couple of mitts and baseballs in there too."

Judith stood. "I'll join you. Can we bring our drinks?"

"Of course." Charlene waited until the kids darted toward the front door to say, "If you don't want to be downtown, I'm sure the fireworks will be visible from the widow's walk."

"That's a good idea, Martin." Judith seemed to be more worried about the possible danger than her husband. "I just can't believe there was a shooting!"

Charlene had learned that all you could do was take precautions, as life was not always kind. "I'd be happy to serve hot dogs and chips—nothing fancy, but picnic fare, in addition to the snacks already planned."

Martin arched an admonishing brow at Judith. "We don't want you to go to any trouble. Didn't you say that dinner was on our own before the festivities?"

"Well, yes, but these are extenuating circumstances . . ." Her guests' comfort was her number one priority.

Judith sighed and crossed her arms. "I'd feel better if they had someone in custody."

"Detective Sam Holden is very good at keeping Salem safe. The police here are top-notch. You saw how quickly they responded, and one of their off-duty officers jumped into action. I wouldn't be surprised if they already have the suspect in for questioning."

Jack materialized behind her with a cold snort. "Yeah, right."

Charlene managed to keep a straight face.

"As you say, we'll know more when the detective gets here." Martin handed Judith her iced tea, and they went outside to join their children behind the house where the swing and games were.

"Should I stay then, Charlene?" Minnie asked with concern. "To help with dinner?"

"Absolutely not! It's two o'clock on a holiday, and you're already doing more than you should."

"I'm happy to help. And you make it more than worth my while." Minnie scrutinized the kitchen one last time, but the dishes were done and the food put away. "I left out a dozen cookies, if you wanted to offer some to Sam."

"Thoughtful, as always." Charlene gave Minnie a side-hug on the way out the door. "I couldn't do this without you." Minnie was a godsend, as was Avery Shriver. Her part-time employee had just turned seventeen and would be a senior in high school this year. Avery worked around thirty hours a week and sometimes more if Charlene needed her.

"Bye now. No more trouble for the day, all right?" Minnie headed for the door, and Charlene followed. Her housekeeper had recently purchased a brand-new Volvo wagon that had room for all her grandkids.

Minnie waved goodbye, and Charlene turned to see Angela and Jackie lazily enjoying the shade beneath the large overhang of the front porch. Glasses dripped condensation by their feet; they each had their eyes at half-mast as the best friends conversed in low companionable tones.

She didn't want to intrude, so she backed into the house. Now, what had happened to Tim? Michelle hadn't yet returned. Charlene hoped she wasn't fretting over the murder—as a nurse, she'd surely learned ways to cope with death.

On her way to her suite, she glanced into the library/reading nook, where Jack once had a piano. She found Tim immersed in a nonfiction book on Salem's history. "So here you are!"

"Do you remember where you bought this volume on Winter Island? I haven't seen it before."

Charlene peered closer at the older book. "Actually, I picked that up at an antique store in town, Vintage Treasures. I try to fill my shelves with anything related to Salem."

Jack appeared to her right. Tim didn't even blink at the blast of cold. "I think I may have found something."

She kept her features in a friendly smile. "Tim, can I get you anything?"

"No, thanks." Tim flipped the page. "I was searching for information regarding the American Revolution. I just can't get over the soldiers marching all that way to find those cannons, only to be blocked by a dismantled bridge." He snorted. "Makes me wonder if they really wanted to have a battle."

"I didn't know about Salem's part in the Revolution

before today, I'm sorry to say. Guess I should have paid more attention in history class."

Tim raised his smartphone. "We have encyclopedias at our fingertips now, so no need to be a brainiac." He set it aside. "Things have certainly changed for the better."

"I agree. Well, I'll leave you to it." Charlene returned to her room and shut and locked the door behind her.

She heard the O'Reilly kids playing outside her windows, but the shades were drawn, the curtains shut. Silva's tail flicked, her eyes closed as she continued to nap on the armchair. Charlene wished she had the cat's ability to relax so completely.

"What did you find?" she asked Jack. He leaned back against her narrow desk as he waited for her.

"It sure was crowded on the Common. Appreciate you taking those pictures and video for me. Someday . . ." He stopped talking.

She knew there was no way he'd ever be human again. He'd never feel a summer's breeze, the grass under his feet, or anything regular people took for granted.

Charlene blinked, cleared her throat, and tapped the laptop. The video, once finished, had reverted to the beginning. "You saw something unusual?"

"I might have—can you fast-forward toward the last ten minutes of the play?"

"We only have until Sam gets here." Charlene sat before the laptop, and Jack looked over her shoulder as she set the recording up. "Where?"

"Past the intermission."

Charlene pressed the button down, speeding forward until she got close, then slowed the images. There was a panoramic view of the crowd; the bandstand, in need of some TLC and wrapped with caution tape; food booths; and Danielle, Neville's wife, chastising Jane. "Almost there."

"The play wasn't that great. Some pretty poor acting," Jack remarked.

"It's a small company theater group, mostly locals. Besides, I guess it's kind of hard to portray a historic incident where nothing bad happens." She grinned. "Maybe a shot *should* have been fired and it would have sped the war along. Too much chitchat."

"Hey now! We Salem natives take pride in our political wit. Men in this very county would have died if they'd been found with the brass cannons." Jack rubbed his jaw. "You don't suppose this shooting was meant to make a political statement, do you?"

"I have no idea." Charlene studied each image. Who knew what was in a killer's mind?

"Charlene. Stop right there. Do you see that flash of light?"

She stopped the video in mid-frame. The light had come from her right, away from the crowd, to strike Madison on stage. Madison's eyes had grown wide as she'd clutched her chest, and then fallen off the stage.

"Well done, Jack, good catch." Charlene rewound it and watched the light flash again.

Jack paced back and forth. "Dropping that musket might have been a distraction. Timed exactly as the handgun fired. It wasn't part of the play?"

"No. The actor's name is Hunter, and he took off after only a few minutes. But he couldn't have killed Madison—the powder they'd used in the musket was fake. He couldn't have been holding a handgun or hiding one in his costume." She stared at the actors on her screen for something, anything, off.

"And the angle is wrong for him to have done it," Jack said. Cold air brushed her ear from his essence—he had no breath. "It had to be someone from the far rear of the audience on the right side."

"So why would Hunter disappear if he's innocent?"

"Good question." Jack tilted his head to watch the video. "The actress is bewitching."

"Madison Boswell." Charlene shifted on the wooden chair. "Funny that you say that—I noticed it too. She's compelling, drawing all eyes to her, and it doesn't even seem to be an effort."

"Actors who appear effortless are usually working the hardest," Jack observed. "She reminds me of Elizabeth Taylor or Marilyn Monroe. They have that special something you can't learn in acting class."

"It's a shame that Madison will never fulfill her potential—though to be honest, she wasn't that great." Charlene sighed. "I wonder if she's got family nearby."

"News of her death will be a nasty shock. At her age, it's likely her parents are still living. Do you know of anyone named Logan?"

"No. Why?"

He pointed to the video. "She cried out 'Logan' to the crowd. Her boyfriend? Husband?"

"That's right . . . but Madison was sleeping with the producer, Neville." Charlene squinted at the screen, searching for the emerald and gold on Madison's finger . . . a possible wedding band or engagement ring—too feminine to be part of the British officer costume. "His wife knows and is furious." Charlene told Jack what she'd overheard in the actors' tent.

"Sleeping to the top." Jack frowned. "It didn't get her where she wanted to go, that's for sure. It's always sad when a person dies this young. No matter what her faults, she had a life ahead of her."

"I wonder why she was *here*? Salem isn't exactly big-time." Charlene pushed her hair off her face. "You know, when I asked Amy about who might not have liked Madison, she became very defensive."

"Kevin's girlfriend? I like her." Charlene had invited some friends over for a summer picnic at the end of June, and Jack had watched from the sidelines. The only way he could. "From what little I saw, she seemed to have more acting chops than all the others. Including Neville."

"Hmm." Charlene shifted on her chair. "I have the same question—why is Amy here in Salem, when she clearly has acting talent? She was good in the movies in LA, Kevin said."

Charlene stared at the stage, the blue fabric for the river, the pieces of bridge. Had this play been worth dying over? "From what we just saw, Madison was an okay actress with immense appeal. Jealousy makes people behave out of character."

"So, who might want her out of the way?"

"One person for sure. Danielle Hampton." Charlene rewound the tape to where Neville's wife yelled at Jane to speak louder. "This woman is furious that her husband cheated, and she's obviously not the wilting violet type."

"Where was Mrs. Hampton when Madison was shot?"

"I lost track while watching the show."

Jack nodded and crossed his arms. His red T-shirt didn't ripple. "She's got a temper."

"I'd love to see what happens behind the scenes at Salem Stage Right."

"Drama on drama. Well, since I can't leave the house, how about I do some research on the theater company while you're gone tonight for the fireworks?"

"If the event is still happening." It had been such a full day that she almost wished she didn't have to leave the house. She'd prefer a quiet night on the widow's walk with Jack.

"As sad as the shooting is, I doubt the city council will let all the money invested in fireworks go to waste."

She heard a squeal of laughter and the rope swing hitch. "The O'Reillys are here for an American holiday— I hope this doesn't completely ruin their vacation. I want to make sure they have a good time and aren't scarred by this."

"*You* are not responsible for what happened, Charlene. Besides, aren't they from Dublin?"

"Yeah—so?"

His dark brow arched. "The Irish are tough."

"We'll see how they feel later." She chewed her bottom lip, concerned over all her guests. Without them, the bills wouldn't get paid. But it was more than that. It was personal.

Jack lifted his head and listened. "I think your detective's here."

"Great. I hope he has good news!"

"Do you think he'll need your computer for the video?"

"I don't believe so. I can email it to him." She sent it off with the press of a button. "Technology is our friend! He doesn't need to know that we've seen it already."

"He'll know you have. Show him the flash."

"I will." Charlene closed her laptop. "Aren't you coming?"

His mouth pursed. Her ghost had an itty-bitty jealous streak, and it was best sometimes if Jack and Sam stayed apart. "I don't know."

"You should," she said. "Sam will be talking about the shooting. You have great instincts for these things, *if* the killer hasn't already been caught."

When he'd been alive, he'd been a smart, caring doctor. Now that Jack was deceased, his need to help was stifled, but she had no problem picking his brain over problems—from the cracked tile in the roof, to managing difficult guests, to helping Sam solve the occasional crime—like it or not.

CHAPTER FOUR

Charlene opened the front door to Sam and invited him in. She regarded the Adirondack chairs on the porch, but Angela and Jackie were no longer lounging in the shade there. "Well, do you have any news? Did you find Hunter and make him confess?" She shut the door once they were both in the foyer.

Jack stood near the kitchen, listening to her and Sam's conversation. She was glad to have him there, so long as her ghost didn't stir things up. He enjoyed making her respond to him in front of people and create confusion now and then. His little joke.

Sam laughed. "You don't waste time, do you?"

"Of course not!" Charlene led the way to the kitchen. "What's the point in that?" She put her hands on the counter and leaned forward. "Can I get you anything? Coffee, iced tea? How about some of Minnie's freshly made cookies?

Chocolate chip, oatmeal and raisin? She also made pea-
nut butter cookies and a tray of brownies."

"Well, that all sounds tempting. A brownie and a cup
of coffee would be great. I missed lunch." He patted his
hard stomach.

She put a brownie and a couple of cookies on a plate—
oatmeal was sorta healthy—then fired up some dark roast
on the Keurig. He sat on a bar stool.

"Missed lunch because you were busy catching the
killer, right?"

She could feel the rush of cold air as Jack materialized
behind her. "Hey, you're talking to Sam here. Not Sher-
lock Holmes."

To annoy Jack, she gave Sam a big smile. "The guests
are all occupied, so you can talk to me privately. Tell me
what's happened! Did you find Hunter?"

"Yeah—we found him." Sam casually stretched out a
long leg. "Officers Jimenez and Blake tracked him down
to the nearest pub." He hooked his boot heel on the rung
of the stool. "They called me after Hunter gave them
some flack about his rights as a citizen—he'd been drinking . . . anyway, I was able to get a statement from him."

"Oh, really!" She shot a *so there* look over her shoulder to Jack. "Good work, Detective. You solved this in
record-breaking time."

"Hunter didn't do the shooting," Jack murmured.

"Not quite." Sam took two bites of the brownie, then it
was gone. He swallowed it down with coffee and wiped
his mouth with a napkin. "Hunter didn't do it."

"I thought he confessed." Charlene ignored the sound
of Jack clapping.

"He gave a *statement*. Someone he doesn't know paid

him five hundred dollars to fumble and drop the musket when Madison yelled for Neville to *yield*."

"What?" Charlene and Jack asked in unison.

"Yep. He was contacted this morning and paid during the intermission. Cash was sealed in a brown envelope on the table in the actors' tent—all handled over an app that blocks the sender's number. Probably a burner phone, but we'll check." Sam smoothed his luxurious mustache. "Hunter claims he thought it was a harmless prank—he needed the cash as a starving artist."

That seemed very shady. "And you believed him?"

Jack, at her elbow, chuckled. "Don't say I didn't tell you so."

"I'll verify his story. He voluntarily handed over his cell phone, saying he was terrified when Madison was actually shot, and worried that he might be next, to keep quiet about the money."

"I guess I can understand that."

Sam shifted, and the stool creaked. "I asked him if he had a grudge against Madison and, thanks to the whiskey, he couldn't shut up about Madison belittling him on stage, not just for this play, but at the theater too."

Charlene refilled her iced tea glass from a pitcher in the fridge. "Which gives him a motive for wanting her dead." She'd witnessed the play, and he hadn't pulled the trigger. "Hunter might not have killed Madison, but he assisted—what's that called?"

"Aiding and abetting, but it has to be with intent, and this kid supposedly just wanted the money to make Madison trip up her lines on stage. Show Neville Hampton, their producer, that she was a lousy actress. Her humiliation would've been a bonus."

She sipped her iced tea, thinking that over. It made sense. "That's a relief—so then what? You patted his head and told him to be on his way?"

Jack snorted.

"Charlene, why do you like to rile me?" Sam lifted the oatmeal-raisin, and before biting into it, gave her a long look that made her heart beat faster. "Kid was sobbing. Figured he'd be going to jail for the next ten years. Hunter's prints are already on file because he used to work as an aide in the public schools."

"What happened to the money?" Charlene centered her iced tea on a coaster.

"We confiscated it—only three hundred left after his drinking spree—and the envelope, and are running forensics to see if they can find fingerprints. If the person's in the system, we might get a match." Sam finished the cookie. "Damn, that Minnie is a gem."

"Yes, she is. More coffee?"

"No, thanks. This hit the spot."

Charlene settled her hip against the counter in hopes that he'd be sweetened up and wouldn't mind answering a few more questions. "Have you interviewed anyone else?"

Sam checked his watch. "Of course. But what kind of detective would I be if I told you who, or what they said?"

She hated when he did that. "You mentioned that Hunter didn't like her because she was mean—Amy said the same, that Madison could be 'cutting' to other actors." Danielle hadn't cared for Madison either, but for a different reason.

Sam's eyes narrowed on her. "I want you to let me handle it."

"He should know better than that," Jack murmured. "He'd never solve as much as a puzzle if you weren't the one with the brains."

Charlene hid a smile by ducking her head. "Before you accuse me of snooping, I was just passing the producer's tent"—*snooping*—"and heard Danielle and Neville Hampton arguing."

"About what?"

"Madison. Neville was sleeping with her, and I think he accused Danielle of having something to do with her death—she seemed defensive about it, saying that if she was going to kill anyone, it would be him."

"That's a serious accusation." Sam scowled. "Anything else you learned during this little chat?"

"His wife has a short fuse, from what I saw with my own eyes. Danielle ripped apart Jane, the announcer, during the show. And she was, more understandably, furious with Neville."

"For cheating." Sam straightened and placed both boots flush to the floor. "What else did your innocent ears pick up while you were minding your own business?"

"Was that sarcasm?" Charlene cleaned the crumbs off the counter with a paper napkin, glancing up at Sam.

Jack's chill got chillier, and a light in the kitchen flickered in warning.

"You just told me that you overheard two different possible motives." Sam stood, and the playful mood between them was gone. "I'd like to speak to your guests about what they saw."

Charlene tossed the napkin into the trash. "The O'Reillys are out back. They're from Dublin and were quite shaken up about today's events. Perhaps you can let them know that it's safe to go to the fireworks tonight?"

"Sure. We'll have extra security to ensure the show goes on as planned."

"Oh, that's good news." Charlene slipped a lock of hair behind her ear. "I'll get Angela and Jackie for you—they must be up in their rooms."

Sam flashed his white teeth, but she knew it was the shark coming out in him and not a smile. "What a terrific idea. Maybe you can learn more about what happened today so I can be spared the trouble."

"Sam, it isn't my fault people talk to me. I don't *force* them . . . How did you get Hunter to talk?"

"Force?" he said in a quiet voice. Too quiet for her liking.

Jack emerged in cold, bright form at Charlene's side. The sheer curtain by the window moved a half inch in an invisible breeze. She worried she might have gone too far with her poor word choice.

"We don't force confessions by physical violence." Sam rocked back on his heels. "We just let folks know it's in their best interests to give information to officers of the law. In Hunter's case, it was getting him a cup of coffee to sober up and listen."

"What brave police work," Jack remarked in a droll tone.

"That was smart." Charlene knew Sam would never be violent for the sake of violence. "Please remember to be that nice when you question my guests, okay, Sam? This is my business."

"And police work is mine. See the difference?"

"Sorry." Sam could be so rigid about police procedure, yet Charlene couldn't seem to stop ruffling his feathers. People confided in her. Was that her fault?

Jack calmed down. "Don't forget to tell him about the video, Charlene. *If* you still want to help him."

Charlene took a drink of her tea. "I sent the video of the play to your office email."

"I saw that, but I haven't had a chance to open it yet. Thanks."

Sam's attitude was borderline chilly, probably because he was upset with her, but this was about finding the shooter and not personal. She touched his hand. "I was watching the recording and saw something that may or may not have any importance. It's a flash of light about ten minutes from the end of the tape. The same time as the musket dropped and Madison was shot. Might have been someone taking pictures, but nobody would need a flash in the middle of the day, would they?"

Sam scratched his smooth-shaven chin as he studied her. "Wouldn't think so. I'll have a look at it."

"I'll go round up the guests for you." Charlene strode toward the sweeping staircase with her head high, just in case Sam was watching, then climbed to the second floor and continued up the next set of steps. The two ladies were in the single rooms, next door to each other. She rapped on the first door.

Jackie answered, her blond hair loose to her shoulders, her nose pink from the sun despite the cap she'd worn. "Hi, Charlene. Your face is red. Is everything all right?"

Darn Sam. "Yes, of course. Detective Holden is here and would like to speak to you about the tragedy at the Common today. It should only take a few minutes. And oh! The fireworks are still on. The city's added extra security, so he assured me it will be safe."

"Have they caught the shooter?" Jackie leaned against the doorway.

"Not yet." Charlene spoke with cool confidence as befitted a business owner whose job was to make her guests comfortable. "But they will."

Jackie poked her head in the hall and pointed to the next door, which remained closed. "Well, I'll let Angela know about the fireworks, and we'll be right down. We were just freshening up anyway."

"Thank you." Charlene descended in a rush, her fingers slick on the polished golden oak. She didn't bother stopping at the O'Reilly suite but ran down the last flight of stairs. Tim was in the kitchen—no Sam. Silva rubbed her furry head against his tanned calves. He knelt down to give her a little kitty love, and she purred her affection back.

"Hey, Tim. Detective Holden's here to ask everyone a few questions."

"I heard him in the living room with the O'Reillys, which is why I decided to wait here." His book on Winter Island was on the kitchen table next to a water bottle he must've pulled from the fridge.

"I have some good news—the fireworks are still on, and we'll be going around six, as originally planned, to get dinner. I'm having a happy hour before we leave. Interested?"

"I'd like that." He uncapped his water bottle and drank. "I was up on the widow's walk, seeing the air show. Used to love that kind of thing. My grandpa was an air force fighter pilot in the Second World War—he lived to be ninety-five, bless him. Anyway, he did a stretch on Winter Island around the fifties and the Cold War. He'd come visit when I was a kid, and man, he could tell the best stories." Tim screwed the cap back on.

"You must've been proud of him." Charlene could hear it in Tim's voice. "Did you ever want to be a pilot?"

"Yes. Unfortunately, I have red-green color blindness, which prevents me from flying."

"Oh, Tim, I'm sorry to hear that."

"It's all right. I've made my fortune with horses—a skill passed down on my other grandfather's side. That and Kentucky moonshine."

Charlene chuckled. What a character.

"I've gotta say, Charlene, that your telescope is first class." Tim snagged a cookie off the serving plate still on the counter. "Great view up there too."

"Thank you. The telescope was one of my better finds from Vintage Treasures—that antique shop I was telling you about earlier."

Shannon raced into the kitchen with a wide grin. "Your turn, Tim!" Aaron, Judith, and Martin chased Shannon up the stairs to their suite, the family laughing, which meant Sam hadn't been too heavy-handed.

"Guess I better get this interview over. What time is this happy-hour shindig?"

The digital clock on the stove read three thirty. "About an hour, in the living room. I want to leave early enough that everyone will have time to eat dinner before the fireworks and wander around town. Salem has so much to see."

"Sounds good." Tim left to speak with Sam.

Charlene pulled her list from the drawer by the silverware. To get people into the July Fourth spirit, she planned to serve red or white sangria, in addition to coffee or tea, and white grape juice for the kids.

Minnie'd left a note below the cupboard where Charlene kept her wineglasses, on top of a recipe book open to the page for party appetizers where she'd circled, in pencil, a hot chicken dip. It was served in a festive red and blue patriotic dish and could be eaten with crackers or crisp celery. The note instructed Charlene to look in the fridge.

Thank you, Minnie!

Charlene pulled all the needed ingredients from the bottom drawer: cream cheese, Miracle Whip, lemon, Worcestershire sauce, and a chunk of chicken breast. The directions were simple enough for even a non-cook like her.

After she had everything set, she returned to her rooms, took a shower, and dressed for the evening ahead. It was still hot, so she put on a pair of white capris and a sleeveless red and blue top.

She hadn't seen Jack since his protective flare-up in the kitchen with Sam. Charlene kept the TV on low and went to the kitchen to find Tim just closing the refrigerator door. He'd also spruced up and had changed into linen shorts and a blue shirt.

"I thought I'd help." Tim pointed at her list she'd left on the counter. "Filled the ice buckets and brought out the sangrias. Is this lemonade?"

"White grape juice with raspberries. I thought the kids should have a special drink too. Tim, thank you." How sweet.

"Least I could do after the detective left—he said he'd call ya later."

"How did the conversation go with Sam?" Charlene made a tray with the chicken dip, crackers, and celery. She created a second platter with red, white, and blue nacho chips and seven-layer guacamole.

"Fine. I told him what I saw, which was practically nothing except watching the actress fall off the stage. I asked him if the musket had somehow been rigged with a real bullet, but he told me no. Even if it had and the fool had dropped it by mistake, what were the odds the bullet would hit the actress in the chest when she was facing the crowd?"

An impossible angle. "Couldn't happen. What gets me is that whoever did this risked being seen in the crowd. They must have been very confident of their shot, right?"

"Buddy of mine was a competition shooter—he was on *Top Shot*. Ever see that show?"

Charlene wiped her hands on a paper towel. "No. And the closest I've come to firing a gun is a water pistol."

Tim laughed. "Those aren't much for aim. Well, he told me that a proficient shooter can draw and shoot his weapon in under one-and-a-half seconds. That's faster than a racehorse on a track—they average six seconds a length."

"That *is* fast." She tapped her lower lip. "And what about the noise? Shouldn't we have heard something?"

Their conversation was interrupted by the O'Reillys clattering down the stairs, Shannon dragging her witch doll by the hair.

"Can I pour you some sangria?" Tim asked.

"Oh, yeah—the white, please." She'd added frozen blueberries and cherries to her white wine and couldn't wait to try it. "But let's bring it in the other room first."

She balanced the food while Tim brought in the drinks.

"It's a party!" Shannon jumped up and down. "Can I have one of the flags, Charlene?"

"Sure! Juice, hon?"

"Yes, please!"

Charlene handed it over and smiled at Judith. "Grown-up juice, Judith?"

"White, please—and a flag." Judith tucked one of the

paper American flags, meant to be appetizer toothpicks, into Shannon's ponytail.

Once everyone had a drink, Tim suggested a toast. "To Charlene!" They all raised their glasses in a salute.

The sangria was cool and fruity—perfect for the hot summer afternoon. "Help yourselves to the dips. Paper plates are on the sideboard there."

Charlene felt a cold draft and shivered. Jack was practically breathing down her neck. "Watch out, Charlene. You've got a new admirer."

She arched her brow, her mouth firm, then stepped forward to greet Angela and Jackie as they entered the living room. "Hi, girls. Can I recommend the sangria? We have red or white."

"White, if you don't mind. It's too hot for red." Angela saw Tim and Martin drinking big pours of red with white grapes and blueberries, and lifted her shoulder. "For me, anyway."

"And you, Jackie?"

"The same. Thank you."

She turned toward the frosty pitchers, but Tim had beaten her to it, offering each woman a tall, clear cup. All three of them sat on the sofa, and Charlene stood behind the armchair to Tim's right. "Charlene and I were just talking about what happened earlier. What did the detective have to say? All I got was that Hunter didn't shoot Madison by accident."

"That's more than he said to us—he was very close-mouthed." Angela sipped her sangria and her face brightened. "Yum, Charlene." She turned to her best friend. "We gave him a pretty good description of the play, but we know nothing about that poor young woman. Couldn't help him at all."

Jackie took a drink, cupping a square napkin around the bottom of the glass. "It was such a shock. In broad daylight—how brazen can you be?"

Michelle must have returned while Charlene was in the shower, and she sank into the armchair with a sigh. The nurse balanced a plate with a little of everything on it. "I told Detective Holden about the pictures I took today and offered to give him copies tomorrow. Is he married, Charlene? I'd reconsider my move to Long Island if I thought I had a chance." The plump nurse giggled to let them all know she was joking.

Charlene rested her elbow on the top of the armchair. "Single. He has an Irish Setter. Married to his job, maybe."

Jack, out of sight but audible to her, huffed. "Sam's waiting for his big chance with you."

She ignored her adorable jealous ghost altogether and focused on her guests.

"Like me," Michelle said. "I decided when I didn't want children or a traditional relationship that my gift with nursing was something that connected me to my human family." She patted the camera bag at her feet. "I get to satisfy my wanderlust without any guilt."

"We're both married," Jackie said. "Our spouses are friends and understand that we need our 'girl' trips— although I'm not sure what mine's going to say about that after this one."

"We'll be sure to make it clear we weren't in any danger." Angela clinked her sangria glass to Jackie's.

The hour passed in a flash, until the last swipe of chicken dip on a celery stick was gone. Not even a blue chip or the guacamole remained.

"Five minutes," Charlene called as she carried the

empty dishes and pitchers back to the kitchen. Shannon and Aaron both helped, so she gave them each another cookie.

Charlene whispered a good night to Jack and petted Silva, then led the group down Crown Point Road into town. Passing Bella's Italian Ristorante, the parking lot empty, the green awning crooked, Charlene told them about the manager, David, who had won the lottery but hadn't lived long enough to spend his fortune.

Charlene kept the tale entertaining, but the empty restaurant made her sad. They arrived at Pickering Wharf with plenty of time to spare before the fireworks at nine, so she suggested places where they might grab a bite to eat.

"The Sea Level Oyster Bar is great, and Finz right here is considered one of the best restaurants around—although a little pricey."

"Which would you suggest, Charlene?" Jackie asked. "Angela and I are ready to sample some Maine lobster."

"Then Finz is your place." Charlene glanced around her red-cheeked group. "Anyone else want a suggestion?"

"Us," Judith answered, her hand clasped with Shannon's.

"Longboards to our right—super casual—or Bambolina's for a great pizza. It's a couple of blocks away, but an easy walk."

"Where are you going to eat, Charlene?" Tim asked. "If you don't mind, I'd like to join you."

"Me too," Michelle said. "But I need to drop my film at a drugstore to be developed, at some point tonight."

"We just passed one a half block back." Charlene gestured behind her.

"Not digital?" Tim asked. "This *is* the twenty-first century."

Michelle rolled her eyes at his teasing. "I'm only going to share the relevant pictures, thank you, with copies."

"How thoughtful of you, Michelle. I'm so pleased we'll be together—I hate eating alone, and now it's a party." Charlene tilted her head and considered their restaurant options. "I've been to them all, though tonight I'd prefer something casual. How about Longboards? It's crowded, but they have great lobster rolls and chowder. Flatbreads too." She glanced at her watch. "Hope we can still get in."

"That sounds good." Jackie glanced at Angela. "What do you think? We can do Finz tomorrow."

"Perfect, if you're okay with us tagging along too?" Angela fanned her hot face with a "Charlene's" brochure.

"Not at all. You good with that, Tim?"

"Of course." Tim wasn't flashy, but a man who'd been around awhile and knew his worth. "Not often that I get to dine with four lovely ladies."

Martin turned to his kids. "You guys ready for an American pizza?"

"Yeah!" Aaron shot a fist in the air.

Shannon jumped up and down. "Pizza, pizza, yummy."

"Guess we won't be joining you." Judith ruffled her son's carrot-top hair. "We'll try to catch up with you for the fireworks, but if we miss you in the crowd, don't worry, we'll cab it back."

"Have a great time." Charlene gave them directions and then gestured to the others. "Longboards, here we come. It's clustered around other shops. You can't see it from the street, but they're adjacent to the hotel on the left."

"That looks like a wonderful place to stay," Michelle said. "The Waterfront. I'll have to tell my nursing friends about it . . . and 'Charlene's.'"

"I hope so," Charlene said, not at all offended. "The Hawthorne is another great hotel, well worth visiting."

Charlene kept a brisk pace toward Longboards. "The restaurant will probably be awfully busy—are you okay with a wait? There are places to walk around."

"Fine," her four guests chorused.

"It's also an excellent spot for viewing the fireworks, if we don't want to be closer to the pier."

When they arrived there was a line, but Charlene put her name on the list for a table for five and was told it could be forty-five minutes.

"I'll go drop my film." Michelle held her camera bag to her side and rushed off.

"Good thing we had drinks already and that chicken dip," Angela said. "It's such a pleasant evening that I don't mind waiting at all." The entire square was decked out with red, white, and blue ribbons; the storefronts also had patriotic flags. Some people stood at the railing, gazing in the direction of a lighthouse, while others peered into store windows. "It's too bad we don't have time to wander through these boutiques—they're charming."

"We can shop tomorrow," Jackie told her. "Before dinner at Finz."

"Now, that's a great plan." Angela patted her stomach. "Lobster two nights in a row, and souvenirs."

Charlene had been given a buzzer, and it lit up after only thirty minutes. Michelle arrived out of breath just as they were seated in a snug booth, which added to the fun of getting to know your neighbor. Tim ordered a local beer and the ladies a bottle of red wine. They talked, they ate, they shared dishes, and they had not one complaint.

Afterward, they found an excellent spot on the grass to view the fireworks. At eight o'clock music could be heard floating over the water, and people around them began to dance. Silence descended when the national anthem was played. At nine the fireworks started, and the crowds cheered with delight as one by one each display outdid the other.

Charlene felt enormous pride in her newly adopted city as the celebration continued, enthralling her guests and everyone watching the dazzling display that lasted for a full hour.

When it was all over, the throng cleared out. Tim and Michelle decided to pick up the film, then go to the Hawthorne for a nightcap, and Charlene hailed a cab for herself, Jackie, and Angela.

The day had been successful despite being tainted by death.

Silva greeted them on the front porch with a meow, as if she'd been waiting up. "She's so beautiful," Angela said as they entered.

"She is, and she knows it." Charlene laughed. "Can I get you anything?"

Angela and Jackie exchanged a look, and Angela said, "I think we're going to share some wine on the widow's walk and then go to bed."

"Make yourselves at home."

"The wine in our rooms is a classy touch, Charlene," Jackie said. "You've made us feel incredibly welcome."

The best friends climbed the stairs, and Charlene, heart warm, went into the kitchen. No Jack at the table.

Silva waited impatiently by her bowl, so Charlene fed the cat her favorite tuna.

"Jack?" she whispered. She opened the wine cellar door and flipped on the light. No Jack downstairs.

He wasn't in his favorite chair near the fireplace either. Or her suite. The TV was off. Disappointment welled. She'd wanted to share the excitement of the celebration—had he watched the fireworks from the widow's walk? She'd also wondered if he'd discovered anything more about Salem Stage Right and the actors.

As she was getting ready for bed, she realized that she hadn't heard back from Sam about the video she'd sent, or the significance of the flash and whether it had been from the gunshot. Charlene sent him a text of the time on the recording when the flash occurred so that he could get straight to it.

Fifteen minutes later, Sam called. She'd been sitting in bed with a good book, to unwind so she could sleep. "Sam! Did you have a chance to look for the flash?"

"Sorry. I've been scanning hours of security cameras around Salem Common. You know what? One of them was vandalized," he growled. "The one that had a perfect angle to see the stage from the bandstand."

"Oh no. But wasn't it off-limits because of the remodel?"

"Yeah—didn't stop the vandal. I promise to look at your *home video* first thing in the morning when my eyes can focus again."

"Well"—she bristled at his tone—"I'm sorry I bothered you. Ja . . . I mean I thought it might be helpful, but clearly I was wrong. Good night!"

"Charlene. Wait! I'm just in a foul mood because we keep drawing blanks. I'm sorry if I sounded ungrateful. It was smart of you to send me this—hmm. You probably weren't the only person in the crowd filming the production."

"Don't forget all the folks taking pictures. Michelle dropped her film off tonight and should have it for you in the morning."

"Someone somewhere might have caught the killer on tape." He groaned. "Which means more hours of poring through them."

Charlene *almost* felt sorry for him.

"That said, if the shooter noticed you, or anybody else, filming, that could be a problem."

A hint of alarm brought her wide-awake. "Geez, Sam. Now you think I could be in danger?"

"It would be a very slight chance. Want me to come over?" His sexy voice made her body tremble and break into goose bumps. She blamed it on fear.

"No, I don't want you to come over. You might wake my guests. And besides, I'm still mad at you. I tried to do you a favor, and you made me feel like an idiot."

"You are not an idiot. I'm sorry. I could make you feel better if you'd let me."

"No! I won't let you. I'm going to stay mad at you."

"Here we go again."

"We're not going anywhere. I'm going to bed."

"Sweet dreams, my fiery friend."

"What's a fiery friend?" she asked.

"Someone who is excitable."

"And you think that's me?"

He chuckled, which made her smile too.

"Good night," he said softly.

"Good night, Sam," she answered and put her head on the pillow. Sweet dreams, indeed!

Chapter Five

Saturday, after a large family-style breakfast, Charlene loaded the dishwasher while Jack sat in his chair at the kitchen table and provided commentary on the killer still being loose. The shooting had received a five-minute spotlight on the news earlier, with the police giving a number to call if someone had information.

Her guests were all out for the day, which left her to straighten their rooms and think about something fun for happy hour, to go with Minnie's sweets.

"They'll catch the person responsible, Jack." Sam hadn't let her down yet.

"Speaking of caught, what do you think about getting a bell for Silva's collar?" Jack stroked his hand over the feline's fur, and it raised slightly from the energy of his palm. Silva was able to see Jack but unable to touch him, which confused the cat no end. At the moment, Silva ignored Jack and lasered large eyes at Charlene while she scraped the bits of egg from a serving bowl to the trash.

Charlene sighed and caved in, feeding Silva a small chunk. "Just a bite, that's all there is." She rinsed the dish and put it in the dishwasher.

Silva washed her paw over her whiskers.

"Why a bell?"

"She captured another bird this morning, and it was all I could do to get the poor thing free before it went to birdie heaven." He grimaced. "Wasn't an easy task."

"Oh no!" What if one of the guests had seen it? Or the kids? "Thank you." Charlene shuddered as she recalled the gift Silva had brought in the house for her last month—a stunned robin that Charlene had been able to set free. She'd had a serious heart-to-heart with her cat, which had gone unheeded.

"Feline instinct," Jack declared. "Silva wants to contribute to the family. She can't help it. If you don't want a bell, maybe call Nikki at the vet to see what can be done. I've heard about cats having their front claws removed to keep from scratching the furniture. Seems a little extreme, I think. Couldn't defend herself from a predator."

Charlene loaded the last cup and shut the door, pressing start on the dishwasher. She picked up Silva and stared the cat in the eye—Silva just purred. "The furniture would've been a deal-breaker, furball. You know how much I've invested in the antiques, don't you?"

Jack chuckled. "She's a very smart cat. I bet she saw the quality of stuff in the moving van and knew her chances of landing in clover were high."

"I got everything cheap at estate sales, so Silva was completely misled." Charlene dropped a kiss between her soft ears and put her down. "No more birds, Silva, okay?"

Silva, being a cat, made no promises as she flicked her tail.

Laughing, Jack said, "That might even be a no."

"All right. I'll get a bell."

Charlene wiped her hands with the dish towel on the stove rack and straightened it. "Hey, did you ever get a chance to research the theater company? I missed you last night."

"No." Jack gave her a sheepish expression. "I've got to work on my precision when it comes to scanning the internet. I tried to mentally search for Salem Stage Right and got into Salem's Street Life—in Oregon. Not pretty."

"Oops!" His ghostly powers were intermittent. They'd tried to see if he could use the voice-to-text feature on her tablet, but it hadn't worked—his tones hadn't even registered, yet he could peck at the laptop keys and operate the television to turn it off and on and change the channels. He loved watching documentaries. His greatest talent was his mind, and he seemed to gain strength from electromagnetic energy—but then, *zap*. He'd be gone.

She'd considered for all of five seconds writing a how-to manual on living with a ghost but realized that if it was found, she'd be considered a nutcase. Not to mention that, other than Jack not being able to leave the property where he'd been murdered, there weren't hard-and-fast rules for his existence.

"You remember how to hit the back button on the laptop if you get to the wrong place?"

Jack flexed his fingers. "As a doctor, my typing skills were limited. My frustration got the better of me, and so, no, I didn't do that."

Which meant he'd disappeared in a foul mood. "I can

help after I finish the upstairs rooms. Michelle is staying an extra night, so I don't have to change linen, only the towels. I think being a traveling nurse is such an interesting way to see the world. On the other hand, it would be kind of lonely—never staying long enough in one place to make friends or build real relationships."

"There're pluses and minuses in every job." Jack stood up, the image catching like a slow-motion picture.

Had he overextended his energy? Did he need to take a break? "I'd think it would be great when you're in your twenties, but if you ever wanted kids and to settle down, that would have to end. Michelle said she didn't want that normal kind of life."

"I thought highly of the nurses I worked with at the hospital," Jack said. "Most of them had their own families at home but worked hard and cared about the patients' comfort and well-being. They were bright and adaptable." He sighed and closed his eyes for a second.

It made her heart ache, knowing how much he missed being part of *life*. "Why don't I set up the internet, and you read about the theater company while I clean? You can give me the highlights when I'm done."

Jack perked up a bit at having a job. "Deal."

They went into her suite—well, she walked and he appeared at her table by the wall in a cool blink. Silva followed them with a meow.

She turned on her laptop and typed into the search bar, leaning over the desk. "Salem Stage Right. Here you go. If you get stuck, come get me." Charlene turned toward the door.

"What should I look for?"

Crossing her arms, she considered and said, "Anything

about Neville Hampton and Madison Boswell. Danielle Hampton. There was a lover's triangle, and now one of the three is dead in a very public way."

"Homicide victims are usually killed by someone they know. It's rare that it's done by a random encounter or that they've been targeted by a stranger. Although mass shootings are becoming way too common." Jack sat down before her laptop and wiggled his fingers over the keyboard.

"Tim said yesterday that it would be possible for a trained gunman to draw, aim, and fire a weapon in under two seconds."

"Whoa—that's fast. Are you thinking a cop?"

Charlene put her hand in her pocket. "That would be awful, and no, I wasn't." She tossed a few ideas out. "Someone familiar with the play. Someone with a grudge against Madison. Hunter said he was told to drop the musket at the word *yield*. Or maybe we should be thinking of who had the most to gain from her death? Her family? Danielle, jealous; or Neville, to appease his wife; or a disgruntled fellow actor?"

Jack swiveled toward her. "This was a one-time-only performance, according to the announcer. Did you get a playbill?"

"Yeah. I might still have it." Charlene searched the pockets on her purse, tugging free a much-folded list of the play's actors, the plot, and other points of interest. She smoothed it flat next to her computer on the table. "Here you go. What's on your mind?"

"If we're searching for who would be familiar with the play, we could be looking at our list of suspects."

She rubbed her arms and studied the smiling faces on the full-color playbill that she'd used as a paper fan during the summer heat. Madison Boswell, Hunter Elliott, Amy Fadar, and Neville Hampton. "I like my lists, Jack, but this might be a bit too on the nose."

"Don't you have cleaning to do?" Jack widened the door for her without even looking her way. "I've got this."

Before Charlene got involved with her chores, she texted Kevin to tell him and Amy that Hunter had been found and questioned. She also said he'd been paid five hundred bucks to drop the musket.

He immediately texted back. **The moron had been whining all over town about how he got framed, that he just took the money 'cause dropping a prop wasn't a crime**.

She laughed at that image. **Seems suspicious to me that an "unknown someone" would offer him so much money.**

He replied, **Amy's coming over with some of the actors around lunchtime. Want to join us?**

She really wanted to, but she had to clean first. Avery would be in at two, but she had other jobs. **Can't. Working.** ☹

CU Later then!

Charlene spent the next hour tidying rooms and replacing towels, then ran the vacuum over the carpets. Michelle had left after breakfast to pick up the prints from the drugstore that hadn't been ready last night, taking her camera with her.

"Should I tell the cute detective hello for you?" Michelle had asked with a wink.

"No, thank you," she'd replied. Charlene swallowed a smidge of jealousy. The nurse was free to flirt.

She brought the stack of towels down the stairs to the laundry room and started the washing machine. Kass Fortune, a local Wiccan tea shop owner, had given her lavender sachets to use in the dryer to make her sheets and towels soft and floral.

No matter how busy Charlene's hands were, she couldn't forget Madison Boswell. Her low laugh, her intriguing eyes as she spoke to the entire audience, making each person feel like she was speaking just to them.

Then the terror as she'd clutched her chest and fallen to the ground.

Dead. The life in those eyes vanquished forever. It was just so sad . . .

Jack popped up next to her, and she screamed, dropping the wicker laundry basket.

"Gotcha!"

"Jack!" She hurried into the hall to make sure she was still alone, her guests out enjoying Salem. "One of these days . . ."

"I didn't mean to startle you . . ."

She arched her brow.

"That time," he admitted with a smile.

"Do you need help with the internet?" Charlene picked up the basket and placed it on the shelf next to the washing machine.

"No—I found out something interesting."

"Oh?" She made a mental note to put detergent on the shopping list.

"Madison Boswell comes from a very, very wealthy family in Boston. We're talking billions." Jack flickered the overhead bulb to make his point.

"What do they do?" She switched off the light and entered the hall.

"Dad is an investment banker, and Mom's a high-profile activist for women's rights. A lawyer."

"Wow." Everything Charlene had thought about Madison changed in that moment. "Madison could've afforded the best acting schools in the world. LA, New York, abroad. With that meal ticket, how did she end up here?" Charlene shrugged. "It might be quaint and charming and quirky—but Salem is small potatoes for the acting community."

"Close to home but independent?" Jack suggested.

"A lot of old money in Boston," Charlene said, thinking aloud. "Especially in the historic Back Bay or Beacon Hill—not that I've been there yet." It was on her list. "A homebody, Jack? I don't know . . . my impression of her was she liked the spotlight."

Jack frowned. "So why wouldn't she jump all over her family resources? Instead, she joins a local theater company—no offense to Neville, but it's second-rate."

"Big fish in a little pond?"

"Could be. She's twenty-eight—kids aren't leaving the nest until later, and why leave at all if your parents are loaded?"

"Don't get me started on reasons why you'd want to move far away from your parents." She blew her hair back in exasperation.

"Now, Charlene, don't pretend you don't love your family, because I know you do. Your dad is a saint, but your mother?" Jack grimaced. "A saint in the making."

"Saint, hardly!" She stayed on topic. "Madison is a mystery. Why she'd be in Salem when the whole world beckons, I have no idea. Who, or what, would bring her here?"

Jack made the motion of rubbing his hands together—not that his palms touched. "We love our mysteries. Want to see what I've found so far?"

"Yeah." She headed through the kitchen to her suite and sat at the chair before her desk, where Jack had an article open to Madison's parents at a fundraising dinner.

Madison resembled her mother, with dark hair.

She scanned the short piece, then did another search on Foster and Laura Boswell. Fourth-generation bankers, the Boswells had a good reputation in their community. "Kids . . ." she murmured, scrolling the headlines. "Bingo." Her pulse raced at connecting one of the many dots. "*Logan* Boswell. Firstborn, only son. Two years older than Madison."

"That's the name Madison called out into the crowd."

Not a boyfriend . . . family. "So, he'd be thirty. Was he there to support her acting career? Maybe they were close."

"Hmm." Jack ruffled the pages of her notepad. "What if he's the shooter?"

Doubt and horror filled her as Charlene recalled the terror on Madison's face before she fell off the stage. "No . . ."

Jack shrugged. "This could be an inheritance issue. Murders happen over money all the time—does he live at home?"

She did another search and clicked her tongue to her teeth, skimming down the headlines. "Oh . . . I don't think so. Father and son had a falling-out when he was still in college. Logan Boswell now works for a competing company to his father's. Just last year he was voted as one of Boston's up-and-coming young professionals."

"Doesn't need his old man's money and has something to prove." Jack leaned against the table. "You know, the internet is amazing when it comes to getting quick answers, but there is more to the story than those little information bites, Charlene. Were Madison and her family tight? The only way to really know that is by talking to people."

She didn't disagree and went back to the Salem Stage Right website, which had an announcement at the top of the page—no performances for Saturday due to the death of their fellow actor, but there would be a fundraiser performance Sunday at five p.m. to endow the Madison Boswell Actors Fund. Tickets would be fifty dollars each, and the intimate theater was sure to sell out at less than eighty seats. She copied down the company's phone number. The contact person was Danielle Hampton.

"Click on the upcoming features," Jack said from over her shoulder.

Charlene did and was taken to a new page. "*A Midsummer Night's Dream* is playing weekends at the theater from June through September. I wonder if that's the play for tomorrow? I'd like to go." To support her friends, of course.

"Call to see if you can buy a ticket," Jack said. "I hope it's not sold-out."

Charlene used her cell phone to dial the theater number—it rang twice before being bumped off due to a full voice message system. She texted Kevin and asked him to call her.

"I just texted Kevin for Amy's number—maybe she can hook me up with a ticket."

"And?" Jack prodded, knowing her so well.

"I also want to ask Amy if Madison had ever mentioned her family, especially her brother, Logan." As she talked to Jack, she clicked on the picture tab on Salem Stage Right's website.

Amy was in costume for a part in *Romeo and Juliet* with Madison looking on. Then another candid shot showed Madison and Neville, exuding passionate love.

"I wonder if this is where Danielle discovered their affair?" Charlene asked. "You can see their attraction in the photo."

"It could be explained by acting. I don't think I'd like being married to an actress. A beautiful woman was difficult enough."

She raised her brow at him. He'd been married to a high-maintenance socialite who'd cheated . . . there was no excuse for that. "You should be able to trust your partner—no matter what!"

The phone rang and showed Kevin's number. She answered and put it on speaker. "Hello, Kev! Is this a bad time?"

"Nope. Just on my way into Brews and Broomsticks to cover for a few hours before I take a tour out tonight. We'll reschedule lunch, if you're calling to change your mind. What's up?"

"Can I have Amy's number? There's a special performance tomorrow at the theater. I tried to call for tickets, but no one answered."

Silence, then, "And you're suddenly interested in Shakespeare?"

"Actually, I'm very curious about what goes on behind the scenes."

"I bet. Does this have anything to do with Madison being shot?"

"Well . . . yes, a little."

"I'll have Amy call you, if she wants to talk about it, okay? She's really shaken up by Madison's death."

"I appreciate that, Kevin." Was there guilt behind Amy's being upset? Or were they the normal emotions of losing a friend and fellow actor? A rival? Since Jared's death, Charlene's curious nature had developed a suspicious edge.

Not all people were who they portrayed themselves to be.

Not everybody was kind.

She missed her rose-colored glasses.

"And before you make anything of it," Kevin continued, "I'm asking you to tread lightly. I know you saw how Amy reacted yesterday, so I'm giving you a heads-up. Amy and Madison had history in LA before landing in Salem. Don't ask her about it—she'll tell you if she wants to."

"I won't. I promise." Charlene switched hands with the phone, her palms damp. Was Kevin covering for his girlfriend? "But why would she want to hide it?"

"I didn't say she was hiding *any*thing. She's already answered questions from the police. Maybe you should back away from this and let Salem's finest handle it. That's what they get paid for."

She drew herself up. "I just want a ticket for the show and a little information."

"Look, I know Amy had nothing to do with it," Kevin huffed. "I'll get in touch with her and let *her* decide whether or not she wants to talk to you."

He hung up, clearly annoyed, which made her feel bad. Kevin had become a wonderful friend, and she hoped her questions hadn't put that at risk.

"Cheer up," Jack said, having heard the whole conversation. "You don't think Amy is guilty either, right?"

"Wrong angle of the gunshot, and we saw her on stage the whole time." Charlene lifted her eyes to his. "Jack, I don't want to be the kind of person that makes her friends run in the opposite direction!"

He shook his head, his smile wavering—she'd learned the signs. He'd used a lot of his energy today manifesting himself for her. "Stop being so nosy, then." Jack disappeared with a haunting chuckle, pleased at having gotten the last word.

"Jack!"

He was gone.

She sat down at her desk and studied the pictures—Amy was girl-next-door beautiful, while Madison had dark hair and mesmerizing eyes. Sultry. Both were slender and tall.

They had some kind of "history," which was probably very normal in the drama community.

Amy was thirty-five to Madison's twenty-eight.

In the acting game, age was a definite factor.

Amy hadn't shot Madison.

But, she knew every part of the play. She was a professional, and much better than Madison, even though Madison had gotten the choice part. Amy had access to the tents, being an actress herself.

Amy could have easily paid Hunter to drop his musket and provide the distraction for the shooter in the crowd to get away with murder.

CHAPTER SIX

Done with her chores by eleven, Charlene had extra time before Avery arrived at the B & B for work today. She trusted the teenager with her whole heart but didn't like to leave Avery alone in the big house. If Jack could, he'd be there, but it wasn't something she could count on.

Lunch had been canceled. Given three free hours, she was tempted to drive down to the theater and dig around Salem Stage Right. Would shy Jane be there, willing to talk to friendly Charlene about Danielle or Neville or Hunter?

She was not going to bother Amy but would wait for her call, as Kevin's friendship was important to her. Minnie had baked extra cookies, and Charlene could bring some down to the theater for the actors to express her condolences.

Pleased with that decision, Charlene showered and dressed in a light skirt and blouse, her long hair piled in a messy bun on the top of her head, perfect for the hot and humid weather.

She fed Silva some tuna. "Here you are, sweetie—now behave!" The feline raised her back, waved her silvery tail, and stared her in the face without a single blink—the cat would do as she pleased, and that was the end of that.

Charlene packed four dozen cookies in a box, then grabbed her keys from the foyer table. She was halfway out the door when her cell phone rang. "Hello?"

"It's Amy. Kevin said you wanted to talk to me?"

"Thanks for calling. I wanted to ask about tickets for the special performance tomorrow—I tried to call but couldn't get through."

"The theater is closed today out of respect for Madison's death."

Charlene reconsidered her plan to drop by the theater and stepped back inside the house. "Will anybody be there at all?"

"I doubt it. Actors are a superstitious bunch."

What did that mean?

Before Charlene could ask, Amy said, "Kevin said you know about Hunter being paid to mess up the show? What an idiot. You should have heard him last night, going on and on about being set up—like he needed his ten minutes of fame. God knows he's not going to get it for his acting skills."

Ouch. "It's likely he didn't know what was going to happen, but the money, combined with making Madison look bad, got the best of his good judgment."

"No excuse in my mind. He should be charged as an accessory!"

"I agree." Hunter had burned his bridges in the Salem acting community. "It makes me wonder about the timing. I mean, the musket going off precisely at the moment the bullet hit poor Madison in the chest." She brought the box of cookies to the kitchen counter. "Unless two people worked together. I guess that's possible, don't you think?"

"I honestly don't know what to think, except I'm glad I won't be on stage tonight, when Madison's killer is still running around. I could be next. It might not be someone who hated *her* at all. For all I know, it could be a kook who just decided he was going to shoot someone because he hates the Fourth of July. Who knows? Who cares? I want the police to find him and get him off the streets."

"I hear you. Salem's unique history brings in unique visitors, which is part of the joy in my B and B."

"That's what I loved about doing the play *Salem's Rebels* with Neville. It showed a unique perspective on what happened before the war, without bloodshed. It's ironic that Madison is dead when the play was anti-violence. Maybe that's what made the shooter mad?"

"Yikes! There's no telling what will spark someone not in their right mind. There's a lot of that going on in the world right now." Charlene scooped Silva up in one arm and snuggled the purring cat. "But it seems personal, not random."

"I'm a nervous wreck—I'd rather that it be a stranger. Imagine if it's someone I know? I could be performing right alongside them and not have a clue. Hey, are you still working?"

Kevin must have told Amy why Charlene couldn't come to lunch. "Finished inside, just now. I haven't got much going on until two."

"Listen, Kevin had to cancel to fill in at the bar, but

why don't you meet me and Kass for lunch? I'm at the tea shop now, and she mentioned that she's a friend of yours too. Salem's a small town, if you haven't noticed." Amy chuckled. "You and I haven't had a chance to really get to know each other, and I'd like to change that."

"Me too!" Charlene immediately thought that Kass and Amy's friendship made sense because of their shared drama background. "Where would you like to meet?"

"How about Cod and Capers?"

"That's perfect." It fit in with her plan too—to find out what Amy was hiding in regard to Madison. "One of my favorite restaurants. I know the manager quite well."

"Sharon's a doll. Meet you in fifteen?"

They ended the call, and Charlene left the house, tossing her keys and catching them. It would be great to see Kass again. She passed Bella's and turned left on Main. As she neared the restaurant, she saw a long black hearse round the corner. Following that was a black town car with tinted windows. Was that the silhouette of a man and woman in the rear seat? It was impossible to be sure.

Her heart fluttered. Could that be Madison's mother and father in Salem to retrieve their daughter's body? Foster and Laura Boswell would take their child to Boston for burial, where Charlene assumed a lavish funeral would be held. It was all too sad.

No parent should have to bury their child.

She drove the few blocks to Cod and Capers, her mind racing. The death was so abrupt, ending Madison's hopes and dreams, as well as her family's. Whoever had done this brutal crime to that vital woman must either be insane or have a strong score to settle.

Pushing the disturbing image away, she entered the restaurant. Sharon lifted her hand in greeting from behind the bar. Charlene joined her and leaned her elbow on the laminate counter. "Hi!"

"Nice to see you, Charlene. It's been a while. How's everything going?" Sharon was somewhere in her forties, with a curvy shape and colored hair that changed from a deep red to orange or strawberry every few months. She always had a smile on her face and a happy disposition.

"Business is good," Charlene answered. "Can't complain there. I'm sorry it's been so long since I stopped by—I'm meeting friends here at noon."

"Oh, don't be silly. There are plenty of restaurants in town . . . I don't expect you to come to Cod and Capers every time you decide to do lunch." Sharon leaned over the counter and lowered her voice. "I read about the shooting in the Common yesterday. That poor woman! And where was security, I want to know! What good are all those street cameras everywhere if they don't work?"

A few of Salem's citizens had been up in arms at what they viewed as a breach of their privacy, but the majority had won.

Charlene whispered, "I was there with my guests to see the play, *Salem's Rebels*. It's shocking to think the shooter was confident enough to commit murder in broad daylight with hundreds of people around." She didn't share about the vandalized camera.

"What is going on in the world?"

She waved her friend closer. "The actress, Madison Boswell, was having an affair with the producer, Neville. Do you know him, or his wife, Danielle?"

"Not sure, unless they're customers, but I don't know them by name."

Charlene briefly touched Sharon's wrist. "I thought I'd ask—you know more people than I do!"

"What do the police say?" Sharon swiped a towel across the counter.

"Not much, but I'm sure the detective will have the killer behind bars very soon."

Sharon dipped her head to a man at the end of the bar. "Can I get you a glass of wine while you wait, Charlene?"

"No, thanks."

"Who are you meeting?" Sharon nodded toward the door. "There's Amy Fadar, Kevin's friend, and Kass Fortune."

"That's them!" Charlene turned and waved. "I'll talk to you soon," she told Sharon and joined the ladies by the podium.

Charlene gave them each a half-hug but linked an arm through Kass's. "It's great to see you!" Her six-foot-tall friend was slender and pale, dressed for the summer heat in a gauzy black skirt and a black silk tank top. Her raven-black hair was mostly straight down her back, with the occasional tiny braid knotted in. Amy was head to toe pink-and-green Lilly Pulitzer, tan skin, and California gorgeous.

Amy slung the gold chain of her purse over her shoulder. "I was picking up some herbal tea from her shop when Kevin texted me, saying you wanted my number. Kass suggested we ask you to join us."

"I'm so glad that you did." Charlene released Kass. "I finished vacuuming early."

Kass chuckled. "I have a hard time imagining you doing chores."

Amy's eyes flashed with humor. "I hire out."

The hostess pointed to an empty table by the window. "Will that be all right?"

The three women nodded and walked to the corner. The restaurant was only a block from Pickering Wharf and had a harbor view. The nautical décor suited the location with gray and blue walls, fishnets hanging from the ceiling, and painted lobster murals. The food was expertly prepared, and she had never been disappointed in whatever she'd chosen.

The young waitress with a nose ring and blue-tipped hair dropped off three ice waters and handed each of them a menu. Her name tag said Lindsay. She couldn't seem to take her eyes off Kass.

When Kass asked her if they could have lemons, the girl nodded and took off like her tail was on fire.

Kass chuckled and lifted her tree-of-life-in-a-pentagram pendant. "She must be new to Salem. I get that expression a lot from our tourists, but people around here are used to me."

Amy tilted her head and scrutinized Kass, admiring the black handkerchief skirt. "You look like a perfectly good witch," she teased.

"Oh, thanks!" Kass had long, slender fingers, with multiple rings on each one. "I can't complain since I am one."

Charlene pursed her mouth, covering a grin. "All you need is the pointy hat."

"Not you too, Judas." Kass leaned her long body back against the chair.

"Here she comes," Amy whispered. "Try not to scare her off. I'm starving. Skipped breakfast and hardly ate a thing last night."

"It's no wonder, after all you went through." Charlene smiled at Lindsay and thanked her for the lemons. The waitress nodded, darted another look at Kass, and scurried off.

The three of them burst into laughter. "My guess is that she isn't Wiccan. Probably a good Catholic girl gone wrong. I'm not the one wearing a gold ring in my nose." Kass squirted a slice of lemon in her water, then dried her hands on a napkin. "So what are we having for lunch besides gossip?"

"Wine?" Amy asked. "I could use a glass right about now."

"I probably shouldn't this time of the day, but oh heck, why not?" Charlene glanced at Lindsay hovering beside the door like she wanted to bolt, and lifted a finger. The girl, head down as if going to an execution, slowly came forward.

"Lindsay," Kass spoke gently. "Please lift your head. I'm not going to eat you. I tell fortunes at the tea shop. Perfectly respectable."

Amy snickered, and Charlene bit back a laugh. "We'd each like a glass of wine—white all right, ladies?"

They nodded their agreement, and Charlene said, "Please ask Sharon for a chardonnay from Flint Wineries. A healthy pour."

The girl nodded. "Okay. Do you want to know what the specials are?"

Kass gave her a brief smile. "Where are you from, Lindsay?"

"Kansas," the young woman muttered.

"Ah, that explains it."

"Explains what?" she squeaked, her cheeks flaming with color.

"Why I frighten you. I could be a wicked witch!" At her blank stare, Kass tried again. "From *The Wizard of Oz*?"

"I've never seen that movie. *Are* you a witch?"

"A white witch." Kass sipped her water. "I believe in love and light."

The waitress relaxed a tiny bit at that.

"Lindsay," Amy said. "Could we please have our wine now? We'll give you our orders when you come back." After Lindsay left, she said, "We better make a decision fast before she freaks out again. I'm not even going to glance at the menu. I love the seafood chowder, and they serve it with a warm slice of multigrain bread."

"That sounds good to me as well." Charlene closed the menu and stacked it with hers.

"I'm going for the crab cakes," Kass declared, adding her menu on the top. "And a fresh pint of blood." She made a face, and the others laughed.

"Behave yourself," Charlene warned. "We want to enjoy our food without worrying about added garlic."

After their wine arrived and the order was in, Charlene veered the conversation to Madison. "Did you know her, Kass?"

"Yes." Kass touched her necklace. "I met her when she moved to town, what was it, four months ago? At the theater."

"Yeah. I've been back from LA for six," Amy confirmed, her mouth tight.

"Time flies!" Charlene said. "It will be ten months in Salem for me. Wait, you're part of the acting troupe here? Kass, I had no idea."

"Of course! I was bit by the theater bug so hard it left a scar!"

Kass had a presence about her that made her a memorable orator—her historical tours were terrific. Charlene had been to three so far and learned something new each time. "But you weren't in *Salem's Rebels*?"

"No. I don't do it full time."

Amy tapped Kass's shoulder. "You're very talented— you could do more if you wanted."

"I have my tea shop and the tours that keep me more than busy. I couldn't commit to anything else. Girl's gotta sleep sometime."

"Sleep is very important." Charlene drank her water. "So, Kass, you told me that you'd gone to college in Boston for theater, but Salem called to you. Did you know Neville there?"

"I'd seen him in a few plays, but he and Danielle started up Salem Stage Right what, eight years ago?" Kass twisted a single braid. "I was disillusioned by the whole business when I moved to Salem. My shop and the fortunes I do, reading tea leaves, makes more money than acting. At least I can pay the mortgage. It was different for Amy, being successful in the movies."

Amy origamied a napkin into a swan. "I made a steady living. Royalties are nice, I don't mind saying."

"From the little I saw, it's obvious that you are more talented than Madison," Charlene said. "You both are!"

"Talent is not all you need in the acting biz. It's luck, drive, perseverance, and a fondness for torture." Kass peered at Amy over her slim nose. "Am I right?"

"One hundred percent." Amy held her hand up for a high five.

"I wonder when Madison and Neville first met?" Charlene looked to the kitchen when her stomach rumbled, but there was no sign of Lindsay.

"Oh, I know that," Kass said. "Ten years ago when he

was still teaching in Boston. Before he and Danielle set up shop in Salem."

Amy glanced at her friends. She lifted the wineglass so fast she spilled a little. "Do you think they had an affair then?"

Charlene did the math in her head. "An eighteen-year-old starlet and a charismatic theater teacher? I wouldn't be surprised."

"It would've been before Danielle," Kass said with certainty. "She isn't the kind to share. And why should she be?"

Amy stroked the stem of her glass. "Well, it's obvious that Madison became his lover soon after she arrived four months ago. And then *wham*, I lost my part in the play to her." Anger furrowed Amy's brow.

Kass took a sip of her wine and put down the glass. "Madison acted like a woman in love around Neville— but she had that gift to make people infatuated with her. It was how she walked and spoke and engaged you."

"It was all an act," Amy insisted. "It wasn't a gift. Trust me."

"I don't know, Amy." Kass shifted on her chair. "Madison said she had the ability to make people see what they wanted to see about her. Maybe that's how she got past Danielle's radar to not only work with Neville again but cast him under her spell."

Amy pressed her lips together. "Overt sexuality is not magic."

"Hmm. Do you think Danielle is the one to have hired Hunter and the shooter?" Charlene asked.

"I can't see Danielle as a killer," Amy stated. "She'd make Neville's life sheer hell. Give him a high-profile divorce and slander him through the mud. Torture him with lack of visitation rights to the kids."

Kass sat back in her seat. "I agree—I bet she made him sign a prenup so she keeps everything. The family home, custody of their two kids, and Salem Stage Right—down to the last velvet curtain."

Charlene broke the contemplative silence at the table a few seconds later. "Did you know that Madison was very, very wealthy? I Googled her. Her parents are billionaires—Dad's in investments, and Mom's a lawyer. She's got an older brother, Logan." She lowered her voice. "She shouted that name before falling from the stage, do you remember that, Amy?"

Amy's eyes widened and shimmered as she swallowed tears. "I . . . I . . ."

"Had she seen him in the crowd?" Kass asked.

"That's what I was thinking." Charlene drummed her fingers against the table. "Maybe he was there to see her perform?"

"Do you know what Logan looks like?" Amy asked. "Not that it matters. I was really into my part, to nail the show for Neville. He thought it would be his big break. The audience was a blur."

"I wouldn't recognize Logan if he sat next to me." Charlene gestured to the empty seat at the four-top. "But as I was driving here, I saw a hearse round the corner, followed by a town car. I wondered if it was her parents bringing her body back to Boston." She sighed. "All the money in the world can't keep you safe from pain."

Lindsay arrived with their meals, putting a stop to the conversation. They made room on the table for their lunches, and Lindsay asked if there was anything else.

They each said no, more interested in filling their bellies than talking.

"Let's eat." Charlene dipped her spoon into the chowder and didn't think she'd ever had a better one. Loaded with shrimp and chunks of lobster, she was in heaven.

"Great recommendation, Amy. This alone makes you a friend for life."

Amy laughed and took a big spoonful herself. "Yum!"

Halfway through their meal, Kass said, "I know you don't want to believe it, Amy, but Madison had something powerful." She cut into her second crab cake and dipped it in the rémoulade sauce. "I've seen her with Neville, but it's also Jane and Hunter and the other actors too. They hung on her every word, even when she wasn't nice."

Amy's brow wrinkled. "Anything is possible, I suppose. Maybe Neville was so far bewitched that she convinced him to ask Danielle for a divorce? She flipped out?"

"*And* paid Hunter *and* set up the shooter?" Charlene asked. "I don't know . . . we saw Danielle the whole time."

Charlene finished her last bite and used the napkin to wipe her mouth before she licked the bowl. It was that good.

Amy patted Kass's ringed hand. "Listen, I don't see ghosts, like you can, and I can't read fortunes." She gestured to herself. "Unlike you, Kass, my only skill is acting. I don't believe that Madison had special powers. Here's why: You know what classes she excelled at in college?"

"Theater," Kass said.

"And . . . *hypnotherapy*." Amy nodded at each of them.

Madison had been a hypnotist? "Her eyes were captivating," Charlene said. "I saw that for myself."

Amy shrugged. "She used them as a tool. Once she told me that she could hypnotize people—this was in LA—I never looked into them again."

Charlene grabbed her water glass and took two large sips—wanting to get the bad taste out of her mouth. Madison didn't need to have talent as an actress when she could entrance the audience. That was some superpower! Had that gift gotten her killed?

CHAPTER SEVEN

L indsay refilled their water glasses and asked if they'd like dessert. No one did, so she left to get the individual checks.

When she was gone, Charlene turned to Amy. "I'm glad they canceled tonight's show. It would have been so difficult for everyone to act as if nothing was wrong."

"We're all relieved," Amy said. "It'll be hard enough tomorrow night to pretend that all is well in the world when someone, perhaps even one of us, wanted Madison dead."

"I hope Brooklyn is ready." Kass smiled at Charlene and explained, "Madison's understudy."

"Tomorrow's event—is it still possible to buy tickets?" Charlene asked. "I would love to go."

"How many do you need?" Kass asked. "Give your name at will call. I'll inform them you're coming."

"How exciting! I didn't know you were in *A Midsummer Night's Dream*." She swirled her soup spoon, then dropped it on the side plate next to the bowl. "But if the tickets are free, I'd like to make a donation."

"I'm sure they'll be grateful for whatever you choose to give." Kass leaned back in her chair. "The summer play is perfect because the shows are only on weekends, and I can rearrange my schedule. I'm not a star like Amy here, but a fairy. A very tall fairy." She laughed. "How many would you like?"

"Two. Not sure who I'll invite, but just in case."

"How about sexy Sam? You can bring him back to my changing room later." Kass's eyes twinkled as she teased Charlene.

"He'll be busy catching a killer—I hope." Charlene turned to Amy. "Did you just say that you knew Madison in LA? In movies?" Oh shoot, hopefully she wasn't treading where Kevin had warned her not to go—but the question had just popped out.

Amy quieted and stared at her napkin.

Kass floated the origami swan at the top of her water glass. "I don't think either you or Madison mentioned that, or maybe I was just oblivious. Totally possible."

Amy glanced at their two faces and released a dramatic sigh. "It's just . . ."

"Just what?" Kass asked. "Does this have to do with Kevin?"

"No, not Kevin. He's the best thing in my life!" Her cheeks paled, and she dropped her eyes.

Charlene's stomach twisted. What secret was Amy about to share?

"This isn't a confession, I hope." Kass bumped her friend's arm, her tone only half joking.

"No." Amy picked up another square napkin and began to fold it. "I met Madison five or six years ago in California."

"I take it you weren't close?" Charlene asked.

"Not exactly. I was living in LA at the time." Amy created a triangle, focusing on her project and occasionally glancing up. "I had several bit parts in movies, no lead roles, but I was earning money, paying my way. Waiting for my big break, you know."

"Do I ever," Kass snorted. "Nothing but walk-ons for years. Not even a line. No wonder I was jaded."

Amy flicked the back, and the origami frog hopped. "Madison wanted to be number one. Some people are driven like that."

"Drive can be very important." Charlene slipped Amy another napkin to see what else she would make.

Amy nodded. "Charlene, you asked if I'd met her in the movies. It was actually a play. I did live theater between the movies, and we were cast members in a remake of *Saturday Night Fever*. John Travolta in that classic white suit?"

Charlene and Kass exchanged smiles.

"I had a decent role as one of the dancers . . . two minutes of fame that led to bigger parts. I remember that Madison had just turned twenty-two. She was stunning, with her long brunette waves and big eyes. Her role was to chat up a bartender—not that she had an actual line. Well, the guy who played Tony Manero fell for her on the spot."

"Mesmerizing men," Kass said. She hopped the frog toward Charlene, who turned it around and scooted it back.

Amy folded and folded. "They dated for a while when

the show was still running, but it didn't help her get a bigger role—she had beauty, but she tripped over her lines. Beauty in LA is mandatory. As an actress you need to be able to emote, sing, and dance, as well as be beautiful."

"I imagine it helps to have connections, right?" Charlene asked.

"Madison had those too." Amy offered Charlene an origami rose. "Her grandmother was Priscilla Phipps, who lived in Beverly Hills. I never met her, but her beauty was legendary. Madison lived with her, and she used to tell everyone about the lavish parties they had. The famous people she'd met. Her grandmother was very well connected. One husband had been a successful director; the other was a head honcho at Paramount." Amy rolled her eyes. "It still couldn't help land Madison a leading role."

"Which is what she wanted more than anything, I bet," Kass said.

"You're right."

"Madison had a charmed life," Charlene murmured. She caressed the paper petal. "What went wrong?"

"Money wasn't enough. She wanted fame. Hey, have you ever seen the mascara commercials, where it's just the large, oval, golden-brown eyes?"

Charlene cupped the rose in her palm. "No way—Madison?"

Amy chuckled. "So she said. It used to make her so mad because they didn't use her whole face."

Kass tucked a lock of hair behind her ear. "She had to have made a fortune."

"Between those commercials and her grandma?" Amy rotated the origami shape to work on the other side. "She could probably have bought her own mansion in Beverly Hills."

Lindsay dropped off their checks, and they slid in their credit cards and waited for her to leave before they resumed talking.

"So despite all of that, she wasn't happy?" Charlene set the rose by her phone to take home and show Jack.

"Nope. She felt like a failure. Madison wanted to be the toast of Hollywood, and when that didn't happen, well, I saw her true colors. Before that, I'd helped her get an audition, putting my reputation on the line." Fold, fold. "She messed it up, then tried to manipulate the other actors and directors to let her try again, even blaming them for not setting her up to succeed. The thing is, film doesn't lie. Madison couldn't pull it off."

"What happened?" Kass asked.

"It was awkward, but I learned my lesson and didn't offer again. Madison had a better chance of landing roles on stage rather than movies, so that's where she expended her energy."

Charlene recalled her and Jack's conversation about her possibly wanting to be the big fish in a little pond. What was Amy making?

"Did you keep in touch?" Kass asked.

"Not really—we weren't unfriendly," Amy told them. "You don't burn bridges in LA. We'd catch up at mutual friends' parties. We talked about her being from Boston, and me from Salem. I sent flowers when her grandmother got sick and passed away. She called me to say thanks and invited me to lunch. For some stupid reason, I agreed. Madison spent an hour letting me know that she'd had to turn down some great roles because she'd had to be a nursemaid. She thrived on my lack of success. She deemed my steady work as not quite good enough for the big time."

"That's terrible," Charlene said. "She was probably jealous."

"With her ego? No. She felt sorry for me." Amy finished her paper project but hid it with her hand. "She made sure to let me know that she'd inherited her grandmother's estate and didn't need to work . . . and to rub it in, she showed me her antique gold and emerald engagement ring from a successful movie agent."

"Who?" Charlene asked.

"Would only tell me his first name, Tyler—as if I'd try to steal her man, what a joke! Anyway, she claimed he was 'the love of her life' and that he couldn't do enough for her." Amy rubbed her bare finger as if imagining a ring there. "It had been his mother's—you should have seen the way her eyes lit up, like she'd won the grand prize. Not love in those golden-brown orbs, something else. Like she . . . this is weird, but it was like having that power fed something inside her."

Amy showed them the diamond ring she'd crafted from a paper napkin.

"That's so good!" Charlene said.

Amy smiled. "Thanks. Helps me blow off steam."

Charlene doodled when nervous, so could relate.

"Did you know she could hypnotize people at that time?" Kass asked.

"Um, I don't remember when Madison told me . . . I didn't think anything of it until the audition she blew, in front of me, and I saw her try to manipulate the director by staring into his eyes."

"Did you invite her to Salem?" Charlene asked.

"God, no. That lunch where she was bragging about

her engagement, she'd asked if I had anyone special. I'm sure I mentioned Kevin as the man I let get away and how Salem was home." Amy admired the paper ring. "I think that lunch might have been the catalyst for me to leave LA."

"That's lucky for Kevin," Kass teased.

"And me! Best decision I ever made. I was here two months when, out of the blue, into Salem Stage Right walks Madison. And who does she laser those eyes at? Neville Hampton. I think for a few days he tried to stop the attraction, but Madison was determined. And if they'd had an affair before, when she was so young? He stood no chance against her as a seductive woman."

Lindsay returned with the receipts for them to sign, then left once again.

"Wasn't she wearing that ring the day of the performance?" Charlene asked. "That emerald really dazzled in the sunlight."

"She wore it all the time." Amy frowned. "Never took it off. But . . . I don't think she had it on . . . you know, after she was. Shot." She swallowed hard as if the reality of *why* Madison had been on the lawn was too much.

"Maybe someone has it for safekeeping," Charlene suggested softly.

"I hope nobody stole it." Kass wore a worried expression. "Where is her fiancé?"

"I cornered Madison when I saw what she was up to with Neville, and she claimed that her ex had become too clingy and she'd had to leave LA. She wasn't in love with him. She'd seen my face when talking about Salem and decided to check it out for herself." Amy shrugged. "I had no idea about her and Neville's previous . . . activities. She lied and told me they'd never met."

"Did you ever meet Logan, her brother?" Charlene asked. "He's got billions, according to Google."

"Nope," Amy said. "Or her grandmother. He lives in Boston, though; I know that much. I don't think she was close to her family on this coast."

Kass lifted her phone and grinned at whatever she was reading. "Logan Boswell is gorgeous and rich in his own right. Too bad he never showed up at the theater to visit Madison—I would have wanted an introduction."

Amy held out her hand. "Let me see!"

Kass turned the phone around. Logan was cute—dark hair, dark eyes—but not Madison's eyes. His gaze held a simmering anger.

"He looks mad. What about Tyler, Madison's fiancé? Do you think he knows what happened?" Charlene asked.

"Madison's murder has been all over the news. Unless he lives under a rock, he'll know," Kass said. "Hey, should I call this Logan guy and find out if he knows the ex-fiancé?"

"You just want an excuse to talk to him." Amy tossed the origami diamond at Kass, who caught it and pretended to put it on.

Charlene's phone dinged with an incoming text. Avery, on her way, riding her bike. "Well, girls, I'd like to stay and chat, but I've got to run. It's half past one already." She dropped the receipt for lunch in the side pocket of her purse next to the rose. "We should do this again."

"For sure." Kass stood up. "I need to get back to work as well."

The three ladies waved to Sharon as they left the air-conditioned restaurant and walked out into the beautiful summer day.

Once on the sidewalk, Charlene paused and gestured to the road with her head. "There it is again. The hearse." She touched her chest. "I saw it just before noon. It must be on its return trip to Boston. I feel so bad for the family."

"Neville told us that the wake and funeral will be Tuesday and Wednesday. He'll make an announcement after the play tomorrow. He's got Jane putting together a video." Amy bit her bottom lip. "Although I'm not a big fan of Madison, I still should pay my respects. Anyone want to keep me company?"

"I'll go," Charlene told her. "Kass?"

"Wouldn't miss it for the world." Kass tucked the origami frog in one of her skirt pockets. "Thanks for confiding in us. Why did you keep it a secret that you knew her from LA?"

Amy glanced at both their faces. "I was embarrassed by her behavior, sleeping with our director . . . and like I said, we weren't friends."

"Like us," Kass said, hugging Amy, then Charlene.

"Good luck with the play if I don't see you before the opening. I really appreciate the tickets, Kass."

"No problem." Kass gestured a slender arm toward the Pedestrian Mall, where her tea shop was located. "What time will you be there, Charlene?"

She thought about her guest schedule, but most would be checked out. "Four thirty or a little after."

"I'll let Susie at will call know." Kass's long strides quickly carried her out of sight.

"Where's your car parked?" Amy asked. "I'll walk with you so we can talk some more."

"That would be nice. I've enjoyed getting to know you better."

"You have guests at your bed and breakfast right now? It must keep you busy."

"They're all out enjoying this beautiful day, but I have to get things prepared for our afternoon happy hour."

Amy chuckled. "I like the way you operate."

They took a few steps in sync down the sidewalk. Tourists thronged the path, folks reading maps as they tried to find the various sights Salem was famous for. "I've been here since September, but there are still things I haven't seen."

"Like what? Besides the playhouse," Amy teased. "You're from a real city, so don't be disappointed."

"I'll keep my expectations reasonable." She laughed. "So tell me, Amy. What's it like to fight for freedom as a colonial rebel?"

Amy's nose flared. "The muskets were heavy. Neville got permission to use actual guns from the Historical Weapons Society. I didn't mind the trousers or shirt, but the hat and gun were uncomfortable."

"Is that where you got the costumes too?"

"Jane made the ones for the colonists, but Neville had to pay a hefty retainer for the rented English officer uniforms from an outfit in New York."

"Jane, the woman who announced the play?"

"She's a Jane of all trades," Amy quipped. "She loves the theater and is a magician with makeup and costumes, but she's too shy for the stage."

Charlene remembered Danielle's treatment of Jane before the play. "Danielle runs things?"

"It's her money behind Salem Stage Right. She has final say on the business end, while Neville has it over the plays."

"Which is how he hired Madison?"

"Yes. Danielle wanted her gone, but that wasn't the deal they made, so Danielle has been more of a presence at the theater than she was before."

To keep an eye on her husband, probably. "Are you glad to be back in Salem?"

"Oh yes. The movies are so much different than acting on stage, which is what I missed while being on green screen. There's a camaraderie on stage with your fellow actors that you don't really have on movie sets."

"Why is that?"

"These days a lot of action happens in separate scenes or against a green background to be filled in later. You can do a whole movie without seeing the entire cast. In a play, depending on the length of the run, those actors become friends and family—at least, they can."

"Are you back for good?" Charlene hoped so, for Kevin's sake.

"Yeah. I've made enough to sock away. I don't live an extravagant life, but I can do it on my terms. And"—she blushed—"I missed Kevin."

"He's a great guy. Were you angry when Neville gave the part of the British officer to Madison instead of you?"

"Not so much for that piddly role. It was a just a one-time thing. I was talking about *Romeo and Juliet*—I starred in that play, and Madison was my understudy, until Neville gave it to her."

"With no reason?"

"It's his show." She averted her gaze. "I knew that if I made a fuss, I'd be out of this one, and *A Midsummer Night's Dream* is one of my very favorites."

"That doesn't seem fair."

"It wasn't, but I had no choice. I wasn't going to sleep with Neville, that's for sure." Amy tightened her jaw.

"What made it worse is Madison couldn't carry the role." She snickered. "Must admit it made me feel a whole lot better when she fell flat."

"Amy!"

The actress crossed her arms. "What? I'm not a saint, but she was no sweetheart either. I'm not a good enough actress to pretend that I liked her. She was evil, and that's the truth." Amy stormed off.

Charlene felt bad that the conversation had turned sour, but she couldn't do anything about it. It was already quarter till two. She hurried to her car and carefully, but quickly, drove home.

She parked in the driveway in front of the house and waved to Avery, who'd ridden her bike from teen house. Avery had leaned the bike against the far side of the porch and was sitting on one of the Adirondack chairs.

"Hi! Sorry I'm late," Charlene said.

"You aren't." Avery ruffled her dyed pink spiky hair, long tan legs in shorts. She pulled her phone from the pocket. "Two on the nose."

"Well, that was a miracle then. I can't believe how crowded the roads are with tourists."

"I wear my helmet when I ride, believe me."

Charlene opened the front door, and the two went inside.

She glanced at Avery. Her guests would all be checked out by tomorrow at one. A couple from California was due in at noon. "Have you ever been to the theater?"

"No." Avery twisted her mouth in a *no, thanks* kind of way. "Why are you asking?"

"You don't want to broaden your horizons?" Charlene teased.

"What horizons?" she scorned. "What are you going to see?"

"*A Midsummer Night's Dream.*"

"Sounds awful. You trying to give me your ticket?"

"No, it's Shakespeare, and I was hoping you'd like to join me. I have two tickets at my disposal."

"You're desperate for a date," Avery decided. "Fine. I'll go. Do they sell ice cream or popcorn at the theater? If so, you're buying."

Charlene ducked her head, finding Avery very amusing. "If they don't, I promise to buy you some once it's over."

"Deal."

CHAPTER EIGHT

Charlene and Avery were greeted by a friendly feline in the foyer. Silva rubbed her silky body against Avery's bare legs, making it impossible to move forward without some immediate attention.

"Hey, sweet girl. Did you miss me?" Avery scratched behind Silva's ears and got a rough-tongue kiss in return. "I guess that means you did, right?"

Silva purred, gazing up at the teenager with luminous golden eyes before daintily parading to her dish, where she waited expectantly. Avery removed a jar of tuna-flavored cat treats from the cupboard and shook five into her dish. Silva, immobile, just stared at the jar until Avery laughed and gave her more.

"That cat is so spoiled." Charlene smiled indulgently as she leaned her hip against the kitchen counter. "Silva practically runs the house." Which made her think of the yard and the bell Jack had suggested to save the wildlife from extinction. Charlene quickly jotted a reminder down on the notepad by the fridge.

"Practically?" Avery snickered. "She's the boss and knows it. Aren't you, baby?" she cooed.

Charlene's heart melted as the cat preened and pranced. "Can you imagine if Silva was in charge of the shopping? Nothing but tuna fish, and not the sushi grade."

"Yuck." Avery made a face as she washed her hands in the kitchen sink and dried them on a paper towel. "What do you have for me today?"

"I already did the vacuuming, but if you could dust the furniture downstairs, that would be a great start—oh, and the hall tables on the second floor."

"Your home is always spotless, Charlene." Avery retrieved the polish and dust cloth from beneath the sink.

"Because somehow, between you, me, and Minnie, we stay on top of it. If a week went by without dusting?" Charlene used her thumb and forefinger to show an inch. "It'd be piled up like a dirty snowdrift."

"Can't have that," Avery joked as she stuck in one hot-pink earbud, the other loose down her shirt front. "Do you still have a full house?"

"Yep. The O'Reillys leave tomorrow—they're out on a boat cruise in Marblehead. It's such a perfect day to see the sights. They should be back in time for happy hour, though."

"I can help, if you want—last week I showed Janet how to do the dip you made, with chicken breast and mayo?" She patted her flat stomach.

Janet was the house mom where Avery and the other teens lived. So patient she was practically a saint. "Easy but delicious." Charlene's preferred cooking style.

"I thought you had a checkout today?"

Sometimes people left tips in their rooms, and Charlene put the cash in a special jar to be split between Avery, Minnie, and Charlene once a week. "Michelle decided to stay another night."

"Cool." Avery tossed the can of furniture polish from one hand to the other. "What does she do?"

Since this was Avery's last year of high school, what to do with her life afterward was a constant topic of conversation. "She's a traveling nurse."

"I don't know if I'd like to be a nurse. Being around sick people all the time would be kind of sad. Of course, there's always a chance to meet a hot doctor." Avery swung the dust cloth over her shoulder. "Did you ever watch *Grey's Anatomy*? Me and Janet were both bonkers over McDreamy."

Charlene recognized the nickname for the handsome star, Patrick Dempsey. "I remember that series! Everyone was sleeping with everyone else. How did they ever save any lives?" She frowned. "Didn't they kill that character off? Derek Shepherd, neurosurgeon—he was one of my favorites."

"Yeah, that sucked. But life goes on—and I better get to work before you fire me."

Charlene crossed her arms and arched her brow for a double whammy denial. "As if I would."

Avery gave her a cheeky military salute and then ran up the flight of stairs. Silva sprinted after her dangling earbud. Laughing at the girl's antics and her high-and-mighty cat, Charlene went into her suite of rooms. Jack was at her desk, busy on the computer. He turned to greet her with his gorgeous smile.

"Charlene! It's good to hear you laughing—I heard Avery too."

"Avery is a constant reminder to not take myself too seriously." Charlene moved toward him. "I was hoping you'd be here." She reached for his shoulder, then stopped short. His essence was freezer-burn cold when she actually managed to touch him—most times her hand went straight through.

"Guess what I found out?"

He was smart, he was dedicated, and he'd been searching the internet for hours. "You know who the shooter is!"

"No." He chuckled. "Not yet. But I have some information on Madison's brother, Logan."

Charlene rubbed her hands together. "Oh, do tell me."

She sat down on the love seat facing Jack at the computer. His knee-length cream-colored shorts showed off his well-shaped legs, slightly tanned, and brown sandals. The blue linen camp shirt, open at the neck, brought out the dazzling turquoise of his eyes.

"You're so handsome, Jack." She appreciated the effort he went to day after day to dress for her. His dark hair was slightly longer than usual, touching his collar, a lock falling over his forehead as he leaned forward, hands clamped over his knee.

"Thank you." He half smiled at her.

She wished she had a magic wand to make him real. *Not going to happen*. Clearing her throat, she asked, "So, what did you find on Logan? Were he and Madison on good terms?"

"I found a few articles dating back to his college days. Logan Boswell was set to follow in his father's footsteps, but then they had a falling-out, and Logan split away from the family business to work at a rival investment company. He's doing very well, already a billionaire at thirty, without Dad's money. There's an interview he gave where he credits his cutthroat upbringing for his success."

Charlene fluffed a cushion on the love seat and put it behind her back. "What did they fight about?"

"I couldn't find anything specific, but the final blow seemed to happen during his sophomore year of college."

"Did Madison go along with her parents' decision to cut him from the family?"

"Don't know." Jack propped his elbow on the desk. "The article didn't mention their sibling relationship, only that he had a sister in California. Maybe they were close behind Mom and Dad's back?"

"It's possible." She brought the afghan over her lap. "Madison lived with her grandmother in Beverly Hills. Grandma died, leaving Madison some money."

"What did Madison do exactly?"

"Amy told me at lunch that she and Madison knew each other in LA. Madison was determined to be an actress, both stage and screen, but wasn't good enough. She had a contract with a cosmetic company and sold mascara—I mean, her eyes were mesmerizing. Use your assets, right?"

Jack chuckled. "It sounds like success. Why quit?"

"I don't know." Charlene smoothed the soft fleece over her knee. "I don't understand why Madison returned to the East Coast. And specifically Salem, not Boston." At least Boston had prestige as a bustling city, but it was night and day to LA.

"Was the fiancé another actor? Seems crazy to ditch a career over a breakup." Jack telepathically snugged the blanket closer to Charlene. "Want your sweater?"

"No, thank you." Jack's chill was a price she was happy to pay for his company. "Tyler was a very successful *agent* to the stars. Maybe that wasn't prestigious enough for her? From what I've learned about Madison, she wanted fame. To be a star. Amy was shocked when Madison showed up at Salem Stage Right. Then to hook up with Neville? Possibly for the second time?"

"Could be that Madison had so much money she didn't need it. If what Logan said in his article is true, and his upbringing was cutthroat, it stands to reason that Madison was raised the same way."

"So she would be motivated by accolades, not cash?" Charlene thought that made sense. "How nice if Madison's death brought the family together again."

"Searching for the silver lining?" Jack asked, flashing his dimple at her.

Charlene's cheeks heated. "It's a tragic waste of a life. If I were those parents, I would want my other child at my side."

"What if one of them did it?"

"Jack! Why? They have billions."

"Which is nothing to a billionaire. Money is always a motivating factor." Jack snapped his fingers without sound. "Did you get tickets for the play tomorrow?"

"I scored! Kass was at lunch today and offered me two tickets. The cast and crew get them for free for family and friends, so I'll make a generous donation on behalf of 'Charlene's.'"

"Two? I wish I could go with you. Who did you invite?" Jack's form quivered out of focus. "Not Sam, I hope."

She waved her hand. "No. I'm taking Avery."

He solidified. "It'll be a great experience for her. I

loved the theater, and Shakespeare never gets old. Always see something new in every show."

Charlene smiled at his enthusiasm. "I'm happy to record it for you."

"That's not necessary. I'm still going through the video from yesterday. I just feel like we're missing something."

"Michelle took some pictures from that morning that might be helpful. She was going to give them to Sam. I hope she got two copies."

A knock sounded at the door.

"I better go." She removed the blanket and folded it, placing the fleece on the arm of the love seat.

"I'll be here—still want me to focus on Logan?"

"Yes, please." Charlene rose. "And see what you can find about Priscilla Phipps's wealth—was it evenly distributed after her death?"

Jack straightened. "You know, the Boswell family is old-school Episcopalian and prominent in Boston. They'll have a big funeral."

She nodded, making a mental note to tell him about her being invited to go with Kass and Amy to the funeral. Charlene opened the door to see Avery, dust cloth in hand, poised to knock again. "Hey, hon! Are you done already?" She checked her watch—three? Sheesh.

"Got all the dusting in the upstairs hall and downstairs. What next?"

Charlene followed Avery to the kitchen as the teen put the cleaning supplies away. "Did you get the mirror over the dining room table?"

"Yep."

"You ready to polish the silver?"

"Ha ha—not."

It was a running joke between them, as it was one of the first things Avery had asked her after seeing the outside of the house. "Want to help me make crab cakes?"

"Ooh, yeah. Can I have one?" Her phone and earbuds disappeared into her back pocket.

"Of course. A cook must always taste-test their food."

"Cool. Bet they're delicious."

"You've never had one?"

"They don't serve fancy crab cakes at teen house. Spaghetti, mac and cheese, beef stroganoff." Avery wore a goofy grin, but Charlene still felt a pang, knowing what a hard life she'd lived.

"I'm not the world's greatest cook, but I can follow a recipe, and I like being in the kitchen, creating. You can be my sous chef." She pulled two aprons from a drawer and handed one to Avery.

"Me and Janet love the cooking shows, but some of the steps seem very complicated." Avery tied on her Kiss the Cook apron.

Charlene, in a boring picnic-plaid apron, showed Avery the list Minnie had left for her. "Easy to follow, I promise."

They tackled the crab cakes first, then spinach and feta puff pastries. By four thirty, Avery set the timer on the oven for the mini quiches and teriyaki chicken wings.

"It smells so good," Avery said.

"It does!" Tim waved from the foyer but went directly up the steps toward his room, carrying a shopping bag.

Charlene and Avery exchanged smiles. "While we wait, why don't you make sure that the plates and napkins are ready for happy hour?"

Avery hurried off as Michelle arrived at the house. The plump nurse had her camera bag over her shoulder and joined Charlene in the kitchen.

"Hi, Michelle! How's it going?"

"Great. Wish I didn't have to leave tomorrow, but I've got friends to meet up the coast. I had no idea there would be so much to do around Salem."

"Then you will have to come again. Can I get you something to drink? We're about set up for snacks."

"I can wait." Michelle took out a packet from the drug-store. "I dropped a set of photos off with Sam."

"That's good—was he able to use them?"

"I didn't stay—he was busy. I thought you might want to look at them too? You're from the area and will understand them more than I."

"I'd love to." Charlene pulled the photos free from the paper pouch. It had been a while since she'd held actual pictures—most things were digital these days. "Thanks."

Jack appeared behind her in a whoosh. "Looks like we're in business."

"I snapped about twenty of the stage and bandstand." Michelle shrugged and stood where Jack was, then stepped back with a shiver. Jack disappeared.

"These are terrific—nice composition." Charlene placed them next to each other on the kitchen table. Was there a connection? A clue that she could find to help nab Madison's killer?

"I completed a photography course last summer. It's a hobby of mine."

There weren't many photos of people, and the ones that had been captured were the actors. Her hopes of finding Logan in the crowd dimmed. Thanks to Kass, at least she knew what he looked like.

"Do you remember Madison wearing a ring, Michelle? She had one on at the beginning of the show . . ."

The nurse tapped her lower lip. "Nothing on her hands or wrists. In the ER it's automatic to search for a medical alert bracelet, or a wedding ring."

The front door opened as Jackie and Angela returned, laughing and talking so fast that it was impossible to understand what they were saying.

"Do you mind if I do this later?" Charlene asked, torn between her duty and her desire to help.

"No—I should have gotten another set." Michelle stacked them together but left them on the kitchen table.

"Thanks. I'll return them before you leave in the morning."

"Okay. I'll be out early—by nine."

Jackie called hello from the foyer, and Charlene joined them as Avery asked where they'd gone.

"Plymouth," Angela said, setting down her shopping bags of souvenirs.

"I'm not the history buff Angela is, but the seaside town is charming—made me want to paint." Jackie elbowed her friend. "We saw the Mayflower Society House and library as well as the Pilgrim Hall Museum."

"The spiel on the origin of the rock was enlightening," Angela said. "I learned quite a few things I hadn't known."

"But the rock itself is slightly underwhelming." Jackie tossed her blond hair back. "You have to admit that, Ange."

"Yes—but it was the beginning of our nation," Angela exclaimed. "Have you seen it, Avery?"

"School field trips. I'm with Jackie." Avery squeezed her finger and thumb together. "It's a little rock."

Angela clasped her hands before her and adopted a dreamy tone as she said, "The Pilgrims were simple men and women who risked their lives on the *Mayflower*, leaving their homes behind to carve out a new life in America—that's just so brave. This small rock was a stepping-stone for the beginning of our great nation."

Avery and Jackie grinned at one another. Michelle chuckled from her spot at the foot of the stairs.

"It was certainly well worth a visit," Angela declared self-consciously.

"I'd like to see the rock too." It was on Charlene's list, but farther down until she had free time. She hadn't even hit Boston's highlights yet.

"The park is lovely, and the town is right on the water—adorable boutiques." Jackie lifted her own shopping bag.

Angela sniffed the air. "What are you cooking, Charlene? It smells wonderful."

"Avery and I put together some crab cakes and other snacks for happy hour."

"We have a dinner reservation at seven," Jackie told her. "At Finz. We've got to have our lobster before we leave."

"We'll go light on the appetizers," Angela said regretfully. "But you had me at crab cakes."

"We barely ate lunch." Jackie shrugged. "I plan on eating till I burst. I can diet tomorrow."

"Excellent. The O'Reillys will be back anytime." Charlene gestured toward the living room. "We'll serve around five."

"Good. That'll give us both time to shower and dress," Angela said. "Charlene, you do such a wonderful job here—we'll be sure to recommend it highly."

"Thanks. That means a lot." Charlene untied her apron. "We have plenty of food, so take your time and come down when you're ready."

The ladies all headed upstairs. Avery gave Charlene a hug. "Thanks for including me. I didn't do much."

"You helped! You deserve the credit as sous chef. Would you mind setting the oven to three hundred so we can warm up the crab cakes? We'll cover them in foil and in fifteen minutes they should be perfect."

Avery got the foil from the pantry.

"I'll be back in a sec." Charlene picked up the package of photos and brought them to her room, where Jack was at the computer. "Jack. Here's Michelle's photos. Good luck!"

"I'll need it. My eyes are crossing."

When she returned a minute later, Avery had put mitts on and slid the baking tray into the warm oven. "They look perfect," she said wistfully.

"Why don't you wash up—we'll be serving soon. I'll make a plate for you, okay?"

"You're the best, Charlene."

Charlene was surprised by the ping of emotion that brought. This young lady had worked her way into Charlene's heart.

The O'Reillys burst through the door, all high spirits as the kids teased each other. "Hi, Charlene," Martin said. He smiled at Avery. "Hello, I'm Martin, my wife is Judith, and these rascals are Aaron and Shannon."

"Pleased to meet you," she said. "I'm Avery."

"I just wanted to say that we had a splendid day at Marblehead. Charlene, if you haven't visited it yet, I highly recommend it. It's well worth a trip."

"I still have so much to explore! I can't wait to hear all

about it over drinks. One day when I have time, I'd love to do more of the local sights. Running the B and B keeps me pretty busy and close to home. How about you, Avery?"

"I went on my share of field trips when Mom signed the permission slips." She ducked her head down.

Charlene wondered how many Avery's mom had forgotten to sign. "Well, when I get a chance to visit, I'll bring you with me, if you want."

"Yeah . . . okay. If I'm not busy."

Shannon shyly studied the teenage girl. "You're pretty. I like your hair."

"Thank you." Avery blushed. "Do kids at your school have a style like this?"

Shannon shook her head no.

Aaron laughed. "I go to a boys-only school—they wouldn't be caught dead with pink hair." He stepped toward her. "Can I see your tattoo?"

"Sure. It's a spider." Avery turned around and lifted her short hair. The spider was done in dark-blue ink in thin, feminine lines.

"Cool!" Aaron said.

"Don't even think about it," Martin told his son.

Aaron stepped back in disappointment. "Everybody has tattoos."

"Mom, can I dye my hair?" Shannon pulled at her mother's sleeve.

"Maybe when you're older." Judith winked at Avery. "Right now, let's get cleaned up, and then we'll be down for drinks. I'm ready for some sherry."

Avery dashed into the kitchen as the O'Reillys climbed the stairs. Charlene went into the living room, where Tim relaxed in Jack's favorite chair with a glass of wine.

"I'll be leaving late tomorrow, if that's okay with you? My flight home isn't until five."

Which meant he'd need to leave about three. "That's fine." That gave her plenty of time to get ready for the theater and the couple checking in from California. She glanced at his wineglass. "Ready for a refill? Everyone is back now and will be descending on us soon."

"Okay. Will you join me?"

"Love to." She took his glass to the sideboard and topped it off with white wine, pouring one for herself. "In spite of the disastrous Fourth of July, I hope you've enjoyed your visit?"

"It's been very informative."

What did he mean by that? She stood before him, and they clinked glasses in a mutual toast.

"Charlene?" Avery called from the threshold. "We're ready."

She couldn't find out more just yet, but Tim looked like the cat that ate the canary.

"Let me help Avery bring in the food, and then I want to hear all about your stay."

She and Avery set the wings, quiches, and crab cakes—Avery loved them so much she had two—on the long, narrow serving table set against the wall. Round appetizer plates were stacked next to napkins and silverware. The tea cart with bottles of wine, and sherry for Judith, was between the yellow-patterned sofa and two plush brocade chairs.

The scent of food attracted the guests better than a dinner bell, and they all descended the wide staircase and entered the living room. Charlene and Avery made sure that everyone had nibbles and drinks, then helped them find seats.

Tim tapped his fork on his glass to command the attention of Charlene and her guests. "Last night, Michelle and I were at the bar at the Hawthorne Hotel. She returned to the B and B, but I stayed to listen to the band. The cast members of the play arrived and sat at the tables next to my bar stool at the counter." His voice quivered with excitement. "I overheard them discussing the murder we all witnessed."

Charlene's ears perked.

Martin and Judith exchanged a parental glance, then eyed their children.

Tim casually crossed one leg over the other as he delivered his bombshell. "Do you know some of them believe that Madison was a witch?"

Michelle, Jackie, and Angela murmured surprise.

"Witches aren't real, sweetheart," Judith said, her arm around Shannon's shoulder.

"They are too!" Aaron argued.

Tim seemed to realize the mixed age of his audience and sipped his wine before continuing. "Madison was very *close* to the producer, Neville Hampton."

Charlene nodded. The affair was out of the bag, if it had ever been a secret. "Was Neville Hampton there?"

"He was—so, I bought the actors a round, complimenting them, and commiserating too."

Nice move to loosen them up, Charlene thought. "Was Danielle there?"

"No." Tim grinned. "Which meant that Neville was free to flirt with the other actresses, waitresses, and guests of the hotel—and he did."

"Madison was bad enough. Now you're saying he's a ladies' man?" Michelle turned her nose up. "What a pig."

Tim smoothed his hand over his graying hair, quite

pleased to deliver such juicy gossip. "After a few drinks, I wondered aloud how they'd get along without their star, and that's when Neville really lost his cool. Pounded the table, spilled his beer."

"I'm sorry I missed this. Wish I'd stayed!" Michelle said. She bit into her half-dollar-sized quiche.

"Does he think she's a . . . you know . . ." Angela asked, her gaze on the kids.

"Neville told me that he believes he was under some kind of spell." Tim lowered his voice. "And it wasn't the first time she'd made him behave out of character, if you know what I mean."

Charlene didn't share what she'd learned today. She wondered how this mediocre actress managed to entice a very married man and father of two, within days of her moving to Salem. He'd already broken Madison's chains once; how could he go back? Were they some kind of aging Romeo and Juliet—and had Neville decided it was till death do them part?

"I can't understand why he'd take a chance of ruining his life and marriage over an affair." Charlene sipped her wine.

"Don't know, but the path of true love never runs smooth." Tim lifted his glass and peered inside as if searching for the truth. "He was teary-eyed and weaving a bit, but he said that his wife told him to *get rid* of Madison, or she'd take the children and leave. When he tried to break it off, Madison had refused to go. I guess she had this special way of looking at him that made him weak. He got physically sick whenever he brought it up."

Get rid of?

Had Madison pushed too hard with her beguiling power? Had Neville snapped and hired someone to shoot Madison in plain sight—where he clearly had an alibi, as he'd been on stage?

Neville had a very compelling reason to want Madison gone, especially if she'd used her hypnotherapy to make him ill.

"What an unlikable twosome! That dashing Neville is not so handsome to me anymore," Angela said.

The ladies quickly agreed, and Charlene brought the bottle of wine around to top off glasses, while Avery helped Shannon and Aaron get more lemonade.

Charlene would love an opportunity to speak to Neville about his affair with Madison—without Danielle around. She might learn more from his manner and his omissions than what he would divulge outright.

CHAPTER NINE

Charlene walked out to the front porch with Avery at six, the happy hour still in full swing. "Ride your bike carefully going home. I'll pick you up tomorrow at four thirty for our date to the theater." She applied a posh English accent to make it sound like *thee-ah-tah* and was rewarded with Avery's laugh.

"Do I have to dress fancy?"

"Not for here—a sundress will be fine."

"I'm hanging out tonight with my friend Tiffany to watch movies. I'll see if she has something I can borrow."

"That sounds like fun—but don't worry. This is Salem. Anything goes."

"It's a plus for living here, that's for sure." Avery strapped on her bright green helmet and rode off with a wave.

Charlene watched until the teen reached the end of the

driveway and turned left, out of sight, before going back inside her house.

When she returned, the O'Reillys were sharing pictures of their boat tour adventure. The subject of the shooting had been put to rest as there was no real news after Tim's bombshell announcement that Danielle had told Neville to get rid of Madison, but that he was under the actress's spell and *physically* couldn't.

Jackie and Angela sat next to each other on the sofa, their wineglasses empty. "Tim, how did you end up here this weekend? In Salem, I mean?" Jackie leaned toward him. "You don't seem the type to believe in witchcraft or haunted houses. What was the draw?"

"You're right about that. I don't believe in all that craziness. I was at the Belmont checkin' out a new filly on the first of July. I've got an eager buyer in Kentucky who wants to add to his stable."

"That's exciting. What did you think of the horse?" Michelle asked. "I've never been to a big race."

"I told my buyer she was the best li'l filly I'd seen in years." He deepened his Southern drawl.

"So it seems you made a sale." Jackie smiled. "Good for you, Tim."

"It's my job, which I hope I'm good at after thirty years." His chest puffed under the ladies' attention. "As far as Salem goes, a friend of mine suggested it for the air show. My grandfather was a pilot at the coast guard base on Winter Island."

Angela's museum-curator side arose, and she straightened as she recited facts better than an encyclopedia. ". . . and the last year of operation was 1970."

He pulled at his chin in amusement. "That's true. I read that in one of Charlene's books."

Jackie gently elbowed her friend. "Angela reads something once and retains it forever."

They all laughed. "Not me," Tim said. "These days I find myself in a room and wonder what I was looking for by the time I get there."

"That's more me," Jackie agreed. "I blame my creative side."

Angela rested her glass on her knee. "Winter Island is supposed to have a very nice campground and park."

"I'll have to check it out." Charlene wasn't into air shows, having witnessed a horrifying crash at one with Jared. The memory had stayed with her for a long time, and she'd avoided them ever since.

Tim gave his smooth chin another tug. "New York isn't far, so I decided to take a few days and see what Salem is all about. Hotels were all booked up. Sure was glad to find 'Charlene's.'"

"I bet," Jack said in her ear, bringing goose bumps with him. She shivered and rubbed her arms.

Jackie narrowed her eyes and stared in Jack's direction. "I think your air-conditioning just kicked on."

Charlene reached for the ladies' wineglasses. "Can I get you another?"

"No, we're ready for dinner." Angela's phone dinged. "That should be our ride now."

Jackie lifted the strap of her purse over her shoulder, the leather bag bulging with various treasures and the brochure for Finz poking up. "This is our last night, so we might be late." She laughed. "*Very* late."

After a hurried goodbye, the friends left, leaving Tim, who had a reservation at a swank seafood restaurant, waiting for his cab with Michelle, who'd decided to join him.

"Would you like me to top off your wines?" Charlene asked.

"Sure, thanks. Our reservation is at seven thirty." Tim checked his watch. "The car will be here in a half hour."

"I'll go freshen up," Michelle said.

Charlene refilled Tim's glass and returned it. Martin stole the opportunity to snag the couch and leaned back. He and Tim started in on a previous topic about horses and betting on the races at Leopardstown, or the seven-day festival in Galway.

"What are your plans for this evening?" Charlene asked Judith, who was doing a puzzle with Shannon while Aaron played his video game.

"Lobster rolls at the pier and then a movie, before or after stargazing on your widow's walk." Judith lifted her head from the joint project. "Is that all right?"

"Sure." Charlene gestured to the parlor area. "There's a TV and DVDs. Make yourself at home. You can bring a movie up to your suite as well."

By half past seven, Charlene's house was empty again, except for her, Jack, and Silva. She made a light dinner of leftovers, poured a glass of her special Flint Wineries summer blend, and sat before her laptop.

"Did you find anything interesting?" Charlene leafed through Michelle's photos as she questioned her room-mate.

Jack pointed at one. "See this? A shadow just inside the bandstand." Sheets of plastic and caution tape surrounded the right-hand side of the structure, and a rope of chain with a Do Not Enter sign closed off the entrance. Anybody could have walked over it—it was a suggestion, really.

"Is that the shape of a person?" Charlene squinted at the picture. *Could be hair, maybe . . .*

"It's hard to make out. I wish we had something concrete. Like a full face with contact information."

"Funny." Charlene sighed. "It's impossible to make this photo bigger. Let's see if we can find that same shot on the video I recorded."

It took a while, but she captured the bandstand. Despite the crowd of people in the Common, nobody was inside it because it was being refurbished. She enlarged the video image and put it next to the photo. "There is definitely something different in the picture Michelle got."

Jack hovered over her shoulder. "Stop! Is that Logan Boswell in the crowd?"

She lifted her finger off the button of her phone and rewound, frame by frame. "You're good at this, Jack!" She studied Logan's facial structure—handsome. Refined. Very well dressed and out of place in Salem Common. "Logan lives in Boston and will be at the funeral. I'd sure like to meet him before then."

"Maybe he'll show up at the theater tomorrow to support the benefit for his sister?"

"That would be too lucky. You know, Madison said that her fiancé was an agent in LA. Tyler. How many could there be?"

"Type in Tyler, talent agent," Jack suggested.

She tried Tyler, agent, California, into the search bar. "There are five of them," she groaned to Jack.

Jack crossed his arms from where he read over her shoulder. "I think you can nix the sixty-five-year-old in Yreka."

Which left four. Smith. Holloran. Cooke. "Here's San Fran—wrong part of the coast."

She scrolled until she recognized the blue eyes. Tyler Lawson Agency for the Stars. "You've got to be kidding me—what are the chances of the guy dumping a Frappuccino on me that day being Tyler Lawson, Madison's ex-fiancé?" Charlene sat back with a sick feeling. Had Madison invited him, or had Tyler tracked her down?

Jack's image wavered to her right. "He was here in Salem?"

Charlene rose from her chair and paced behind the love seat. "Yeah—see what I mean about how much he looks like Leo DiCaprio?"

When she turned to see his answer, Jack was gone.

Had they been pushing his energy too far? What happened if he used it all? Charlene couldn't think about that and fired up the video, fast-forwarding to the crowd, where she then put it on slow motion.

There was the bandstand.

There were the food vendors.

She found Logan in the crowd and then widened her search for the mysterious Tyler—she'd had no idea who he was. She owed him a thank-you for buying her lemonade.

Charlene sat forward and zoomed in as close as she could, making the man's features a blur—but that shirt she recognized, blousy over white pants. Ray-Bans, Rolex—Tyler. He stood near Logan, who wore plaid golf shorts and a polo, with a lightweight beige vest that had a lot of pockets—was that a fashion statement? She scanned the physical distance between the two men. Two feet. Maybe three. It could go either way—friends or strangers.

Did they know each other? It was possible that Logan, friends with Madison behind their parents' backs, knew about her fiancé, Tyler. Charlene copied down Tyler's business phone number, since his personal number wasn't listed.

Her phone rang, and she jumped. "Charlene's."

"I was wondering if you had a room available for September tenth? We're driving in from New York."

She turned back to her laptop and got down to business. "Of course. Can I get your name?"

Charlene dressed casually for the local theater production of a *A Midsummer Night's Dream* in a sleeveless floral-print sundress and low-heeled sandals. She carried a shawl in case the theater was cold. Her plan yesterday had been to go early to the theater, with cookies, to talk to the people behind the scenes; but with the extra guests to check in and the stream of guests checking out, she'd had to wait.

She'd texted Amy to let her know that she was bringing Avery and to ask about going backstage. She would apologize for being too pushy in person when she saw her friend.

Avery was waiting outside with Janet when Charlene arrived at four fifteen.

Parking the Pilot, Charlene got out to speak with Janet for a minute. "Who is this gorgeous lady?" she teased.

Avery smiled shyly and touched her pink mouth. "Too much?" Her short, flouncy skirt and pink T-shirt matched her hair—the spikes had been tamed into crimped waves.

Charlene blinked her eyes clear at the effort Avery had gone to. "You look perfect."

"Janet helped."

Janet shuffled on the lawn before the house, blue toe-nails visible in her flip-flops. Shorts and a tank top completed her summer ensemble. "My pleasure. Let me know how the play is. I might want to take some of the other kids."

"Sophie's in drama class," Avery said quickly. She held a light pink clutch with a thin silver strap. "That's all she talks about."

Charlene jiggled her keys. "You ready?"

"Yes!"

"Bye, Janet." Charlene got behind the wheel and turned to Avery, who was buckling her seat belt. "Are you familiar with the play at all?"

"Me and Janet read about it on Wikipedia so I wasn't totally lost," she said with a nose-crinkle.

"Smart! So, fill me in on the way. I saw it many years ago, but my memory is rusty."

"Okay—this duke wants to marry the queen of the Amazons. She's got a funny name, Hippo, Hippa?"

"Hippolyta."

"Yeah. Anyway, they're going to get married, and they're having a big party, right? There's a girl named Hermia—I only remembered because it's like Hermione from *Harry Potter*—and she has two boyfriends. Her dad wants her to marry one, but she's in love with the other guy; I can't remember *their* names."

"I'm impressed. But don't worry—most places hand out a program so you know who the actors are, and we can follow along."

"You've probably been to a ton of plays," she said.

"Not really—I like movies better. But I did see a few great productions in Chicago. *Les Mis*, *Phantom*, and when I was ten, my parents took me to Radio City Music Hall in New York to see the Rockettes."

"That sounds pretty cool."

"Hey, I almost forgot. What movies did you see last night?"

Her eyes widened. "Charlene, when I told my friend Tiff that we were going to the play because of the dead girl, she told me about a movie called *Ghost Light*—have you seen it? It's hysterical but sort of scary. It's a spoof."

"About what?"

"Every theater is supposed to have a ghost light."

"What is that?" Charlene pulled into the lot of the historic two-story brick building.

"It's to find the ghosts before they find you!" Avery curled her fingers toward Charlene. "Bwahahaha."

Her old response would have been that ghosts weren't real. Now she knew better. "What happens if they don't have the light?"

"There's a curse. Everybody is going to die." Avery fake-groaned like a ghoul as she collapsed against her seat.

"All the actors?" She darted a quick peek at Avery to see if she was actually scared or playing it up.

"And some of the audience. We stayed up way late watching it at my house—she slept over; otherwise, I wouldn't have made curfew, but Janet's awesome."

"That she is. But you know that's just a scary movie, right? No need for a ghost light. We'll be safe." She turned off the engine and pulled the keys from the ignition. "Are you ready for Shakespeare?"

"Yeah, but if it's really bad? I want to leave during intermission and go for that ice cream you promised. Two scoops. Is that a deal?"

"You have very low expectations," Charlene said as they walked toward the front entrance. "Just you wait!"

Salem Stage Right was printed in old-fashioned letters across the top of the door. Amy hadn't texted her back about the backstage visit.

Charlene opened the door, and a musty old-building smell escaped.

Avery waved her hand beneath her nose. About a dozen folks milled in the lobby, but nobody that Charlene recognized.

"This way." Charlene headed toward the window that read WILL CALL.

"This is cool," Avery said in a wide-eyed hush as she took in the old Broadway show posters framed in gilt on all the walls. Mirrors gave the room depth and made it seem bigger than it was.

Danielle Hampton, impeccable in a navy dress, sat behind the window.

"Mrs. Hampton!" Charlene recalled the last time she'd seen Danielle, arguing with Neville in their tent.

The woman's eyes went icy cold, making Charlene shiver and toss her wrap over her shoulders.

"Our regular girl quit this morning. Scared silly, foolish thing, all due to a broken lamp. So here I am, doling out tickets when I have box seats waiting."

"Sorry to hear that. I'm Charlene Morris. Kass Fortune reserved two tickets for me?"

Danielle's brow lifted as she tried to place Charlene. "Free tickets you mean? This is supposed to raise money for an actors fund in Madison's name." Her nostrils flared as she said *Madison*.

"I'm donating to the cause." Charlene handed over a business check for one hundred dollars.

"Thank you. Would you like to purchase a program? Ten bucks, but a great souvenir for your daughter."

"We'll take two." She didn't correct Danielle's impression as she paid and handed a playbill to Avery.

Danielle softened a little as she spoke to Avery. "You can get autographs afterward if you want."

"Thanks." Avery clutched it to her chest.

Danielle's chin went up as she studied Charlene. "You seem so familiar."

"From Fourth of July," Charlene said softly, not wanting to bring up the murder in this setting.

"That's right. You were in the crowd at *Salem's Rebels*." Danielle's lips tightened into a thin red line. "You wouldn't think that finding a shooter in the middle of Salem Common during the day would be so difficult, now would you?"

Her sarcasm could melt iron.

"No. I had my video camera, as did so many others. I'm sure it's just a matter of time before the person is caught." Charlene glanced behind her, but there was no one else in line. "Thank you for the tickets. I hope you get to see the play."

"I've seen it more times than I can count."

Avery stepped up to the window. "Do you have a ghost light?" she asked brightly—innocently.

Danielle's mouth twisted. "Of course—that is what went out overnight and why that twit Susie quit." She made a sweeping gesture with her hand to encompass the whole building and gritted out, "I dare Madison to haunt this place. I'd buy some sage and burn this theater down. Good riddance."

CHAPTER TEN

After finding their seats, Charlene and Avery only had a few minutes to check out the audience before the lights went down and the orchestra began to play. "There's Alice!"

She and Avery waved to the director of Felicity House for Children, where the younger kids in need of adoption lived. Charlene had been working with Alice and her staff on an awareness campaign for funds over the past six months, and it had been through Alice and Felicity House that Charlene had met Avery.

The small theater, built in the eighteen hundreds but renovated a few times over the years, maintained the authentic mood and ambiance of a quaint, cozy playhouse. The orchestra below the stage consisted of six people: four playing strings, one a piano, and the other had a harp twice as big as she was.

A purple velvet curtain that had to be as old as the theater itself remained closed, but Charlene and Avery heard the rustling sound of movement from behind the fabric as the actors took their positions.

"This is exciting, isn't it?"

Avery nodded, on the edge of her chair.

Four box seats overlooked the stage like balconies, two on the right, and two on the left. Danielle and two children sat in one, and across on the other side she noticed Brandy and her mother, Evelyn Flint, with a handsome man by her side. Charlene recognized their good friend Lucas Evergreen, who owned the witchcraft bookstore in town.

Both women would be striking even wearing brown sacks, but they were dressed more in keeping with an opening night on Broadway than a small local production. The gentleman wore a formal dark suit, Evelyn a maroon silk dress that complimented her silver shoulder-length hair, and Brandy was stunning with her auburn hair falling in waves down her low-cut—front and back—fitted dress. Where was Theo Rowlings, Brandy's lover?

"Who's that?" Avery asked.

"The two ladies own Flint's Vineyard, where I buy my house wine. We're on friendly terms, at least most of the time"—she laughed—"and I'd like to keep it that way."

"Wow. They're knockouts. Kinda dressed up, aren't they?"

"They like to make a statement everywhere they go. Even Danielle Hampton can't take her eyes off them." She squeezed Avery's hand. "She was certainly in a mood this evening, wasn't she?"

"If I were Madison and somebody killed me, I'd haunt

the theater just to get even. Besides, I think it would be fun to be a ghost and float around scaring people." Avery turned toward the stage as the curtains began to open, then whipped her head around and said, "Boo!" in Charlene's face.

A startled burst of laughter from Charlene had people putting their fingers to their lips and shushing her. She had to cover her mouth to smother a fit of giggles. "Behave," she whispered to Avery, who couldn't stop laughing. Luckily, the music covered their mirth. The stage had transformed into a green forest with fairies in the trees, teasing each other as they flitted about, and all attention was drawn to them.

Charlene enjoyed watching Avery's reactions to the characters on the stage, and noticed how her breath caught when the nobleman, Egeus, threatened his daughter Hermia, saying if she refused to marry Demetrius she'd be punished to the full extent of the law. In a booming voice he warned her she'd either be sent to a convent or executed. Egeus was getting married this weekend, and there were many festivities surrounding the important event. Before he tied the knot, Hermia had to decide.

Avery, face pale, murmured to Charlene, "That's so unfair."

"'All's well that ends well,'" she whispered back. Avery, not understanding the quote from another of Shakespeare's plays, merely shrugged, then leaned forward in her chair, watching the stage with a rapt expression.

When Hermia and Lysander decided they'd have to escape Athens and elope, Avery clapped with enthusiasm. The couple managed to sneak away later that night and entered the woods. They ran into a band of fairies, and the magic, the mayhem, the wit of Shakespeare had the entire audience applauding. Avery, too, was enthralled by the story and laughed at all the jokes, even if she didn't understand them.

When the first act was over, they had a brief intermission, and Avery's grin reached ear to ear.

"Well, what do you think?" Charlene asked, though she could see for herself. "Should we ditch the play and go get ice cream?"

"No way—this is so much fun. Much better than I expected."

"Guess we'll just have to do this more often."

"Can we?"

Charlene didn't get a chance to answer because Amy and Kass peeked out from behind the curtain, and when they spotted the two of them they beckoned for her and Avery to come forward.

"I think we're getting invited backstage," Charlene told her young friend. "Would you like to go?"

"Are you kidding? Of course!"

Charlene could barely keep up with Avery as she ran toward the stage. Kass pointed to the side where they could enter.

"Hey," Charlene greeted Kass and Amy. "Are we allowed back here?"

"Not for long—but we have twenty minutes." Amy glanced at Avery, and Charlene made the introductions.

"So how are you enjoying it so far?" Amy asked. Amy's light brown hair was down in waves, with a pearled circlet on top. Her arms were bare in a Romanesque gown.

"It's amazing." Avery pointed to the program. "You're Hermia, right?"

"Yes, but I'm Amy Fadar in real life—pleased to meet you."

Avery gushed, "I hope you get to marry Lysander. He's nicer than Demetrius, and he's in love with the other girl anyway."

"You've been following along!" Amy sounded impressed.

"I have—which actress are you?" Avery turned to Kass, swathed in purple and pink tulle with glittery wings.

"I'm the tallest fairy," Kass said. "I don't have any speaking parts in this play."

"You can do that? Just dance around?"

Kass put an arm around Avery's shoulders. "Looks like we might have another possible theater fan. Want to try acting?"

"I couldn't do that," Avery said in a guileless manner, "but I do love to sing."

"Even better." Kass shook her wings. "Follow me."

Kass and Avery strode ahead, and Amy dropped behind. "Sorry I got annoyed at lunch yesterday, but it's been stressful. Madison's death. It wasn't a random accident, you know? Somebody chose to end her life."

Charlene touched Amy's bare arm. "No, I'm sorry. I sometimes get single-minded." She changed the subject. "Thanks for inviting us back here."

"I can't get you into all the rooms, of course, but I can show you the fairy costumes and how things are orchestrated back here. We'll have to hurry."

They passed a few of the actors' dressing rooms on the way to the costumes. Charlene noted that Neville had a big star on his door, and Amy's was slightly smaller but still very important looking. When they got to the costume room, Avery enthused over each of the fancy ball gowns and fairy costumes. Kass suggested she could try one on.

Charlene excused herself for a moment and ducked down the hallway, hoping to encounter Neville. As luck would have it, he stood outside his door, speaking with someone in harsh terms. She recognized Hunter as the man brushed past her in a fit of anger. She thought about retreating, but it was too late.

"Can I help you with anything?" Neville's expression was anything but pleased as he realized he had a witness.

"I didn't mean to intrude. I'm a friend of Amy's. She and Kass invited us to see backstage. It's pretty impressive."

"Do I know you? You look familiar."

"I'm Charlene. I own the bed and breakfast on Crown Point."

"Oh, right. Old Strathmore place."

Charlene shuffled her feet. Should she bring up that she'd seen him and Danielle argue after the play? "Yes, that's correct."

"It was empty for a few years. Rumor had it that the place was haunted. Was it?"

She gave a nervous cough, then relaxed when he chuckled.

"Theater humor—you should see the pranks that happen when we do *Macbeth*. Sorry," he said.

"It's fine."

He tilted his head. "Were you at the Common to see *Salem's Rebels*? Second to front row?"

"I was. My guests and I took up two benches. Such a tragedy, what happened to Madison Boswell."

He wiped a hand over his mouth. "Tragic. Awful. Hopefully our offering today will appease her restless spirit."

Charlene tucked her hands in her pockets. "Danielle

mentioned a broken light and somebody quitting. Do you really think Madison is haunting the theater?"

"Don't look so shocked—there are things of this world we cannot know." Neville forced a laugh. "But of course not."

She wasn't quite certain she believed him. "Was that Hunter just now?"

"Yeah. I fired him and sent that fool packing. How dare he take money to ruin my play? *My* play? The one I wrote? Directed? Bled over? *Salem's Rebels* was *my* chance to be remembered in Salem as a worthy playwright."

Neville was no Shakespeare—not even close. "I'd heard he was upset with Madison," Charlene murmured.

"Who wasn't?" Neville's breath grew ragged. "She played us all, and dear God, I'm only human." He checked the time on his phone, then tucked it out of sight in his regal robe—Theseus, naturally.

"You knew her from when she was your student in Boston, isn't that right?"

He focused on her, and Charlene shivered, wrapping her shawl around her. Neville had a lot of reasons to want Madison gone from his life. "Briefly. Why all the questions? You should get back to your seat."

Charlene swallowed to wet her dry throat, the sounds of Avery, Kass, and Amy so close making her brave. "One of my guests last night overheard you and your actors at the Hawthorne Hotel bar."

Neville winced. "We were just letting off steam. One of my actors is dead, so we cut loose—that's no crime."

"You had an affair with Madison when she was in college, didn't you?"

Neville's first reaction was shock, then surprise, then

self-righteousness. His put-upon sigh could have parted the Red Sea. "Before I tied the knot and settled down."

"I don't understand . . ." She kept her body language open, doing some acting of her own when she conveyed empathy.

His voice roughened, and Charlene could tell he didn't want to answer her, yet his large ego meant he had to try to justify himself. "Madison waltzed into the theater, and it was like yesterday—she had me ensnared with a siren's glance."

Charlene shifted a half step away from the perturbed director and flicked a gaze down the hall, which remained empty. "Were you in love? Is that why you risked your marriage?"

"Love? No." Neville's handsome face soured in humiliation. "The woman was a witch. A sorceress."

Neville's voice caught. His jaw clenched, and his fist curled. Fury emanated from him. According to Tim, he'd referred to Madison as a witch last night at the Hawthorne Hotel as well as just now. Was it easier to believe that than accept his weakness toward the starlet?

"I see your disbelief, but you have no idea what Madison was like. I tried to break it off when Danielle discovered us. Madison had a power over me—she had it then, and now." His voice cracked. "She refused to go, and whenever I tried to bring up the subject my stomach churned like I was about to hurl." Neville brought his knuckle to his lower lip, then whirled and bolted inside his dressing room, slamming the door.

Charlene stared at the gold star. Neville Hampton. Producer. Actor. Murderer? One way to free himself from Madison would be her death.

Kass stepped out of the costume area, her fairy wings as wide as the hall. "You okay?"

Charlene tightened her shawl around her shoulders and smiled as if her nerves weren't stretched tight. Had Neville lost his temper with Madison and paid Hunter to find someone to shoot his lover? Hunter had stormed off, angry. "Yeah." Amy and Avery joined Kass. "Did you have fun, Avery?"

Kass raised an eyebrow but said nothing.

"It was a blast!" Avery cried excitedly.

"Thanks for showing us around." The lights dimmed twice to signal intermission was just about over.

"If you're not in a hurry, you could join us after the show." Amy shrugged. "I told Kevin we'd go the bar later."

"Yeah! You should meet us there for a cocktail," Kass seconded.

Tempted, Charlene shook her head. "Avery and I have a date with ice cream, and then I have to get home to my guests. Another time though." She tapped the teenager's elbow. "Guess we better hurry to our seats. Good luck, Amy, Kass, with the rest of the show. Break a leg."

When they were out of hearing range, Avery asked, "Why would you tell your friends to break a leg when they were so nice?"

"It means good luck in this business. Not sure why. Sorry I missed you in the costume. How did it look?"

"Ridiculous," she said with a pleased expression, "but Kass didn't think so. I had her take a picture of me to post on Facebook."

"I want to see!"

Charlene knew that Avery hung out with Tiffany and

Jenna, but didn't have a boyfriend—yet. Senior year, things could change.

Avery was more confident by the day. "Okay—I'll send it to you."

Charlene checked her phone as it dinged. "Ah!" Avery made an adorable fairy, complete with large eyes and pouting lips. "Hey—would you be interested in taking acting classes? You just had a birthday, and I'd love to give that to you as a gift."

"In June. You bought me music already!"

"This is different. If you're interested, let's check it out."

"Nah. It would be a waste of your money."

"No, it wouldn't. Or singing classes? Just think about it."

Avery glanced up at her. "Why are you always so nice to me?"

"Because I like you, that's why." And Charlene did— Avery was a special person in her life. They reached their row and slid by some people to take their seats. "We better be quiet, or we'll get shushed again."

Avery's eyes twinkled. "That was so funny, wasn't it?"

"Super funny."

The orchestra played the light and airy music, the prelude to the next act as the audience settled in their seats and the heavy purple drapes slid away. The room darkened, and the theater became quiet.

A second later, Charlene heard a rustling around her— she searched but didn't see anything unusual. A chill crept down the back of her neck.

Neville had hinted that Madison's spirit had needed to be appeased—because she'd been murdered by one of her fellow actors? She rubbed her arms.

Before Jack, she'd never seen a ghost in her life, but the very first night in her new home, she'd seen him as clearly as she did Avery, sitting right next to her.

"Do you hear that?" she whispered.

Avery shook her head no and put a finger to her lips, effectively shushing her.

Charlene bit back a laugh at the same time she felt as though someone had walked over her grave. She looked left toward Brandy and noticed a flickering light attached to the wall like a sconce. A woman's shape appeared. Brandy was oblivious as she watched the stage, the apparition vibrating in the air.

Ghost light! Was Madison here?

CHAPTER ELEVEN

Charlene blinked quickly to try to bring the eerie feminine image into focus, but it was gone. Brandy and Evelyn remained unaware that anything had happened. She nudged Avery. "Did you see anything over there a second ago?" She spoke very softly and nodded toward the flickering light.

Avery gave a little head shake and a questioning brow.

Kass had told her months ago that she saw ghosts everywhere in Salem. Charlene would have to ask the actress later if she'd seen Madison, or another ghost, in the theater.

The actors on stage commandeered her attention. She recognized Amy, beautiful and ethereal as Hermia, crying by herself after Lysander claimed to love Helena. The fairy Puck had placed a magical potion on both Lysander's and Demetrius's eyes, and they had each fallen in love with the first woman they saw—who happened to be Helena. Helena feared the men were mocking her when they declared their love. Secretly, she'd always loved Demetrius.

Neville, playing Theseus, the Duke of Athens, was positioned to the right side of the stage with Hippolyta, the Queen of the Amazons. His betrothed. The part was to have been played by Madison Boswell. Her understudy, according to the program, was Brooklyn Thomas, a graduate from the Aquest Actors studio in Salem. This was her first role. Charlene could see she was nervous, wearing an obvious wig similar to Madison's long hairstyle.

Jane was on the sidelines, flashing cards to remind her of the lines. Normally, the prompter would be out of sight, but Brooklyn required constant help. If Neville thought he'd be fooling anyone that their star was still here, he was mistaken.

The music set the mood, Charlene noticed. When she and Jared had been to the theater in Chicago, she hadn't realized how much the orchestra was part of the play itself. Theseus and Hippolyta danced to the fairy's music, when Hippolyta tripped over a piece of the scenery. The audience tittered as Neville caught her by the arm and tried to play it off by embracing her close. The brunette wig tipped backward.

"That poor girl," Charlene murmured. "Her debut, and she's the star."

"I feel so bad for her," Avery said quietly.

"Me too." Charlene winced as Neville tried to casually right the hairpiece before it fell off.

"At least it's a comedy." Avery glanced at Charlene with a small smile.

Charlene somehow managed to keep a straight face. "Probably not what Shakespeare had in mind."

Kass's slender height was easy to identify as she danced among the flowers, her body graceful and glittery. Next was the scene where Puck tried to undo his terrible mistake of placing the magic potion on Lysander's eyes before Demetrius's. A distraught Hermia challenged Helena to a fight.

"Who is playing Puck?" Avery asked. "I think it's a woman but supposed to be a man."

"It's possible. They did it with *Salem's Rebels*, too." Charlene had her playbill open in her lap. Glancing down, she read Salem Stage Right had fifteen actors, some who were also members of the board or wore different hats, such as set director or marketing director. Jane Wallace's title was costume coordinator, but from what Charlene had witnessed, the young woman took care of many things.

Of the fifteen photos, ten were female, five were male. "Yeah, Puck is played by Lissa McKinnon."

Avery checked out the photos. "Lots more women."

Neville was in charge of the hiring and casting and obviously had a preference for the ladies.

The music slowed and Helena, Hermia, Lysander, and Demetrius all fell asleep, and Puck fixed his mistake. Oberon and Titania, king and queen of the fairies, watched anxiously from the sidelines.

Theseus and Hippolyta, Neville's arm firmly through the young lady's, entered the forest where the lovers were all sleeping. He woke them up to take them back to the palace in Athens.

The curtain closed at the end of the mystical scene to

rowdy applause. The locals stood and clapped, showing support for the theater and their friends.

Charlene looked around in the dark theater, the sounds of wooden sets being dragged across the floor a reminder that it wasn't all magic but hard work. Thin ropes hung from the ceiling above the stage. The steps were dark. It was, in fact, dangerous.

It would have been much easier to kill Madison in this setting and try to make it seem like an accident, she thought.

Madison had been shot in broad daylight. Deliberately.

Charlene rubbed her arms and shifted toward the stage as the curtain opened to Athens and Theseus's palace.

"No more fairies," Avery said sadly.

She glanced at Avery. "Back to the 'real' world, in a palace. Not such a bad thing."

"True. Who will Hermia pick?"

"Just watch." Charlene leaned forward in anticipation.

The actors separated into three couples: Theseus and Hippolyta, Helena and Demetrius, Hermia and Lysander, and were wed in a triple ceremony.

"Perfect!" Avery clasped her hands, enchanted.

When the scene was over, Puck bowed before them and apologized for the misadventure, then begged the audience to remember it as *all just a dream*.

Neville called to Jane, then walked to the front of the stage, his head held regally as if he still played his part as king. "Thank you all for coming to this show, dedicated to the life of Madison Boswell. All proceeds of today's performance will go to the Madison Boswell Actors Fund." The light flared dramatically, then returned to normal. "I've spoken with her family, and there will be a wake Tuesday at Trinity Church in Boston, and the funeral service on Wednesday." Neville bowed his head as if overcome with sorrow. "Jane?"

Behind him a movie screen lowered in jerky stops and starts.

Jane hunched over a laptop near the orchestra pit. She fumbled with the remote control but eventually hit the play button. Neville watched from the sidelines and shook a finger at the young woman. Perhaps she was a relative, and that's why the Hamptons kept her on?

Madison's face loomed in gigantic living color on the screen, her gorgeous brown-gold eyes luminous, her smile enchanting. The date of her birth, July fifth, then her death, July fourth. To not have made it to twenty-nine? Charlene gripped the armrests, watching the slideshow of pictures from the theater, which had been taken over the last four months. The romantic photo of Madison and Neville wasn't shown.

Charlene turned toward where Danielle sat with her two children. The woman was stone-faced and rigid, her hands clasped in her lap, obviously fuming. But who could really blame her?

A movement behind Danielle caught Charlene's focus, and she gasped. Was that Tyler Lawson?

The man's attention was locked to the screen, the shining glisten of tears in his eyes clear to Charlene as he watched the pictures. She recognized the expression of true grief—there was a man who'd lost the woman he'd loved—nothing like Neville's anger and resentment.

Would Logan be somewhere in the audience too?

She scanned the whole theater, dimly lit, but didn't see him. The light above the box seat where Brandy and Evelyn sat flickered again.

Charlene waited and held her breath for the ghostly image to reappear. Nothing.

She turned back to the screen. There was a picture of Neville and Madison, standing before a door that had a star that read *Madison*. She was beaming—in her element. Though a small stage, she'd earned a star.

The final picture was of Madison, Amy, Neville, Hunter, and Danielle from an after-party shot where everybody was all smiles . . . Jane was to the right, as if not quite part of the group, her smile uncertain.

The lights brightened, and Charlene glanced to where Tyler had been.

He was gone. Charlene wasn't surprised.

"Can we have the actors sign my program?" Avery asked as they both stood up.

"Of course!" They gathered their handbags and moved down the aisle. "Did you have fun?"

"Yeah, even the newbie's acting didn't make it bad." Her eyes shone with excitement. "Brooklyn was so lucky to get this part, but it's awful, too, knowing it was only because the real actress was killed. That kinda sucks."

Charlene slipped her arm around Avery's shoulders. "I understand what you mean—it's hard to balance life with death. I learned that you have to take each day as it comes. Some days are easier than others."

Avery, having been bounced around in her own uncertain childhood, didn't take anything for granted. Charlene led the way, and they followed the people from the seats to the crowded lobby.

The actors were all present, speaking with their fans and ready to sign autographs. They stood in line and chatted with the other people in the audience. Brandy and Evelyn were gone, but Alice mingled with a male friend.

When they reached Neville, he ignored Charlene but signed the program for Avery. Kass wasn't there.

Amy was the last signature that Avery wanted, and the actress signed with a flourish. She gave Avery a hug. "It was really nice to meet you. If you ever have any interest in acting, let me know."

"Thanks!" Avery embraced the book of autographs to her chest as if it were a treasure.

"Where's Kass?" Charlene wanted to talk to her about the apparition she'd seen. "I'd like to say goodbye."

"Go on back to the dressing rooms. She's changing— there's a shortcut down this hall to the left. If you get lost, shout for Jane, she'll help you."

"Thanks."

Charlene and Avery went down the shadowy hallway away from the fun until they reached a door that read STAGE. She twisted the knob and it opened. Muffled laughter echoed toward them.

"This is spooky," Avery said, glancing nervously over her shoulder.

"I half expected the door to be locked." Charlene chuckled.

"Right?" Avery kept her program close.

The door opened into a "hall" made of unused props, like giant trees, tall posts, mannequins, dolls, stuffed animals, and trunks. Someone with a warped sense of humor had created a path that you had to travel while being watched.

"It feels like they can see me." Avery shivered.

"It's pretend," Charlene assured her, not liking it either. "We'll just be a minute." It was important to know if Kass had seen Madison's ghost.

The back entrance passed a large laundry room, a restroom, and the makeup area. Here the mannequins were all dressed in fairy costumes and masks. It was a relief to hear voices from an open dressing-room door.

A tall figure popped into the hall from behind an open door, in her customary black on black, her body loose and graceful, her hip-length hair in several braids and loops.

"Kass!" Charlene said. "Just who we wanted to talk to."

Kass whirled with a smile. "Hey—what are you two doing here?"

"We wanted to say goodbye, and I had something to ask you . . . in private." She whispered the last words, tilting her head toward Avery, who was digging through her pink purse.

"It's scary back here." Avery had found a pink pen and used it to gesture at the path behind them, the props bulky and creepy. "Where are we?"

"These rooms are farthest from the stage, where the peons have to dress," Kass joked. "No stars on the doors here."

Two other girls now in street clothes also left the room. "Not yet," the bleached blonde said. "But I have hope! I know I wouldn't have bombed as bad as Brooklyn."

"Madison's understudy," the redhead informed them, "was a joke!"

Kass bit her lip at the woman's snarky comment. "She was nervous, that's all."

The bleached blonde rolled her eyes. "Madison's probably spinning in her grave. She detested Brooklyn anyway."

"Not to speak ill of the dead, but Madison was a snob." The redhead slung her backpack over her arm. "I heard from Lissa that Brooklyn refused to get ready in Madison's dressing room."

"Why's that?" Charlene asked. Lissa was the talented young woman who had played Puck.

The blonde hunched her shoulders. "I heard the ghost light was out this morning when they came in. Susie quit then and there."

"Does she think it's haunted?" Charlene peered at Kass to see if she knew anything.

The redhead glanced behind her down the hall before she murmured, "Brooklyn's kind of a dimwit. I wouldn't be surprised."

The blonde added, "I know for a fact that Neville had the light on yesterday—it's a theater thing. Double trouble, I bet, because it was Madison's birthday."

"I just saw the movie *Ghost Light*," Avery said, her eyes big. "Is the play cursed now?"

"No!" Kass glared at the two actresses. "It's a superstition, that's all."

Charlene knew that Kass could see ghosts, but now wasn't the time to ask about Madison. She needed a moment alone with her.

"What about you, Kass? Why don't you ask if you can take over the role?" the redhead asked. "You're more experienced and a way better actress than Brooklyn."

"She never expected to be on stage as lead," Kass said in Brooklyn's defense. She shrugged and tucked her hands into her pants pockets. "This is a hobby for me—I like background roles that if I can't make it, don't affect the play."

"Whatever floats your boat," the redhead said with a grin, pulling on her friend's arm. "Come on, or we'll be late for our dates. We snagged twins; can you believe it? Models. So what if they're short?"

The blonde looked up at Kass. "They're about your shoulder height, but what do we care? They can dance! See ya!"

The two women hurried down the hall and out of sight.

"Kass, will you sign my program?" Avery asked.

"Sure!" Kass scrawled her name beneath her picture. "Let's walk out together. This exit leads to the parking lot." She pointed to the doors on either side as they went. "The closer to the stage, the bigger the stars. See the size of Neville's?"

Jane burst from a half-open door with Madison's star on it, her plain face pale. In her arms was a costume from the play . . . an orange cape. Her eyes widened when she saw Kass. "I can't fix this," she said. "Someone's cut Madison's Hippolyta costume to shreds. Trashed the room! This isn't funny at all."

Charlene, Kass, and Avery exchanged looks.

"Who would do such a thing?" Kass held out her arms to take the garment. "Is someone trying to frighten us, or is this a real threat?"

Jane whisked the cape back and peered fearfully into the room. "Do you think Madison's ghost is here?"

"Don't get melodramatic, Jane." Kass was a pillar of strength as she pointed to the torn cloth. "A person did this, not a ghost."

"I'll have to make another costume." Jane's hands shook. "Danielle is going to fire me; I know it. Hunter got the axe already."

"Why would she? You didn't do this." Kass touched her wrist. "Chin up, Jane. You've fixed many a calamity before. Neville and Danielle need you."

"Thanks for your vote of confidence, Kass. You're one of the few actors to be nice to me. You and Amy." Her lower lip trembled, and tears filled her eyes. "It's . . . it's not just the costume, the room's been torn up."

Charlene stood close to Avery in alarm. "Have you called the police?"

"No, I'm afraid to." Jane looked down at her feet, and Charlene was reminded of when Jane had done the same thing while announcing the play, *Salem's Rebels*. "I'm responsible for keeping the costumes in pristine shape. Someone must have snuck in. If I can clean it up, then nobody needs to know."

Putting Avery behind her, Charlene shifted to see inside the dressing room. *Witch* had been scrawled along the mirror in red lipstick. The costumes had been tossed from the hangers to the floor, the upholstered bench in front of the vanity shredded like the cape.

"This is more than vandalism, Jane. Someone is seriously unhinged." Charlene pulled out her cell. "I think you should call the police and file a report. Want to use my phone?"

Jane straightened. "No. Please don't! I'm begging you."

"You have to tell Danielle. And Neville," Kass said in a soft tone.

"And then I'll lose my job." Jane sniffed. "This may not seem like much to you; you've got another business, Kass, but this is all I have."

"I'll go with you," Kass offered. "Is Neville in his dressing room?"

"No. He's still signing autographs. He's the star." Jane lowered her head. "He's upset with me already because of Madison's tribute. He gets a tic in his cheek when he's angry, and I saw it clear as day."

"Did you put that tribute together?" Charlene asked. "It was lovely." She tucked her phone in the side pocket of her purse.

"It was very nice," Avery told Jane.

"Yes, thanks." Jane continued to peruse the floor instead of their faces. Charlene wondered what had happened in her past to make her so unsure of herself.

Kass blew out an exasperated breath as she read the mirror. "Witch. Geez. Not very imaginative. Is Danielle in the office?"

"Don't know. Danielle was breathing down my neck the whole time I made it, literally." Jane smoothed the costume. "She said we had to do it right."

"Right? What did she mean by that?" Kass jutted her hip out.

Jane lifted her gaze to Avery, then back at Kass. "Considering, you know . . ."

The affair between Neville and Madison.

"Everybody knew about them," Jane continued. She shifted the weight of the fabric in her arms before she dropped it, the gold ring on her index finger snagging a jagged piece of orange.

"Let me help you," Kass said.

"No. That's okay. Danielle told me to clear this room. It's like she wants to erase Madison from the production company as if she never existed."

Charlene eyed the room with photos of Madison. "Can you send her personal things to her family? Her parents live in Boston. She has a brother, too."

"Her parents came by already. Yesterday afternoon.

Neville met with them—the light was working just fine. I was here preparing the video."

"Was her brother there, too?" Charlene hoped for a family reunion.

"The Boswells, Laura and Foster, were here, but not Logan." Jane's nose twisted. "Madison despised her brother."

"She did?" Charlene had to adjust her thinking. "Do you know why?" Madison must have chosen her parents' side in whatever had gone down in the Boswell household.

Jane shook her head as she answered Charlene. "Madison never talked to me much. Not nicely anyway. But you know how it is; every family has their secrets."

"Hey—do you know a Tyler?" Charlene knew she was pushing, but she might not get a better opportunity.

"No, don't think so." Jane narrowed her eyes in thought. "Is he an actor?"

"He was Madison's ex-fiancé." And had been at the theater to mourn his love.

Jane scoffed. "Madison had many admirers, but in the four months she'd been with the company, I only ever saw her with Neville." She shrugged. "Even *after* Danielle warned them to call it quits. Madison had him in her web."

On Kass's urging, Jane went to find Neville to reluctantly give him the bad news. Charlene and Avery followed Kass out the side door, and they all walked to the parking lot.

"That was very weird." Avery held her purse and her program stacked together. "Do people really think the theater is haunted? I peeked into the room, and the ruined stuff everywhere just seemed like somebody who was mad. A person, not a ghost."

Charlene agreed.

Kass glanced at the theater exit. The evening sky was twilight, and some of the outside streetlamps were coming on. "Jane's having a terrible night. I don't envy her having to take on Neville and Danielle. Who would do such a rotten thing?"

It was on the tip of her tongue to say *someone who had hated Madison enough to shoot her*, but she didn't.

Charlene used the fob to open their car doors, and when Avery jumped inside, Charlene turned to Kass. "I saw something at the beginning of the second act. The lights flickered, and I swear there was an apparition near the Flints' box seats. It was the figure of a woman, Kass, like a . . . ghost. Did you see anything unusual tonight?"

"No, but I was busy flitting around the flowers. You think you saw a ghost, Charlene?" Rather than laugh or say it wasn't possible, Kass patted the top of the Pilot. "I wouldn't be surprised if it was Madison."

CHAPTER TWELVE

Charlene stopped at a drive-through for Avery's ice cream and couldn't resist ordering a cone for herself. White stars twinkled against the dark night sky. "Want to park here?"

"Sure!"

Avery had chosen two scoops, one chocolate fudge, the other cookie dough. She had napkins draped around the large waffle cone but still licked the occasional drip from her hand. She talked nonstop about the show and how happy she was that Hermia got her man.

Charlene savored her single scoop of butter pecan, making sure not to get sticky fingers on her steering wheel. "So what about you?" she asked between bites.

"What?"

Avery, despite her rough upbringing, had an air of innocence that could be attributed to her finding a home at teen house. "You got your eye on some cute boy?"

"Nah." Her nose scrunched. "They're all too weird."

Last year, Avery'd had a small crush on a boy named Dillon, which hadn't gone anywhere. Charlene nibbled the edge of her cone. "Boys at that age are weird—they grow up though." She hoped her young friend would find someone to treat her like a princess. "Want to take that cruise around Marblehead with me next week? I've had quite a few folks recommend it."

"Yeah." Avery finished the cookie dough scoop and was down to the chocolate fudge. "I forgot to tell you— Janet said there's a new internship program to be a dental assistant. I'd start taking classes in January and be able to get a job after I graduate."

A job not at the bed and breakfast. Charlene cleared the clog in her throat. She knew it was in the girl's best interests, but she would miss her. Very much. "That could be good . . . does it sound interesting?"

Avery peered at Charlene with wise eyes over her chocolate ice cream. "I need a career to support myself, and I could start off at thirty-two thousand a year."

That wasn't a lot, but to Avery it would be independence. "Nice money for a first-time job."

"Second job—I work for you." Avery kept her attention on her ice cream. "I have to make a decision to enroll by the first week of August."

"Four weeks away." Charlene had been blessed with parents who'd saved for her college, but she'd also had a strong work ethic and had earned scholarships. She chewed her cone—the last cookie triangle filled with melted butter pecan was delicious. "Would you rather go to college and get an associates degree? You can be working in two years. Or a bachelors. I'll help you."

"Thanks." Avery twirled her cone as she considered this. "I can get school loans, too, but I'd rather work until I know what I want to do with my life."

It killed Charlene to keep her mouth shut and not nag, like her mother would have done to her. She would be supportive of Avery's choice and make sure that there were options for the teenager. Just because she'd been raised in an environment where a traditional post–high school education had been important, didn't mean that Avery wouldn't figure it out. She kept the tone light. "And what would that be?"

Avery grinned, chocolate on her lips. "Besides the next Taylor Swift?"

"Yeah. A real job," Charlene teased.

"I took one of those dumb aptitude tests for careers. I could be a nurse or a teacher, but I'm not feeling it." Avery finished her cone. "I like my dentist and the hygienists, though. It might not be so bad."

"Maybe you can spend a couple of days in the office with them before you decide." Charlene started the car.

Avery wiped her mouth with a napkin and perked up. "That's an amazing idea. I'll ask Janet about it. Thanks, Charlene."

"My pleasure—I love brainstorming ideas to address a problem." It had made her good at her marketing campaigns and served her well at her bed and breakfast. And the occasional case with Sam.

After buckling up, Avery sent off a text. "Letting Janet know we're on our way."

"Thanks!" Charlene put on some upbeat music that she knew Avery liked, so the teen could sing along.

Of their own accord, her thoughts returned to Kass saying that the ghostly figure Charlene had seen could well have been Madison.

But what had it been, exactly? Pale face, long hair . . . a feminine silhouette.

Jack appeared to her as a man . . . not a shadow person. Was there more than one type of ghost? It was totally possible, so she didn't discount the idea.

It had come as a surprise to her when Jane said Logan and Madison hadn't gotten along. Did Logan have any family ties after the falling-out with his father?

What about the grandmother in Beverly Hills? Had Madison gotten his share of the woman's estate, by being there as her nursemaid?

That might make a young man angry, especially one who'd already been cut off. The question remained, why had Madison cried out her brother's name the moment she was shot? To let people know that he had killed her? He'd been standing in the back of the crowd wearing a vest with pockets. Pockets roomy enough to hide a gun in . . .

Avery stuffed her napkins into the cardboard container between them on the console. "You're quiet, whatcha thinking about?"

"Sorry!" Charlene turned the volume on the radio down. "Madison. It was a beautiful tribute, but it's still . . . sad."

"Madison was awful to try and take Neville from his wife, even if Danielle Hampton is a nutcase. And those actresses dissing Brooklyn were not at all nice. Kass and Amy are awesome though, and super pretty. Still." Avery glanced at Charlene. "If that's the theater, I might just stick to music."

"Too much drama in the theater? Who woulda thought?" Charlene turned her blinker on, to go right.

"Hey," Avery said suddenly. "Do you think Danielle might have—you know—*killed* Madison?"

The last thing Charlene wanted to do was give the teenager nightmares about a possible murderer this close to home. "I don't think so," Charlene told Avery, imbuing confidence in her tone. "Danielle might have a reason to want Madison and her husband apart, but he's the father of her children. She's got a lot to lose."

Avery pulled a stick of gum from her pink clutch. "Yeah, I suppose. Besides, being his wife, she'd be the number-one suspect. Want a piece?"

"No, thanks. I'm sure Danielle's too clever to hire someone"—especially someone as nervous as Hunter—"to shoot Madison in front of everyone." Madison could easily have had an accident at the theater.

What was she missing? Charlene shook her head to clear her brain. Why the Fourth of July play? Was she overthinking the timing?

Neville had been very proud of his show—he certainly knew the exact moment a distraction would have been needed. She'd watched what she'd videoed a few times now, as had Jack, and Neville hadn't given anything away that they could tell.

"I sure hope the cops find who did it soon. Gotta admit that it makes me a little freaked out that someone with a gun is wandering around Salem." Avery blew a bubble and then sucked it back in.

Charlene's fingers tightened on the wheel—nobody should have to feel unsafe, especially not this adorable teen. "The Salem police are very good. They'll be caught soon. Sam hopes by the funeral Wednesday."

Avery blew another bubble within a bubble, then popped it.

All that sugar tonight made a trip to the dentist's office a great idea. Avery would do well at whatever she chose to do. "You're pretty good—I used to do that when I was a kid."

Avery smacked the gum in preparation for another masterpiece. "You were probably one of the cool kids, huh? A cheerleader."

"Nope! I was more of a geek. I loved reading or going to museums with my dad—he was an art professor, so he knew all of the history. Mom wasn't interested, so it was 'our' thing. Afterward, we'd stop and get an ice cream float, if it was summer, or a hot pretzel with mustard if the weather was cooler." Charlene pulled up in front of the teen house and smiled at Avery. "Here we are!"

Avery reached for the door handle. "I like your dad. You're so lucky that he was there to do things with." Her voice hitched.

Charlene realized that her memory might have caused Avery pain and immediately jumped out of the car to give Avery a hug once she was out too. "I had the best time today, and I think we should do it again. We can have our own ice cream celebrations."

"Yeah?" She cracked her gum and blinked until her eyes were clear. "Sounds good to me. Thanks for everything."

Charlene walked Avery to the door, and Janet opened it right away. "Did you have fun?" she asked. The house mother, though it was just nine, wore a lightweight robe and fuzzy slippers.

"It was amazing," Avery told her. "We went backstage

and met some of the actresses. The show was really funny."

"We had a great time," Charlene added. "I offered to buy her acting classes for her birthday, or singing, whatever she wants."

"Wow!" Janet turned to Avery. "What do you say to that?"

"I'll think about it." Avery lifted the program with pictures and autographs. "Thanks so much for taking me. It was awesome to meet your friends—especially Kass. She looks a tiny bit like a witch. A pretty one."

Charlene laughed. "I'll tell her that."

"No, don't!" Avery put a hand over her mouth.

"No worries, we tease her about it all the time. And I highly recommend getting your tea at Fortune's Tea Shoppe, if you drink it."

Janet put an arm around Avery. "I watched that movie, *Ghost Light*. It was hokey, but funny. Did you see a light at the theater?"

"They really had one, and someone broke into Madison's dressing room. I got to try on two fairy costumes."

"Come in and tell me all about it. How about you, Charlene? Want to stay a few minutes?"

"Another time. I need to get home and take care of my guests. I told them I'd be back around nine and offer after-dinner drinks and dessert for anyone who wanted it." She stepped backward. "See you tomorrow, Avery!"

It didn't take Charlene more than ten minutes to get home. She let herself in, a sense of purpose enveloping her as she listened to her four guests in the living room make conversation. Drinks at Brews and Broomsticks would have been fun, but this was better.

"Hello!" She joined the two couples with a friendly smile. "I hope you all had an enjoyable day. I'm so glad you're getting to know each other."

James Stewart rose at her entrance and reached out to shake her hand. "Thank you, Charlene—we did. Penny and I visited Marblehead and got back to Salem around sevenish. We dined at Turner's Seafood and had a marvelous meal."

"Yes"—Penny also stood—"thank you for the recommendation. The oysters on the half shell were delicious, and James and I each had a full lobster." She moved next to her husband. "It's a treat for us, coming from Ottawa. Of course, we have good restaurants there as well, but nothing beats fresh Maine lobster."

When they'd checked in earlier, James told her he was a member of Parliament, and his wife was a historian. Both were tall, slim, and well-dressed. James had thinning brown hair starting to gray along the sides. His crisp white shirt was tucked into camel-colored dress slacks. Penny was a strawberry blonde, with soft waves to her shoulders. She wore a lime-green sleeveless blouse, a free-flowing skirt to her knees, and jeweled sandals that revealed her ankles.

All four of them were drinking white wine.

"I hope you don't mind, but we opened a bottle. It was engraved with your name on it." James raised his glass and swirled the wine. "A local brand?"

"Yes. Flint's Wineries. They created a special blend for me. How is it?"

"Delicious," they all said at once.

"I'm glad you had a wonderful day, and the wine is for everyone." She turned to the other couple. "So tell me about your day, Carrie. Did you do the tours that you had in mind?"

Josh and Carrie Franklin were professors from California and had on matching knee-length shorts and pale-blue cotton shirts.

Carrie spoke first. "The weather was so glorious that we took a boat cruise down the river, then walked around Pickering Square. I bought the most beautiful orb; it's this lovely round glass ball in sea-green colors. It'll be a nice souvenir."

"They're called witch balls," Charlene said with a laugh. "Perfectly Salem. I have a couple of them outside." And Jack stayed clear just in case. "I plan on the sailing trip next week—I don't have time to do half the things I want." She checked everyone's glasses to see if they needed refills, but they were all around the half mark. "We have a small local theater where I saw *A Midsummer Night's Dream* tonight. If you get a chance, try to take it in—they only do weekend performances."

"We appreciate the pamphlets you left in the room," Josh told her. "We had a chance to read them and made a list of things to do next. I don't think two days will be enough. Marissa, our oldest grandchild at ten, wants to hear all about the witch trials."

"Come back again and bring her." Charlene clasped her hands. "So, is anyone interested in dessert? Minnie, my fabulous cook, prepared an apple spice cake. She also made a platter of different flavored cannoli."

"Well, I probably shouldn't," Carrie said, "but how can I refuse? The cannoli sounds great."

It was an hour before Charlene could escape downstairs, hoping to find Jack.

She saw him at once. His smoking jacket over a white shirt and jeans made her laugh and reminded her of when they'd first met and he'd held a pipe. "Good evening, Doctor Jonathan Strathmore," she said formally. "What a wonderful host you are. Already have a glass of wine poured and waiting." She grinned. "Where did you get that jacket?"

"I manifested it for you, madame." She took the glass and had a sip, her eyes on his face all the while. He was a great conversationalist, clever, thoughtful, and kind. If only he weren't dead.

Death seemed to have followed her to Salem, and she had no idea why. Yet, solving the mystery of Jack's death had brought them closer together, and now they were linked in an inexplicable way.

Nobody else could see him or communicate with him but her. When the angels had come for him, he'd given up salvation to stay with her. They were quite a team, him teasing her, her making him jealous—their affection for each other undeniable.

Jack's medical background and intelligence assisted her in occasionally helping Sam with a crime. Not that Sam was grateful, but it pleased her and gave Jack a purpose.

"Come upstairs to my suite with me—I have news and questions."

He joined her upstairs—she actually walking up them while he was in the wine cellar one second and gone the next.

"Good night, everyone," Charlene said to her guests. Seemed she had another terrific group of people.

Still carrying her wine, Charlene sat next to Jack on the love seat and told him all about the play, the ghost light, seeing an apparition, and the damage done to Madison's dressing room. "I asked Kass if she'd seen anything during the performance because she can see ghosts." She finished her merlot.

"Do you think that she could see me?" Jack patted his chest.

"I'm not willing to take the chance, Jack." What would she do if Kass knew about Jack? Her ghost belonged to her, and she liked it that way. "Are you?"

"I suppose not. Well, what did she say? Is Madison haunting the theater?" His tone held levity.

"Kass was busy on stage and didn't notice—but she said if there was a ghost, it could be Madison . . . she had a reason to be angry with Neville and Danielle, and she was murdered." Charlene tucked her loose hair behind her ear. "Brooklyn, the understudy, and Jane both believe in the paranormal—ghosts especially. Although, the word *witch* was written on the mirror." She tapped her finger on the couch cushion. "If it was a haunting, why not the word *ghost*?"

"Would Madison consider herself a witch?" Jack asked. "It has a derogatory feel to it."

"You're right. More like an insult—so, who from . . . a jealous lover? Jealous actors? Those two fairies that were cast with Kass were awful. Mean girls. And Neville has referred to her as a witch twice that we know of."

"And Hunter." Jack stretched his legs out to rest his heels on top of the coffee table. "Well, we have a lot of suspects for who might have killed Madison, but little proof."

Charlene sighed. "We know that Hunter was paid to distract the spectators, but who hated her enough to want her dead? In addition to the Hamptons, there is Logan

Boswell. He and Madison were not close. Tyler, her ex-fiancé? Think they were in cahoots?"

Jack cupped his chin, leaning forward in thought. "I'd think by now the police probably have the surveillance videos picked to pieces. They likely have both men on tape. Were they talking? Did they appear friendly?" His laugh held a note of sarcasm. "If only we could call Detective Sam Holden and ask."

"Very funny." Charlene relaxed against the cozy sofa. It had been another long day. The ice cream, cannoli, and wine had made her drowsy.

Jack lifted a finger. "The police know the type of bullet and capabilities of the handgun. From what we've seen on forensic shows, it's likely they've deciphered the distance the bullet traveled and the trajectory, which would nearly pinpoint the exact place the shooter was standing."

"The surveillance camera that recorded the bandstand and stage was broken, remember?" She scooched her back to get comfortable.

"That's very suspicious." Jack rubbed the back of his head. "This was a calculated act by a person willing to aim and shoot a weapon with hundreds of possible witnesses."

"How could they know whether or not the whole crowd would look at the stage when Hunter dropped the musket?" She tugged her earlobe. "What about the noise?"

"It takes a certain type of person to take such a risk," Jack determined.

"Especially when this kill could have happened someplace less obvious, like in that darkened theater. Ropes, wires, props. Eerie corners." Charlene forced her eyes to stay open as another thought occurred. "It was such an arrogant act that it makes me wonder if they wanted to be caught."

Jack began to fade but then grew clearer. "That's interesting. Someone suffering a guilty conscience? Better yet, someone who thinks they would *never* get caught. Ask Sam about that. It would be something for the police profiler."

Charlene stood up and crossed her arms. Her downy bed beckoned. "I can just imagine that conversation," she said tartly.

Jack chuckled. "You look ready to topple over, Charlene. Let's talk about this some more tomorrow. Invite Sam for coffee in the morning. You can casually bring the subject up."

The idea made her smile. "Thanks for the advice, Jack. I can see Sam now. Crimson ears, quivering mustache, and then he'd get quiet." She put her shoulders back and spoke in a deep voice, "*Charlene. Thank you so much for your help in solving this case. A profiler! None of us at the station ever would have thought of that.* Then he'd give me a lecture on minding my own business, and I wouldn't speak to him for another few days."

Jack's merriment turned into full-on laughter. "Now you really have to do it. I want to watch."

Charlene would have punched her ghost in the arm if she could've. Instead, she leaned against the threshold of her bedroom door. "Jack—dear, dear, Jack. What am I going to do with you? You just can't leave Sam alone. He's not a bad guy or an ineffective detective, as much as you prefer to think of him that way. His office wall is loaded with awards and commendations."

"I don't want you to be *too* impressed with him."

Jack's form went from color to sepia, like an old photograph. She blew him a kiss. "Good night, Jack."

The last words she heard were, "Call Sam."

And tell him what?

He hadn't been in touch with her regarding the case, or her video.

Even though it stung her pride, Charlene sent Sam a text to invite him over for coffee in the morning—if he had the time.

CHAPTER THIRTEEN

Monday morning, Charlene woke with the sunrise and dressed in shorts and a T-shirt, then brought her coffee to the back porch. Silva joined her for a quick leg rub, then stalked regally around the oak tree. The cat pounced on a grasshopper but didn't seem too put out when the insect hopped away unharmed.

"I'm buying you a bell today." Charlene lifted her mug toward Silva in acknowledgment of her feline hunting skills. "Will told me that the birds need the bugs to eat—you have tuna, spoiled cat."

Silva slow-blinked her half-lidded eyes in the sunshine, her purr a loud rumble of contentment.

Charlene's phone dinged with a text, and she pulled it from her shorts pocket to read a message from Sam.

Her text last night had been to see if she could tempt him with Minnie's pastries and a cup of coffee. She'd left out the part that she'd be digging for an update on the murder.

I can stop by at eight thirty before I go into the station.

Her heart skipped—it was now seven thirty—she had time to brush her teeth before he arrived. They weren't in the habit of kissing, but it had happened once or twice, and her lips warmed at the memory. One thing she knew for sure—coffee and morning breath did not spell romance.

She texted back a thumbs-up emoji.

Charlene finished her leisurely cup of coffee, knowing that once she started her day, it would be nonstop.

She had folks checking in from Connecticut on Friday. Her Monday morning website updates for the Felicity House GoFundMe, which was halfway to the goal of a hundred thousand dollars toward a new addition, were due. Alice was thrilled by the progress and Charlene had let her know that come October, she'd give it another big push.

She also needed to add new pictures to the "Charlene's" website. The glorious landscaping and flowers in full bloom enhanced the property enormously, making it more appealing than the barren winter shots she'd had before. Judging by the recent number of bookings, the summer photos were a big plus.

Back in Chicago, she and Jared had had normal household chores with time for themselves leftover on the weekends. Running Salem's classiest bed and breakfast took a great deal of work, even with both Minnie and Avery doing their utmost to keep everything operating smoothly. Would Avery be able to work in the fall with her senior year's studies? Charlene would give the teen-ager whatever hours she wanted.

The last sip of coffee was cold, and a prod to stand up and stretch before returning inside. She'd put the TV on low for Jack, but her ghost wasn't around. "Sam's coming over." Still nothing.

She silently wished him a good morning and got to work in the kitchen. During the week, she offered light breakfast fare for her guests to help themselves to in the dining room, so she set out a coffee carafe, hot water for tea, fruit, and Minnie's pastries, warming some blueberry muffins in the oven for her and Sam.

Five minutes later, she opened the door before Sam could knock and ushered him inside, peering sideways at him to take him in. His broad chest was welcoming, a man to lean on. He made her pulse race, even in khakis and a short-sleeved polo for the office, tucked in to reveal a weathered brown leather belt.

What Charlene really admired him in were jeans. Some men were just built for them—she could see Sam on a Levi's billboard.

"Let's visit in the kitchen," she said. "Minnie won't be in until ten today."

"And good morning to you too," Sam said with a tug of his mustache.

Her stomach jumped. "Coffee? I'm warming blue-berry muffins."

"Yes to coffee, yes to muffins. And Charlene, I know what you're up to."

She glanced innocently over her shoulder as she reached for a mug. "What can you possibly mean?"

"You want to know what's going on with the case."

She pulled the muffins from the oven with an oven mitt and set the fragrant pastries on the counter. "Only if you want to tell me, Sam. Butter?"

Sam chuckled. "No to the butter, and *we'll see*, in regard to what I tell you."

She liked his playful mood this morning. Charlene offered him a plate with two steaming muffins and set his coffee on the kitchen table. "That means you know something!" Had he found the killer?

"Mmm-mmm." Sam's brown eyes twinkled as he teased her and sat down, his elbow on the table by his coffee. He rested the plate by the mug and reached for a paper napkin in the center. "Join me?"

How could she resist? She put one muffin on a small plate and sat opposite him with her breakfast. "Definitely. Hey, what do you know about Episcopalian funerals? I've been invited to the wake and funeral for Madison Boswell."

"Where is it held?"

"The wake will be on Tuesday afternoon, the funeral Wednesday, both at Trinity Church—I've heard the architecture is museum quality." She gave her fresh cup of joe a cautious sip. "In Boston, of course. I'm sure you're aware that's where the family is from."

"I am—how did you manage to get yourself invited to the wake?"

She didn't take offense but shrugged. "Through Amy and Kass—the actors were all invited, and Amy included me."

"And you just had to say yes?"

"As a friend of a friend!" Madison had died before her eyes. Her interest was genuine.

Sam finished his first muffin and swallowed it down with coffee. "Please be careful, Charlene. If it was an open invite to all the actors, well . . . Hunter Elliot is missing in action, and I have some further questions for him."

"Oh—I overheard Neville fire him for taking money to drop the musket and ruining his show." He was probably long gone.

"And being an accessory to his star getting shot?" Sam's tone went down a dangerous octave. "How did you acquire this information?"

Charlene blushed. "I spoke briefly with Neville at the theater yesterday—Salem Stage Right donated all the proceeds toward a new Madison Boswell Actors Fund, so I took Avery to see *A Midsummer Night's Dream*. She'd never been to a play before. Kass and Amy let her try on a few costumes."

Sam drank from his mug, his gaze on hers over the rim. He lowered the cup. "And you just so happened to see Neville backstage, or were you in line for autographs?"

"Backstage with Avery. It was, what do you call it . . . serendipitous. Especially because I learned all about a ghost light, which is supposed to appease any ghosts and keep them from haunting the theater."

His brow lifted. "And did you see a ghost?"

She thought of the apparition of the lady behind the Flints' box seat. "I may have seen something."

Sam laughed outright. "Still believing in ghosts, Charlene? Especially in a theater set up for illusions?"

Charlene swallowed a plump blueberry, unable to tell him that he was wrong. "You have to keep an open mind about these things, Sam." She toyed with ways to bring up the subject of what kind of person it would take to shoot someone in broad daylight, but then recalled Jane

and the torn cape—an easier topic. "Hey, did you get a report about some vandalism in the theater yesterday?"

"I don't think so—why?"

"Well, someone broke into Madison's dressing room,
tore up her costume and wrote *witch* across the mirror in
red lipstick. Both Jane and Madison's understudy, Brooklyn, were worried it was Madison's ghost."

He tapped the table with amusement. "And you
weren't?"

"Not really—would Madison have referred to herself
as a witch?" She shook her head. "I don't think so."

"Ghosts and logic don't belong in the same sentence."
Sam pushed his plate back and didn't bother to hide the
smile beneath his glorious mustache.

Was he mocking her? If only he knew about her Jack,
he'd be singing a different tune. "Want more? Or a refill
of coffee?"

"No, thanks—no need to get up."

Charlene settled back in her chair. "I wonder if it was an
actor, or one of the backstage crew? No one seemed to like
her much. And Hunter wouldn't be that dumb, would he?"

"Madison Boswell is dead, and he's partly responsible.
If the guy had any sense, he'd be laying low until this
case is over, not adding to his crimes with vandalism."
Sam shrugged. "I'll ask to see their security footage."

"Jane was going to tell Neville about it. She's the
woman in charge of costumes and set stuff." Charlene
crossed her ankles and tucked them behind the front legs
of the chair. "Amy said Jane wanted to be an actress but
tripped over her lines, so Neville has her working behind
the scenes. Her video homage to Madison last night was
very artfully done."

"Amy is the one you plan on going to the funeral with?"

"Her and Kass, yeah." Charlene wished she had more time in Boston to see the sights, but it was impossible to get away from the bed and breakfast for that long. If only Jack could check people in and out. She pinched the bridge of her nose and banished the thought.

"Tell me about Brooklyn," Sam said. "I haven't interviewed her personally yet, though I've read the notes from Officer Blake."

Charlene shifted on her seat. "Madison's understudy . . . oh, Sam, Avery and I felt so bad for her yesterday. She completely bombed during the performance, and it was her first big role."

"Having to step into a part after her lead actress was shot," Sam said. "No mystery there on why the girl might fumble a few lines. How did Neville handle it?"

"He was supportive and tried to cover Brooklyn's mistakes."

"How was Mrs. Hampton during all of this?"

"She was quietly angry rather than shouting. I forget where I heard it now, but Danielle might have a prenup that excludes Neville from getting a penny if he cheated in their marriage."

"Really? Hmm. These days anything's possible." Sam patted his chest where he normally kept a pocket with an old-school tablet, then reached for his slacks pocket instead. "We're re-interviewing everyone at the theater today."

"Is that why you're looking for Hunter?"

"I told him to stay in town. His cell phone is in evidence, and he's not answering his home phone." Sam's brow furrowed with frustration. "Police work requires a lot of patiently uncovering partial facts. Like, Hunter's prints were on the money we confiscated—no surprise. But there's another partial print smudged on the edge of one of the hundred-dollar bills. If we can make a match, we might have our killer."

"That's wonderful."

Sam's voice resonated slightly with the thrill of the chase. "I'd like to find the guilty party before the funeral, to ease the family's grief. I met with them briefly when they came to pick up Madison's body."

"I saw the hearse on Saturday with a town car following it and wondered if that was them. Are they nice, Sam?"

"The Boswells are an old family in Boston—very proper. Not Irish. You should be all right."

"What do you mean?"

His mustache twitched as he hid his grin. "Sometimes these wakes can get out of hand. Alcohol mixed with grief. Emotions explode, especially among the family members. Murder is one of the worst deaths a loved one has to face. Anger, injustice, questions, and frustration, all this turmoil mixed with booze has a tendency to cause problems."

Charlene empathized on a *been there, done that* level.

His phone rang and he answered, "Detective Holden. Uh-huh. I'll be right in—thanks." Sam hung up and rose fluidly. "Duty calls."

Charlene got to her feet. "Thanks for stopping by." She would have to find a way around the whole profiler thing another time.

"Keep your wits about you at the wake tomorrow, all right? Are you staying in Boston for the night?"

"No. It's not that far."

"Too bad. It's only a forty-five-minute drive, but there are a lot of things to see that would be of interest." He tugged a loose strand of her hair to her shoulder. "Maybe one day we can escape Salem for a few days and I can show you around."

She pressed her hand to her warming stomach. "I can't leave with you overnight."

"Yet?" he rumbled.

"Ever!" Her cheeks had to be cherry red. "Who would be responsible for 'Charlene's'?"

The light in his gaze turned serious. "Until we find the shooter, and the motive, well . . ."

"I'll be safe." Charlene, flustered at his bold suggestion, walked him to the door as Josh and Carrie Franklin descended the stairs—each holding a railing. "We have work to do! Bye, Sam."

She closed the door and faced her guests, Sam out of sight and her thoughts. "Morning!"

"I smell blueberry muffins," Josh said with a jovial grin. "My nose has never let me down." He went right into the dining room.

Charlene laughed. "Help yourself—I can warm them for you, if you'd like?"

"No need to do that," Carrie insisted, eyeing the selection of teas on the sideboard. "What's all this?"

"If you're interested in making your own tea blend, or getting something local, I recommend Fortune's Tea Shoppe at the Pedestrian Mall. Kass does readings with the leaves if you buy a cup in her shop."

Carrie elbowed Josh. "We need to do that. How fun!"

Josh tugged his collar. "All right—but you know that's all a bunch of baloney, right?"

"Being a professor doesn't mean you know everything," Carrie teased her husband as she fixed a cup of orange spice tea. "As educators we owe it to our students to see the world and be open to learning new things, right?"

Charlene wished Sam could have that world view too.

James and Penny ambled in, dressed casually but impeccably. Not a wrinkle to be found in their pressed shorts and designer shirts.

"Good morning!" Charlene gestured to the sideboard. "There are muffins, which I can warm for you, or cinnamon buns and fruit."

"Smells wonderful." Penny's thin mouth didn't back up her words. "But would it be too much trouble to get plain wheat toast?"

That might explain Penny's slim figure. "I can check in the pantry to see what we have. Shouldn't be a problem."

James smiled at Charlene with a politician's charm. "White would be fine, too, if that's all you've got."

"It's a bed and breakfast, James." Penny's tone was heavy on the breakfast. "Thank you, Charlene."

She got the feeling that the two hadn't started off the morning as peacefully as she had, and hurried into the pantry.

"Bless Minnie!" There was a loaf of store-bought wheat that Charlene remembered she'd used for grilled cheese sandwiches a few days before.

She put two slices in the toaster and got out a dish and butter for the side, just in case. When she returned, the four were all chatting amiably. Penny peeled an orange while the others ate muffins.

"Here you are, Penny." Charlene set the plate down. "Can I get you anything else? As stated on the website, we offer a full breakfast on the weekends. Assorted pastries and fruit during the week."

James dipped his head at his wife, who put a little raspberry jam on the corner of her toast. "It's no bother. We're here for a low-key week of summer weather without any stress."

"You don't have to remind me." Penny bit into her toast. "The doctor also recommended long walks in the fresh seaside air."

Charlene studied Penny again. A current of cold air brushed behind her, and Jack appeared. His gaze was intent as he perused Penny from head to toe, then went to James.

"She's thin, but not unhealthy—him, too, though his job in Parliament might be causing stress, maybe on their marriage. I heard them bickering earlier."

Charlene nodded but kept quiet about his observations. "If you have any questions about things to do in Salem, let me know!"

"We check out tomorrow," Carrie said. "What time, Charlene?"

"One in the afternoon." She'd have to find out the exact time of the wake and make sure that Minnie was here to help them. Avery would be in to clean and reset the room for the next guests—Charlene didn't need to be here, but she liked to be.

This was her home, and she'd only been away overnight once . . . not by choice.

"Perfect—our ride will be here at twelve thirty." Josh stood and brushed his hands over his empty plate. "C'mon, Carrie, we have a lot to see."

"Don't forget the tea shop, Josh," Carrie said, stacking her plate on top of Josh's.

Charlene reached for them and took them toward the kitchen. "Have fun, whatever you all end up doing. I'll have a happy hour today at five."

"We'll be back," Carrie said. "That white wine last night was fabulous."

"You can buy it at Flint's Vineyard. In fact, I think if you tell the owner you're from 'Charlene's,' she might give you a discount."

Jack waited in his chair at the kitchen table. "I hope Brandy appreciates how much business you send her way."

"It's a two-way street—I know we've gotten guests from Sharon, Brandy, and Kass. It's word of mouth and good reviews online." Charlene put the dishes in the sink. "My favorite is the one that went on and on about how cozy we are even though the house is huge."

She'd had one bad review about her claim of being close to town center . . . it was a mile walk, but the customer, an overweight man in his forties, had found it misleading. Charlene had refunded the two-night stay and made the mile-distance in a bigger font on the website. She wanted to make her guests happy so that they would return and tell other people.

"Were you talking to me?" James entered the kitchen with his and Penny's plates and cups.

"Myself," she said, glaring at Jack, who grinned. "Let me get those! You didn't have to do that."

"I wanted to apologize for my wife's attitude. She thought a spa would be better than a B and B. It was my turn to choose our vacation, and I found your place— excellent pictures of your property that remind me of my childhood home."

That explained *why* her bed and breakfast out of all the options in Salem.

"These two are on completely different pages," Jack said. "Not good for the marriage, in my opinion."

"How long have you been married?" Charlene added his dishes to the others in the sink to rinse them.

"Five years. Second marriage for each of us. Is there a Mr. Morris?"

"There was for a long time—unfortunately, my husband passed."

James tucked his hand in his shorts pocket. "Sorry to hear that."

"Thanks . . . If you're looking for something romantic, the sunset cruise is lovely and comes with a full dinner, which I've heard is good. Music, dancing under the stars . . ."

James backed up. "That sounds great. I think we'll head down to the wharf. The best thing about places like these is being able to walk everywhere."

"There's a lot of shopping and restaurants. Ice cream. Coffee. Quaint bars with fun drinks. Try the Hawthorne Hotel." Charlene turned off the water. "It's supposed to be haunted—ask at the front desk."

"I don't believe in paranormal activity." James puffed his chest. "I pride myself in being a man of education."

Jack shimmered behind him, floating a paper napkin over James's head.

Charlene put her arm through James's and got him out of the kitchen before Jack proved otherwise.

When she returned to let her spectral roommate know she wasn't pleased, he was, of course, nowhere to be found—though his laughter echoed around her in the kitchen.

CHAPTER FOURTEEN

Charlene's cell phone rang around eight Monday evening as she and Jack were watching a documentary on paranormal photography in her suite. Most of the images were easily debunked, but not all, and that gave Charlene and Jack hope that he wasn't the only spectral being out there.

Carrie, Josh, James, and Penny had all gone out on the dinner cruise and wouldn't be back until late, so she was in her pajamas with an afghan over her lap. Her roommate was better than AC in the hot summer months.

"It's Amy," she told Jack, and muted the volume on the TV. She placed her phone on speaker and set it in the middle of the coffee table.

"Hey! How's it going?"

"Charlene, I was talking with Kass, and we booked a room for Tuesday night in Boston."

Bummer—she'd hoped they could all ride together, and now she would have to take her Pilot separately. "Okay. Sounds like fun."

"Even better. I have points for a suite at the Hyatt from my LA days."

"Nice!" She crossed her legs and adjusted the blanket. "What time will you be going to the wake? I'll meet you there. I'd feel funny arriving without you both."

"You misunderstand, sugar pie," Amy said in a Southern drawl. "You're comin' with us."

"I can't leave my guests." Her mind went down her list. "Carrie and Josh are checking out around one, but I still have Penny and James."

"Surely you have household staff that could step in just this once? Kevin said your housekeeper is a real peach."

"You've been planning this with Kevin?" She smiled at Jack and then at the phone. "Why doesn't he go?"

"He doesn't want to do the funeral thing, dahlin'. It's not like he knew Madison, but Kass and I are sorta obligated."

Charlene laughed. "Can't blame the guy. So why stay the night?"

"Why not? We can get massages and be totally pampered in their spa. Take a lemon situation and make spiked lemonade fizzes."

Jack chuckled. "I like her."

Charlene nodded, then shook her head, then sighed. "It's really thoughtful of you, but I just don't know if I should."

"How about if we see some things to recommend to your guests, like Fenway Park or the Cheers bar?"

She had been meaning to spread her wings but hadn't had the chance.

"You should go," Jack encouraged.

"Really?" she mouthed.

He waggled his black brows. "See the sights. You deserve a massage with all the work you do around here."

"You're considering it, aren't you?" Amy said.

"Maybe . . ." She held Jack's gaze. It seemed so frivolous. Was that wrong?

"I owe Kevin five bucks." Amy lost the Southern drawl. "He said a massage wouldn't be the temptation, but if I dangled some sightseeing, *for your guests*, you might allow yourself to be swayed."

"Not just the business," Jack said, "but to observe Madison's wake and funeral. I can watch over things while you're gone. Not physically, of course."

Charlene kept to herself Sam's invitation to sweep her away for a few days of sightseeing and pleasure. Jack was being so sweet, and it hurt her to know he was housebound.

"Let me call Minnie and ask if she and Will wouldn't mind staying over for a night—but just one, all right? What time is everything?"

"The wake is at the chapel in Trinity Church and will be open viewing from noon to six. If we can get there at four, that should give us plenty of time to do something touristy for tomorrow night. The funeral will be Wednesday at the church at three, then graveside, which we might be able to skip. We'll see. So, will you?"

She hesitated, torn between responsibility and what might be fun. "I'll call Minnie right now."

Minnie agreed right away, saying that it would be jolly

good fun to stay in the best room of the bed and breakfast, overlooking the oak tree.

Will grumbled in the background about his own bed until Minnie let him know he could sleep in it without her; she was taking the gel foam mattress . . . then Will had a change of heart. How could he get along without Minnie beside him?

Jack sat back in the armchair and floated her phone before her. Charlene snagged it from thin air.

"Thank you, Minnie—and Will! I'll see you tomorrow, then. Noon is fine."

She ended the call and glared at Jack. "My phone is not a cat toy." Nerves made her stomach whirl. "It feels strange, but I know the bed and breakfast couldn't be in better hands. Minnie knows what to do, and it will only be James and Penny. And as you said, you will be here."

Charlene got up to make a note that Minnie and Will were not to feel obligated to entertain, then she went into her room and pulled out a small wheeled bag from the closet to pack for an overnight stay.

She thumbed through her black dresses for the wake, not finding one she liked for a summer service. Jack stood at the threshold between the living room and her bedroom, mumbling the whole time.

"What did you say?" Charlene turned toward Jack.

"That Minnie's an excellent sport, but what do you think about Will? I can try a few tricks to convince him the place is haunted."

"Don't you dare!" Charlene placed a pair of black shoes alongside the leather bag. "You wanted me to go, so you have to behave yourself."

He levitated her two-piece floral print pj's from the

edge of her bed and floated them over the cat. Silva, who'd been curled on the comforter fast asleep, blinked her golden eyes, then jumped off to the carpet, tail sticking straight up in the air. Her whiskers quivered, and her head bobbed about as if she'd had too much catnip.

"Not funny, Jack." She tilted her head and arched her brow. "You frightened poor Silva."

He waved his hand in front of the Persian's face, and Silva batted at it, her back hunched, her silver fur standing on end.

Charlene watched, amused, then clapped her hand to her forehead. "The bell!"

Jack patted the love seat for her to join him. "Come finish watching the documentary before you leave me for a whole day and night."

She closed the closet, glad to wait until tomorrow to choose her clothes. Picking up Silva, Charlene settled back on the love seat. Jack brought the afghan over both of them.

He sat down, folded one leg over the other, and pouted. "I'm going to miss you, you know."

"I know you will and I'm sorry for that, but you can keep busy for just one night. Maybe you can even find our killer on the video? But if that's too boring without me, why not practice your precision in searching the internet?"

"Talk about *boring*. It would be more fun to spook Will . . . or how about that Penny woman? She's a little uptight and a good scare might make her realize that life is short and she should smile more."

"She doesn't seem very happy, but no fright therapy while I'm gone, Jack."

He exhaled loudly—just to show his annoyance at her

rules. Then he added, "Be safe, Charlene. There might be a killer in your midst."

She knew plenty of folks who hadn't liked Madison. Tomorrow she planned on meeting the family, talking to them, and discovering more of Madison's life before her career in the theater. She hoped to eliminate people from her list.

"I'll keep my eye out for danger—but nothing is going to happen at a wake or the funeral. It'll be a bunch of staid folks showing up to show their respects for the Boswell family. Just like me."

"I hope so. I'll worry about you until you come home again." Jack raised the volume of the documentary and changed the subject. "Do you think I could learn to take pictures?"

"Sure. Why not?" With all the technological gadgets available, they could find something that worked.

Jack's voice grew animated. "I know, when you get back, why don't you try and take mine? We could make our own documentary."

Charlene raised her gaze to the ceiling. Heaven help her if Jack was ever truly bored!

By quarter till two the next day, Charlene hadn't heard from Jack at all—was he trying to show his displeasure at her for going? Or was he just . . . away?

She scrutinized her image in the full-length mirror in her bathroom and smoothed her hand over her hip. The sleeveless black dress fit a bit snugger, thanks to Minnie's cooking. Black heels she hadn't tortured her feet with since working at the ad agency. Her heart-shaped diamond earrings from Jared, and a simple diamond necklace that had been his first anniversary gift. She rarely wore it anymore, but for most of their marriage, she'd hardly taken it off.

Charlene gave a half turn to view the back of her hair—she'd twisted her long dark locks into a braid and clipped the thick mane in place. Hazel eyes, her skin tan from being outdoors. She was mostly the same, but there were changes.

Her stomach jumped to remind her that this was her first funeral since Jared's. They'd had a simple service for family and friends that she barely remembered, having been in a state of shock.

Tyler's grief on Sunday had been plain to see, and she'd recognized the sorrow. Would he be at the wake today?

Her phone dinged with a text from Amy—five minutes away.

"I'm coming, I'm coming."

Charlene stuffed her black Kate Spade clutch with her cell phone, lipstick, and credit cards, then zipped up her small overnight bag and left her suite with a last look back for Jack. "Bye!" she whispered to no one.

She walked into the kitchen and gave Minnie a hug. "I'm less than an hour away. If you have any problems or a question at all, please don't hesitate to call. I'll have my phone with me at all times."

"I'll be fine, honey. You go and enjoy yourself. It'll do you good to get away for a night. I've got my Will to keep me company in this big old house."

"Carrie and Josh are gone, so that just leaves Penny and James. You don't have to entertain them, all right? It's just important to have you here in case they need something."

"We'll be fine."

Her phone dinged, the sound muffled in her clutch. "Amy's here."

"Well, off you go then." Minnie waved her hands in the air to scoot her toward the door. "Funerals are sad, but they also remind us to celebrate life. It's okay to enjoy yourself with your friends—don't worry about a thing."

"Thanks, Minnie. You're a treasure."

"I know." She fluffed her gray curls. "It's my curse."

Smiling, Charlene let herself out to the front porch. Silva lazed on the railing in the shade. She blew the cat a kiss and brought her bag down the steps toward Amy's red Camaro convertible.

The top on the car was down, and Amy wore a bright turquoise scarf around her head. She pressed a button, and the trunk door opened. "Put your bag in and get in the back. Kass needs the leg space up front—she's waiting outside her apartment. We'll pick her up and be on our way."

"Cool car," Charlene told her. She stowed her overnight bag and climbed into the back seat.

"Thanks. Bought it when I lived in California. Not really great for our seasons here, but hey, it's a beautiful sunny day, so let's enjoy it."

"Is this scarf for me?" Charlene pulled a wrap-around burst of yellow silk from where it had been tucked into the seat pocket.

"Yes. I have one for Kass as well. We don't want to arrive with our hair a fright, but I figured this would be fun."

Charlene felt a little like Audrey Hepburn, head wrapped, big sunglasses on, being chauffeured around town. As promised, Kass was standing on a street corner. She stuck out her thumb and showed her leg when she saw Amy's car. Amy veered over, and Kass slammed her small bag in the back and jumped into the front seat with a "Hey, girl—glad you could make it" to Charlene.

The wind in her face caused Charlene to only catch bits and pieces of the conversation going on in the front, but all three of them were in high spirits—even if they were going to a wake. It helped that none of them had been close to Madison.

An hour later, they had three room keys for their suite in the Hyatt, bags unpacked, and the car parked in the underground parking lot. They easily walked the few blocks to the church.

"I went to college here," Kass said. "Trinity Church is a must-see for any visitor—no matter the religious affiliation."

"We're in Copley Square, Charlene," Amy added. "So you have a frame of reference for your guests when they ask."

"Thank you." Trees lined the streets, providing shade from the summer sun. Blue skies and white clouds were at odds with all of the people wearing black going in and out of the church.

Charlene shivered in anticipation. The architecture of this grand old building was extremely beautiful, if ornate.

"It's recently gone through a forty-seven-million-dollar restoration," Kass said, naturally acting as tour guide. "Interior murals cover nearly every wall, hand painted by a team under the direction of an American artist."

"When was it built, Kass?" Charlene asked.

"The original church was on Summer Street, but it burned down in 1872. So, they decided to move and re-build. Henry Hobson Richardson, the architect, had been inspired by ancient churches in southern France and created his masterpiece with a nod to them rather than the prevalent Gothic Revival style that was popular."

Charlene leaned back to take it all in. "Magnificent." What secrets lived inside these walls? It was a fortress.

As they crossed the street, several young men and women exited the church, laughing and holding hands as they headed down the sidewalk. Madison's friends? Friends of the family? Madison's parents and close relatives would probably be here throughout the six-hour viewing. Would Logan show up, despite the bad blood between him and his dad?

Charlene wasn't sure what to expect. Would Madison be in a coffin, dressed like a perfect doll, as one by one each person who entered said their goodbyes? They hadn't done that for Jared.

She followed Kass and Amy into the lobby. Stunning stained-glass windows allowed sunshine through and cast a golden glow inside the cathedral.

"Sheesh, will you look at this!" Amy whirled around with an astounded expression. "Almost worth dying for."

Charlene didn't agree but didn't argue. The artwork was phenomenal, and she immediately wanted to bring her father when her parents came to Salem at the end of the month.

"Hush, we're here to pay our respects." Kass spoke in a low, dignified voice. "Aren't we?"

"That and more," Charlene said softly, a little awed with the place. Having seen a great many museums with her father, she was familiar with beautiful buildings and exquisite designs, but this was one of the finest she'd ever seen.

With a nod toward the welcome center, Charlene led

the way. "We are here for the Boswell wake," she informed the hostess politely.

"That will be in the Rose Chapel. Here's a brochure as your guide."

The three of them took their time to reach the chapel, taking in the opulent windows, the murals, architectural design, and every exquisite detail along the way.

The door to the chapel was open, and one by one they walked in. There had to be close to a hundred mourners seated on the pews. A short line of perhaps twenty waited along the left aisle to say a final goodbye to the young woman in the coffin next to the pulpit.

A lady with a flowing mane of blond tresses, dressed in a white silk gown, was the perfect ethereal vision as she sat near the organ playing a harp. Gentle music created a somber but peaceful mood.

The three of them joined the line, and as she did so Charlene glanced around at the people seated in the wooden pews, hoping to catch sight of some familiar faces. She knew the first row would be Madison's immediate family, Laura and Foster—and there was Logan. Would Madison's death be what the family needed to heal?

That brought other suspicions to mind.

She followed Amy and Kass toward the coffin, her stomach fluttering. Charlene hadn't known Madison at all and felt a bit like a fraud being here, saying a prayer for the woman's soul, and yet she wished her no harm and only wanted to help solve her murder. Madison had paid the ultimate price for her sins.

Amy bowed her head, folded her hands, then closed her eyes and whispered a few words to the captivating, seductive sorceress who had stolen her leading role, a married man's heart, and broken her engagement to the man who'd loved her.

Kass did the same but didn't close her eyes. She studied Madison's body as if trying to peer beneath her waxy flesh—to see if her spirit was intact, perhaps? Or had her soul already gone to wherever her final journey would take her? Was Madison haunting Salem Stage Right, trying to discover for herself who had fired the fatal bullet?

An eerie feeling crept over Charlene as she stepped up to the coffin. She gazed down at Madison, who exuded beauty even in death. She quickly said a prayer for Madison's soul, feeling as though all eyes were upon her. As she walked away, she caught Logan's stare. His gaze passed over her to settle on Kass.

Amy perused the room and led the way to benches in the middle of the chapel, behind a trio of gossiping women. They had their heads bent together and kept their voices low, but not low enough to disguise their subject matter—Madison and Logan.

Charlene leaned forward to hear, hiding behind a pamphlet with Madison's image and a prayer for her everlasting life. "And . . . then . . . Logan. Set up."

Madison had set her brother up? With what? How?

Amy noticed that Charlene was listening, and winked, then introduced herself to the three women.

"I'm Amy Fadar—here with the theater in Salem. How do you know Madison?"

The woman with dark blond hair, who'd been whispering the loudest, said, "I've known the Boswell family since the kids were in preschool. Dina Prentiss. Teacher."

Amy batted her eyes and lowered her head. "It's such a shame."

Charlene gave a wan smile. "I see that Logan has joined the family again?"

Dina snorted her indignation. "Logan was the sweetest of the two Boswell siblings, responsible for his sister . . . and she turned on him like a viper."

Kass used her chin to point toward Logan. "What happened? I heard rumors . . ." she drawled, playing her part of grieving friend.

A younger redhead giggled, then put a hand over her mouth to whisper, "She told their parents that he was selling drugs at school. He was in his second year at Columbia. I had the biggest crush."

"Was he selling them?" a skinny brunette asked in a hushed tone.

"Of course not," Dina and the redhead said at once.

"Madison was jealous, plain and simple, that Logan was doing so well. Why, with his money and smarts, would he risk everything to sell drugs?" Dina's nostrils flared.

Amy leaned forward. "I heard that Madison used her beauty to get her way. I saw it for myself at the theater."

Kass nodded and dabbed her lashes with a tissue. "Poor Logan."

The redhead, the brunette, and Dina all nodded furiously. "Even as a child Madison used her eyes to get the other children to do what she wanted." Dina flicked a glance toward the oblivious family. "She ruined her family out of spite."

"Was Logan arrested?" Charlene asked. A criminal past would be something she could research online, if needed.

"He was on college probation for two years," the redhead said in a dreamy tone, peeking toward the front of the church and Logan. "He and his father really got into it, and I heard he'd been kicked out of the family. I don't know for sure though."

The skinny brunette raised a scrawny finger. "I think he hit rock bottom before finding his way out. I'm amazed he's here at all."

Kass put her pale hand to her chest and sighed. "How awful. I can't imagine forgiving something like that! Not from a family member."

Charlene agreed—would Logan have taken his revenge in his own hands? Why now? Had her move to Salem been a catalyst to the family?

Dina said, "Some people are just born bad. Madison was one of them. She appeared like an angel, but would cry and tattletale to get her way. That girl could lie with a straight face. Her teachers used to all talk about it."

"An actor was the perfect job for her," the skinny brunette said.

And yet, according to many sources, Madison hadn't been able to act. Had she been the kind to lie to herself so well that it became the truth?

Charlene watched Laura, Foster, and Logan. Laura wore a veil over her face and repeatedly brought her embroidered handkerchief to her mouth. Logan appeared to be dozing upright, with his shoulders relaxed and eyes closed. Foster was red-faced, sitting on the opposite side of his wife, far from Logan, as he glared at the coffin.

Amy murmured, "She was awful, but surely, murdered at twenty-eight is too harsh a punishment. Who would do such a thing?"

"I wish we knew," Dina said emphatically. "It's tearing the family up, and she's already done enough damage."

After a good half hour of gossip, Charlene learned that

Madison had gone to an all-girls school and discovered acting. Her parents hadn't approved. Dina had lost track of her for the most part when Madison had moved to Beverly Hills to be near her grandmother. They didn't know she'd been engaged.

The women left and Amy, Kass, and Charlene went to give their condolences to the Boswells, still seated in the front row.

Charlene recognized them from when she and Jack had done some research online, but both had aged ten years in the last week. Foster was a fourth-generation banker, and Laura a savvy women's lawyer and activist. Logan was a gorgeous mix of both his parents.

Amy started with Logan to shake his hand, then Laura, then Foster, and stepped back. "I'm so sorry for your loss," Amy said.

Laura flipped her veil up, wiped tears from her eyes, and crushed a cloth handkerchief. "How did you know my daughter, dear?"

"We first met in LA a few years ago. Acting is its own world."

"Madison adored it." Laura dabbed the end of her nose.

Charlene got the undercurrent that perhaps her family had never come around to supporting Madison's choice. Would they have considered her career a taint on the prestigious family name?

Amy gestured to Kass, who was in line behind her and had shaken Logan's and Laura's hands already. "And we were in a local play together, in Salem."

Charlene had barely clasped fingers with Logan. There were so many things she wanted to say to him, to ask, but now was not the time.

"Yes." Foster spat the word out. "Where some criminal had the goddamn nerve to shoot my unarmed daughter right through the chest. I hope he fries for this!"

Logan, straight-faced, leaned across the pew to tap his dad's knee. "Dad. Remember where we are."

Public? Church? What did Logan mean?

"I will tell the truth, and I don't care where I am," the heartbroken man spoke louder, then his shoulders slumped, and he began to cry.

Logan handed him a stack of tissues, which he blew his nose into but continued to sob. His wife rubbed his back, making soothing sounds.

Charlene stepped away from their grief, stricken with a reminder of her own, and into the aisle toward the exit. Amy again was in the lead, then Charlene, with Kass bringing up the rear.

She was ready for a large drink and that massage to take away the bone-deep sorrow this had brought on.

"Wait!"

The three of them turned at the exit of the Rose Chapel. Logan grabbed Kass's arm.

Kass's ebony brow arched in admonishment, and yet there was an instant spark even Charlene could see.

Logan released her but didn't step back. He had brown hair with blond streaks, deep brown eyes, and a smooth-shaven, strong jaw.

"Kass, right?" He was a very attractive man, as seductive in his own way as his sister. "Wait," he said again.

Kass's tone was sultry. "For what?" Her body language was relaxed and fluid, her long limbs loose.

"My parents are hosting a smaller gathering at the house following this ridiculous wake. Starts at seven."

Kass said nothing.

"I'd like the three of you to be there." Logan tossed a glimpse over his shoulder to where the black-clad mourners sat. "You'll liven up the place."

"Well"—Kass made her voice extra husky—"we'd have to be invited."

Logan dug around inside his black suit jacket. "Here's my card. A valet will park your car, and the butler will let you in. Don't worry. I'll tell him three gorgeous women are showing up, and he'd better see you to the gardens. It'll be poolside, around back."

The three of them exchanged glances. They all wanted to know more about Madison, just as Logan was curious about them. Charlene offered her hand. "I'm Charlene. If you're sure?" This would be a golden opportunity to see how Madison had grown up. Tyler hadn't been at the wake. Would he be at the home?

"I'm Amy. I was in the play with Madison."

"Yeah. *The Rebel Rousers*, was that it?"

She laughed softly. "No. *Salem's Rebels* was the name. I'm real sorry about your sister."

"Don't be. I'm not."

He turned to Kass and took her hands. "You must be an actress too. You have that whole Cleopatra thing going on."

Kass gave a husky laugh. "Never heard that line before, but I kind of like it."

Charlene examined her friend. Her hair was slightly different. She had thick bangs, her raven hair straight to her hips, heavy blue eyeliner. She wore a long, black, layered skirt and a black silk top. She had a light black wrap draped across her shoulder.

Cleopatra, huh? Whatever it was, Kass rocked it.

CHAPTER FIFTEEN

Charlene couldn't help but smile at how enthusiastic Kass was about Logan Boswell the entire three-block sojourn to the Hyatt.

"Did you see his dimples?" Kass gushed. "Outrageous. Why is that man in banking? He could steal the screen and be a millionaire."

"Probably because he's making billions with his hedge fund company?" Amy quipped.

"Oh that . . ." The three of them laughed and entered the hotel. Charlene had never heard Kass so talkative, and found it adorable.

Once inside the suite, Charlene put her hands on her hips as she stared at her black dress for tomorrow's funeral, hanging up; her jeans and casual blouse; and then scrutinized the black sheath she wore already. "Will the occasion be dressier than any of what I brought?" she asked Amy and Kass.

Amy joined Charlene to peruse her clothes. "My closet is just like yours . . . black, black, jeans. Kass?"

Kass twisted her long ebony hair into a side braid over her shoulder. "Same—except for my jeans are black too. Listen, I want something to wow Logan with—anybody feel like shopping?"

"That's a great idea." Charlene immediately recalled her limited selection to choose from and squashed a spurt of guilt.

"Let's ask at the front desk for something close by." Amy turned her back on the closet. "Unless you know of one, Kass?"

"When I lived here my budget was thrift shop only." Kass picked up her black slouchy leather purse. "I still love them, but thankfully my *fortunes* have improved."

"Don't think I missed the toss-in of your name." Amy shook her head and ushered Kass toward the door, both giggling.

"Let's go!" Charlene hadn't shopped for herself in a long time. She'd made many purchases, as her bank account could attest to, but they were usually business related.

"Copley Place mall has high-end shopping," the clerk informed them moments later. "Just a few blocks away." He gave them a map.

"What time is it?" Amy asked as they shuffled away from the desk.

Charlene checked her phone. "Half past five. Should we eat dinner first?"

"I don't think so," Kass said. "I bet there will be a bunch of food. I still can't believe we're going to their house. The Boswells are well-known for their charitable events and mansion on the hill. It's one of those that tourists drive by."

They avoided the name-brand stores for a boutique shop with silks and satins, so they could find something unique. Charlene explained to the saleslady about the evening, and the woman suggested summery dresses—not quite mourning but not a dance club either.

"Well, darn it," Kass said, dropping her arms to her sides. "That ruins my whole plan. Hot-pink sequins."

The saleslady glanced at Kass in alarm.

"She's joking," Charlene assured the woman.

Amy elbowed Kass. "I'd love to see you in hot pink."

"That's more your color, Amy," Charlene said.

The saleslady raised her hands to resume control of the conversation. "We have long dresses to the right and shorter styles to the left. Would you like to browse?"

They each went a different direction. Charlene found a soft silk dress the color of tangerine, piped in black, which flowed beautifully right above her knees. The deep V-neckline showed off her diamond necklace, and the saleslady found a black clip to hold her hair off her neck. Kass, between trying on dresses, arranged Charlene's hair into a classy updo—Jared's diamond earrings sparkled all the more. She already had black heels on. "Done!" Charlene pronounced.

Another saleslady helped Amy, who was on her fourth dress, three others in a forlorn heap over a chair.

"Well?" Amy floated from behind the curtain in a cerulean blue off-the-shoulder dress that flattered her slender figure.

"It's perfect for you," Charlene said. "Want me to take a picture to send to Kevin?"

Amy winked. "Yeah—let him know what he's missing. Oh, Kass. That is dynamite. Logan will be a puddle of mush when he gets a look at your legs."

Kass stayed true to her dramatic black in a dress with a front-and-back plunging neckline that draped over her slim hips and had a slit up to her thigh. The saleswoman found her gladiator sandals and a wide onyx choker. Cleopatra had nothing on Kass.

"Logan doesn't stand a chance," Charlene announced.

Kass nodded at her reflection and looped her arms through Charlene's and Amy's. The saleslady snapped a few shots for them that Amy sent to Kevin.

"What's the plan?" Amy asked as they returned to their hotel to pick up Amy's car from the garage.

"To seduce Logan?" Kass twirled her hair around her finger.

"That's *your* plan, and we will help," Amy assured her, "but I was talking about the 'discover things about Madison' plan."

Charlene intended to use the evening for exploration. Did Madison have any true friends, or had she burned all her bridges? What had she been like as a kid? "We need to be aware of anything that might lead to who killed Madison."

"I'll keep Logan occupied." Kass smirked and fluttered her fingers. "You guys do whatever you have to do."

"I'm very interested in how come he and Madison didn't get along, and why he was at the Common to see the play." Charlene got into the back of the convertible.

"Good. That's very specific." Kass sat in the front passenger side. "I can do that."

Amy climbed behind the wheel. "I once played this young woman who was killed by her own dad. He'd abused her, and when she started fighting back, he ended things permanently." She slashed her finger over her throat, then started the car.

"I really hope that Madison wasn't killed by anyone in her family, but we can't cross it out," Charlene said.

"Way to land an arrow into my cupid's heart." Kass drew a heart in the air with her fingers and settled back against the seat for the mile ride from the hotel to the Boswell mansion.

Would the killer be here tonight? Goose bumps dotted Charlene's skin. Wouldn't it be just the cat's meow if she could return home, call Sam, and tell him she'd solved the murder? What would her detective say to that?

They waited in line in a long circular driveway. Once the car ahead reached the valet, the driver and passenger would step out, and then the line would move forward another car's length. "Is that a Wahlberg brother who just got out?" Amy asked, leaning over the dash for a better look.

"Told you," Kass said. "The Boswells are a key part of the Boston community."

When it was their turn, Amy handed over the keys for her Chevy Camaro, not seeming to mind the dent in the rear fender. The other cars were Bentleys, Mercedes, Jaguars, and Porsches. Charlene knew that both Amy and Kass had learned the same as she that money did not guarantee happiness.

The butler, a silver-haired man in his sixties, greeted them in the marble foyer like old friends. "Mr. Logan directed me to show you to his table. This way."

Kass hooked her arm through the surprised butler's, and Charlene and Amy followed behind. Charlene couldn't help but be in awe of the stately home, the enormous chandelier in the entranceway that glittered like a thousand diamonds, the gold-framed paintings on the walls, which were surely collector's items and not from a thrift shop like Vintage Treasures. The gorgeous white sweeping staircase led to the second floor—Charlene could only guess at how many bedrooms.

It was an impressive abode, but she wouldn't trade "Charlene's" for it, or a dozen more.

They stepped out to the vast garden and pool, with the city backdrop in the distance. Bubbling fountains around the aqua water appeared centuries old, and a gold cherub peeked out behind huge pots of flowering plants.

Beyond the sparkling resort-style pool was a cabana with a bar, where attendants served guests food from individual stations. Several people stood in line holding white china plates, balancing their drink in the opposite hand. Outside the cabana, a trio played low music that allowed for conversation.

Logan held court at a round table for six draped with black linen, a bottle of champagne on the table, his flute full, three more empty. The butler paraded Kass on his arm. "Your guests," he said to Logan with a dip of his head.

Kass grinned. "Well, hello there, Mr. Boswell. Nice digs."

"Welcome!" Logan didn't stand but waved his hand. "Have a seat. I hope you like champagne?" Dom Perignon nestled in a crystal bucket of ice. "There's plenty more where this came from."

Charlene and Amy sat across from Logan, and Kass chose a chair right next to his. He stood and poured. "Let's have a toast." They all raised their glasses. "To my dear sister Madison, who brought us all together. May her soul rot in hell."

Charlene froze. She couldn't drink to that. "Uh, I would prefer just the first part."

Logan's jaw tensed as he stared at Charlene in challenge. His brown eyes filled with anger, but then he let it go. "Fine." They all touched glasses, and as she raised hers to take a sip, she saw a man with longish blond hair slicked back from a handsome, tanned face. Tyler.

"Do you know him?" she asked after they'd sipped and put their flutes down.

Logan followed her head tilt. "I just met him a few days ago. Tyler Lawson—Madison's talent agent and supposed fiancé, but it was the first I'd heard of him." He drank. "That doesn't mean anything since we weren't close. Mom and Dad, however, welcomed him with open arms for the few minutes they were home on Saturday. They had to deal with funeral arrangements on Madison's birthday." His jaw clenched.

"How awful," Charlene said, shifting her gaze from Logan to Tyler, then back.

"This whole thing's been hell." Logan shrugged and gestured for the butler to bring another bottle of Dom. "Tyler showed me a picture of their engagement dinner. Seems he'd given Madison his mother's emerald ring— then Madison suddenly split four months ago, with the ring and no word. He doesn't know why."

Charlene expelled a breath. She couldn't say *how awful* again, but that was exactly how she felt.

"I asked my parents about the ring, but it hasn't turned up with any of Madison's things. Not at her apartment in Salem, or the theater." Logan raised his filled flute toward Tyler. Tyler nodded but then turned his attention to the food line.

"This must be very difficult for him," Charlene said, wondering what had happened to the emerald. It hadn't been on Madison's finger when she was shot. Neither Amy nor Michelle had seen it. And yet, she remembered her up on the stage addressing the audience, and how the sunlight had shone off a large flashy ring.

"Yeah. I told him if I found it, I'd let him know. He gave me his business card, and I looked him up. Lives in LA, a big shot agent to the stars. His social media page is all about his famous clients—my sister wasn't listed, which probably sucked for her—and his fancy cars. Little flashy if you ask me." Logan gave Charlene a knowing smile. "Want me to introduce you?"

"No, thanks. I bumped into him that day at the festival. Or he actually bumped into me. Splashed his frozen Frappuccino on my arm but then paid for my drink. Doesn't he look like Leo DiCaprio?"

"Definitely," Amy said. "I've heard of Tyler Lawson—he reps one of my friends in LA and got her a movie deal. Madison never told me his last name."

"Seems like a golden opportunity for Madison to hook up with a guy like him," Charlene said. "But her name wasn't listed on his website as a client, Logan?"

"Madison couldn't act," Amy said. "Not his fault."

"Tyler said he still loves her, even though she broke his heart. Par for the course with my dear sister, but I didn't tell him that. She probably dumped him when he didn't make her a star." Logan radiated tension as he balanced his chair on the two rear legs, then righted it again. "I bet she stole that ring to get back at him. She was cruel and petty like that."

Amy lifted her head. "She slandered me after I couldn't help her, so I wouldn't take that bet."

Logan's gaze glinted in the light of the tiki torches, and Charlene glimpsed danger.

According to the ladies at the chapel earlier, Logan had been to rock bottom and clawed his way up to the light, kicked aside because of Madison. Charlene couldn't put her finger on what she saw in those orbs, exactly. He was arrogant, yes, privileged, for sure, but there was more to the picture . . . darkness lurked inside. She'd like to warn Kass, but she knew her friend wouldn't listen or care.

Kass had her own dark secrets and was more than a match for Logan, if you took out the money factor to even the playing field.

"I say we change the subject away from my sister before we lose our appetites." Logan leaned forward slightly, his forearm on the table. "They're carving up some prime beef or racks of lamb with plenty of sides. Another station has the seafood—shrimp, oysters on the half shell, lobster tails. Salads and desserts are set up just beyond."

Charlene and Amy stood up. Kass set her wrist on her armrest and winked at them. "I think I'll wait a while."

Logan poured her more champagne. "I'll keep you company."

Well played, Kass.

Logan and Kass had chemistry, and she just hoped her friend wouldn't get hurt.

"I'm a lobster girl," Charlene told Amy as they entered the large sheltered area next to the house filled with delicious smells. "How about you?"

"Haven't met one I didn't like." They joined the end of

the seafood line as a bartender floated by with a tray of drinks.

"Ladies, would you like a glass of red or white?"

They both chose white and enjoyed the crisp wine as they waited their turn. "What do you think of Logan?" Amy asked.

Her first response was that he seemed dangerous, but she kept that to herself. She would hate to be wrong, as sometimes happened in her quick judgments. "He's got a dynamic personality."

Amy moved forward a half step. "Specifics! What does that mean? Is our Kass going to get burned?"

Charlene sipped the chardonnay. "I think Logan's been raised in luxury and has a high opinion of himself"—she thought of the butler directed to bring them to his table, where he'd waited confidently with Dom—"yet he's just as competitive as his family, in his own way. Dismissive of anyone he believes beneath him."

"Well, if we're talking money alone, that's what—ninety-nine percent of the population?" Amy's long light-brown hair slid down her arm as she shrugged.

Charlene laughed. "He's the top one percent and knows it—and wants everyone else to be aware of it too. But Kass is a confident woman; she's unique. Challenging. I think she can hold her own in whatever immeasurable test he's got in his head."

"Agreed. It's great to see her having fun tonight. He doesn't like his sister much, does he?" Amy stepped closer to the array of seafood. "But since he's not worried about telling us, perfect strangers, his feelings, he couldn't have set up the hit. Only a fool would be so openly hostile, right?"

"Or," Charlene countered, "he's extremely clever and

making it obvious that he hates her, so we and the rest of the world will believe him innocent. It could go either way."

"He is clever, and I suspect conniving as well." Amy frowned. "We should warn Kass not to let down her guard."

"Let's try." It was their turn at last, and Charlene handed her plate to the attendant in a white chef's uniform. "I'll have lobster, please, and a few shrimp and oysters."

"Certainly, ma'am." He turned to Amy. "And you?"

"I'll have the same," Amy told him with a smile.

They brought their plates of grilled lobster to the table. Kass leaned toward Logan, laughing low and trailing her finger over his forearm. Logan was focused on Kass, completely enthralled. Obviously, flattery from an attractive woman made even a man with his ego and money feel like a king.

"That looks pretty good," he said jovially as they sat down. "Kass, you ready yet?"

"I'm ready for anything." Kass stood, and her black dress parted to reveal a length of thigh.

Logan was up in an instant and slid an arm around her waist, murmuring something in her ear. Charlene exchanged glances with Amy, and they both hid their smiles.

They dived into their juicy lobster tail and melted butter, enjoying the rich, full flavor. "This is so awesome to be invited here tonight. I wasn't sure what we'd do about dinner." Charlene savored another bite.

"I was thinking we'd definitely have seafood, and there are plenty of amazing restaurants around our hotel. Luke's Lobster, Island Creek Oyster Bar. But nothing beats this." Amy licked butter from her upper lip.

"Price is right too."

They clinked glasses.

Charlene squirted lemon over her shrimp and oysters, complete with horseradish sauce. "Mmm, this is so good. Imagine living like this all the time."

"It would get old quick," Amy said.

"Right. Of course it would." They shared a laugh.

"Wouldn't it be nice if Kass married him and invited us over all the time?" Amy said, watching the crowd, resting her chin in her hand.

"Nice thought, but here they come. Should we leave them alone?"

"After one more glass of that delicious champagne."

Charlene glanced at Kass's plate when she elegantly returned to her seat like she'd been born to be a lady of the manor. "What? You went for lamb instead of lobster?"

"I went to college around here, remember? And this tender rib is going to be delicious." Kass shrugged and peeked at Logan from beneath her bangs. "Besides, maybe Logan will feed me lobster later."

Logan pushed his plate of lamb away with a grin. "I'll order two to go, with extra butter, this instant."

"To go?" Amy asked.

"I'm staying in the guest house." He jerked his thumb behind them. "Would you join me, Kass?"

"Of course." She slid her knee next to his. "Later."

Conversation as everyone finished eating was kept casual. Answering a question from Amy about the famous bar, Cheers, Logan said it was one of his neighborhood pubs. They discovered he was a devout Red Sox fan and had season tickets for the Bruins.

"I'm ready for something sweet." Amy pushed back her chair.

"Dessert is that way." Logan pointed to his right at a cabana lit in blue.

"I'm going to wash up first," Charlene told her friend.

Logan waved toward where they'd entered. "Follow the lights," he instructed before returning his attention to Kass. Charlene made her way past the pool and entered the double glass doors where the butler had escorted them.

She looked from right to left and entered the parlor. Chatter and laughter sounded from the kitchen, and on impulse Charlene took the grand white stairs, quietly making her way to the second floor. If someone stopped her, she'd say she was lost, searching for a restroom. The only thing on her was her Kate Spade clutch. Couldn't steal the crown jewels with that.

Upstairs was a large open foyer that shot off in either direction down luxuriously carpeted halls. On the far wall was an enormous mural of a tree, with leaves and branches. At the center were framed photos of Laura and Foster Boswell. To either side were their parents, and above them, more leaves and branches with names. Logan and Madison were below their parents. The frames were works of art.

Madison must have been about sixteen in her photo. So very pretty, her expression sweet as candy. Had that also been an act?

Logan, two years older, would probably have gone to Columbia that fall. He had a look of innocence too. His hair was long and shaggy, his smile infectious, slightly mischievous.

But it was his sister who'd deliberately broken the family branch. Madison had lied about him dealing drugs, according to Dina Prentiss, and destroyed his family relationships as well as his reputation.

What would her motivation be to do such a thing to her only brother? How had Madison gained from bringing him down? Alienate him, so that she'd receive all of her parents' love? If he'd been stricken from the will, she'd get the bigger share. Was her plan all about the money?

That didn't fit with what she'd learned so far about Madison. Her driving need was to be the star. Perhaps the family had favored their son when they were both small children, and Madison had to do something to get their notice. By discrediting her brother, she'd stepped up a notch and grew in power. She could win people over with a brilliant smile, entrance them with her golden-brown eyes. Her family might have been her first experiment in controlling other people, making them her first victims.

From the Boswells' display at church, they loved their daughter very much. Had that always been a fact, or had she stolen their affection by destroying Logan so that she had all of their attention?

Charlene had no idea what she hoped to find, but since she was already upstairs, she might as well take a look. Gingerly, she crept down the right-hand hallway.

As expected, the doors to the bedrooms were closed, each empty when she peered inside, but at the end of the corridor was a game room. Comfortable chairs and sofas were sorted around a giant eighty-five-inch TV. In one corner of the room was a billiard table with a set of Royal Crown billiard balls, framed by a triangle. Hanging on the wall were four cue sticks in a rack, a bridge stick, and two brushes. On an opposite wall was a mechanical dartboard. Next to it was a bar.

Tyler sat at it with a drink, thumbing through a photo album. He turned when he realized he was no longer alone.

His blue eyes glinted with unshed tears.

Her heart raced. "What are you doing here?"

"I could ask you the same thing." Tyler closed the photo album and walked toward her, his beer in hand.

"I was looking for a restroom, then I saw the pictures at the top of the stairs. I couldn't resist a quick peek." Charlene wished she hadn't been quite so curious. She hoped Tyler wouldn't say anything to Logan—but she was probably safe, as Kass had his undivided attention. Safe for tonight anyway.

"You expect me to believe that?" Tyler held his arm to his side as if to say, *Come on, lady.*

"Yes, why not?" Charlene lifted her chin. "I have an old mansion that I run as a bed and breakfast, and curiosity got the better of me. Comparing one grand estate to another."

"Did you come to any conclusions regarding whatever you'd hoped to find?"

Charlene gripped the strap of her clutch. "I wasn't searching for anything in particular."

"I wasn't implying you were. I fear the woman doth protest too much." Tyler spoke theatrically.

"Are you an actor too?"

"I'm a talent agent in LA." His shoulders relaxed slightly.

"Logan mentioned that. What were you doing here?"

"Unlike you, ma'am, I'll give an honest answer . . . I was hoping to find Madison's room. To see what her life was like before . . ." Tyler swallowed, but she saw the hint of grief. "When she was a kid. She was so cute, even then." He pointed to the album he'd left on the bar top.

"I'm sorry for your loss. I know you were once engaged."

"You probably think I'm a sucker, being here, crying over her. That woman broke up with me without a word, and left for Salem." Tyler pinched the space between his brows. "I want my mother's antique gold and emerald ring. It's an heirloom."

"I suppose it was worth a fortune."

"No. Market value of less than a grand."

"Not worth stealing for a woman who already has a healthy bank account." Charlene held her purse closer to her body. Logan had assumed that Madison would have taken it just to be cruel. "I don't understand why she wouldn't just give it back."

"Madison? You didn't know her very well. She collects things . . . people. She had me at her feet the first time I saw her smile—she was at her grandmother's for a party. We had an instant connection."

Charlene hadn't known her at all, but she didn't give that away. "She was bewitching." She wondered how many people Madison had used her hypnotic gaze on. Was that the instant connection he'd felt?

Tyler passed by her, out of the room to the hall. "Logan said the family's private rooms were on the third floor. Want to tag along?"

Oh yes, she did, but it would be wrong. "No, thank you. I'll get back to the party."

"Do me a favor and don't mention that you saw me . . . and I won't mention that I saw you, either."

Her cheeks flamed. He had her there.

"I'm sorry that you got caught up in her ways. It seems that she hurt a lot of people. Sad to say, but I suppose you were a victim of hers too."

"I'm nobody's victim." Tyler moved down the hall to the far right where a smaller staircase was. He climbed them two at a time. "C'mon, Charlene. Sure you don't want to join me?"

Charlene went the other direction before she changed her mind. "Good luck," she said. "Finding the ring."

He wouldn't find it here. Madison had been wearing it the day of the show and it had gone missing afterward. She didn't bother trying to be stealthy as she rushed down the hall to the center foyer and staircase, entering the room with the family tree on the wall.

Laura Boswell, impeccable in her designer mourning clothes, whirled, a whiskey tumbler in her hand.

Empty.

"Who are you? What are you doing here?"

Charlene wished the carpeted floor would open up and swallow her. She waited and nothing happened.

Raising her chin, she stepped forward, her hand outstretched. Good manners, her mother always said, can see you through anything.

"Hello, Mrs. Boswell. I'm Charlene Morris."

CHAPTER SIXTEEN

Caught. Guilty. Would Laura Boswell have Charlene arrested? What would Sam say to her then?

Charlene was shaking so bad she had to brace her legs to keep them from buckling. And then . . . Laura's eyes welled, and she clasped Charlene's fingers.

"I remember you from earlier today . . . you're an actress. Logan invited you to the house. Why aren't you outside, enjoying the dinner with my son?"

Charlene chose to evade the question. She didn't correct the woman's idea that Charlene was part of the theater with Amy and Kass, either. "I'm sorry to bother you. I didn't mean to intrude. Someone mentioned your family tree, and having an interest in genealogy, I had to check it out. I hope you don't mind." It was partly true. Her father had done the whole MyHeritage.com thing, and knew the history of their ancestors, and had shared a wealth of information with her.

"It's fine, I suppose." Confusion crossed her face. "I'm Laura, but you already know that." Laura brought her empty glass to her chest and faced the family tree. "Do you have children, Charlene?"

"No."

Laura glared at the artistic rendering with curlicue green ink leaves off a central brown trunk. "My daughter will never have her own branch."

Charlene felt the sting of that personally. "You'll miss her a lot. Were you close?"

"Madison was far from perfect, but she was my only daughter and I loved her." Laura's lip quivered as she stared at their portraits. She hadn't answered Charlene's question either.

"Of course you did." Charlene reached for Laura's arm but drew back—her natural instinct to offer comfort might not be welcomed.

"Foster, my husband's side of the family was quite prolific—he's one of four. Two sons, two daughters, all who married properly and added to the family wealth. They did their duty." There was a catch in her voice as she said this, her body swaying.

"Can I get you a chair?" Charlene scanned the room for something in case the woman collapsed—from grief or drink, it didn't matter. This wasn't a space for sitting but for admiring the Boswell family.

"I'm fine." Laura curled the tumbler closer to her bosom. Tears spilled. "Foster never fails to point out that my side of the family is where all the problems derive. He used to call me determined, but now I'm stubborn. He used to admire my drive, but now he considers me hard." She swallowed and dabbed at her eyes with the napkin from the whiskey glass.

"I'm so sorry." Charlene knew she would never get another chance like this, so she asked softly, "Do you have your family around?"

"My mother, Priscilla Phipps, was divorced several times. She moved to Beverly Hills twenty years ago to marry her plastic surgeon. On my inheritance."

"Oh . . . that's terrible. How could that have happened?"

"She was my trustee and over the years emptied my account, even though she had plenty of money of her own. *Family* money. Both my parents are dead now."

"I'm so sorry. Madison moved to California. Were she and your mother close?"

Laura's cheeks turned bright red as she swayed left to right, cradling the tumbler like a baby. "Yes. I can't begrudge either of them a relationship, though it should have been Madison and me. A mother loves her child with all her heart, and that child . . ." She hiccupped. "That child can break it without a second thought."

Charlene couldn't help but pat Laura's shoulder. "Madison's death broke your heart."

Laura glanced guiltily behind her to make sure they were alone. "It wasn't just her death. My heart was crushed many times. Children do that from time to time." She sucked in a breath. "Forget I said anything. She's my daughter, and I love her. But both she and my mother stole from me. That's the bitter truth. Do you think it was me? Because I was too hard?" The glass slipped from her fingers, and Charlene caught it before it hit the carpet.

"Is there someone we can call to help you to bed? Your husband maybe? A maid?"

"Take me to the elevator," Laura ordered, her mouth in a thin line. Charlene guessed her to be fifty, but her face was without wrinkles. What elevator? She spun around but saw nothing.

A young woman wearing a white apron and cap darted out from the warren of doors and halls and stopped in surprise. "Oh! Mrs. Boswell?"

"Get Sheila," Laura ordered. "I'm ready to retire for the evening. I can't . . ." Tears dripped as steadily as a rainstorm. "I can't."

Charlene stepped away, and the maid hurried forward to lead Mrs. Boswell down a hallway behind a wooden door. She studied the pictures of Madison and Grandma— the golden plaque read Priscilla Phipps. The elderly woman was beautiful in a fun-loving kind of way, as if she knew how to laugh. How to love. And made no apologies for it.

Laura didn't have the same expression—she exuded confidence but not joy. If she'd understood Laura correctly, Madison might have managed to get her mother's fortune.

Where would that go now that Madison was dead? Did she have a will? If not, wouldn't her parents and Logan, the closest relatives, inherit all that she had?

The maid returned. "Can I show you back to the party? This part of the house is for family, ma'am."

"My apologies." Charlene handed the maid the empty glass. "I was looking for the restroom . . ."

The maid brought her to the staircase and gave precise directions to the ladies' lounge downstairs. After freshening up, Charlene went outside to find Amy, Kass, and Logan, still at the table, the mood subdued.

"Hi! I was starting to get worried about you," Amy said.

"I got lost!" she said.

"Oh, really?" Logan asked, turning from Kass. "Where did you wander off to?" His voice hardened, and he studied her with suspicion.

As he had every right to do. "Logan, I just saw your mother, in the room with the family tree."

"Is she all right?" Logan straightened, all signs of relaxation gone in a snap.

The sleeping tiger ready to pounce. Charlene touched her earrings and sat in her chair. "She called for Sheila, and a maid brought her to her room."

"Her maid. God, I don't blame Mom if she takes a Xanax and crashes. This is bound to be hard. Madison was a bitch, yes, but . . ." He shrugged. "A mother's love."

"Should you go to her?" Charlene glanced over her shoulder to the mansion, lit up like Christmas though it was July.

"Me?" Logan scoffed and reached for his champagne. "I lost my golden-child status about ten years ago. Mom and Dad both turned their backs on me. Never their precious Madison, who could do no wrong in their eyes. Mom won't want to see me now. My parents and I barely speak, only to keep up appearances."

Kass snuggled close to him. "I understand about that."

Charlene wasn't sure how to answer and so decided that she would just keep quiet about her adventures in the house.

"Charlene, let's get dessert for the table," Amy said. "I took one look at all the choices and couldn't decide, so I waited for you."

Kass kept her hand on Logan's forearm. "That's a great idea."

Charlene put her purse on her chair and followed Amy to the blue cabana.

"What did you find out?" Amy asked her once they were out of earshot.

"Laura Boswell is truly grieving. She knows her daughter's faults but loves her regardless. It's sad that Logan doesn't get to be part of that or feel welcomed by his own family."

"True—he didn't have much nice to say about either of his parents or his sister. You caught him in a weak moment when he showed compassion just now."

They reached the buffet of tarts, pies, chocolate, and ice cream.

"So we meet again," Tyler said as he joined them by the stack of white plates.

Charlene ducked her face, but her hair was in a clip and wouldn't hide her blush. "Did you find what you were looking for?"

"No. And who is this?"

"Amy Fadar," she said, shaking his hand. "An actress friend of Madison's."

"Tyler Lawson. Agent for the stars." His brows came together and then relaxed. "I know you . . ."

"I recognized you too. Not at first, but then it came to me." Amy gave a modest smile. "I was Nathaniel in the play, the day Madison was shot."

He winced. "Not from then—I didn't stick around after the play started. No, what else have you been in?"

Amy listed her movie credentials, and Tyler snapped his fingers. "That explains why you outclassed everyone else on that stage. And I saw you at the theater for Madison's actors fund."

"I was Hermia."

"Why did you give up LA for Salem?" Tyler exuded confidence. Arrogance. A man who knew he had it all and had been blessed with Leo's looks. The universe had stacked the odds in his favor, but that could be said of many of the people here tonight.

"I know it seems crazy, but my boyfriend is in Salem," Amy said, letting Tyler know that she was spoken for and not interested, in a classy way.

Charlene put four strawberry tarts on her plate along with some fresh fruit.

Amy took four eclairs and four mini cheesecakes.

"You ladies must have a sweet tooth."

"We're bringing dessert for everybody," Charlene said. "Want to join us?"

Tyler looked back to where Kass and Logan sat, engaged in conversation. "I think I'll pass. It's close to midnight, and I want to get a good night's rest before tomorrow. I can't believe that Madison will be gone. All that beauty, buried in the dark." He choked up. "Forever."

Charlene set her plate down to pat his arm. "I'm sorry."

"At the wake, seeing her, you can imagine that she's just sleeping, but tomorrow . . ."

Once the coffin was in the ground, there would be no waking up.

Amy nodded, her eyes filling. "I haven't lost anyone close to me, but I get where you're coming from. This party seems almost out of place. A celebration of her life, perhaps? A way to ease the pain of tomorrow?"

"Will you go back to LA right after the funeral, Tyler?" Charlene asked, retrieving her desserts.

"I fly home on Friday, after the reading of the will."

Tyler tugged at the back of his blond hair. "I'm hoping her lawyers will have my mother's ring."

"I hope so too." Charlene lifted the tray and stepped toward the table.

"It was a pleasure to meet you," Amy said. "Even under these circumstances."

Tyler bowed his head. "See you tomorrow."

He left, and Amy nudged Charlene. "He's really cute. You should have flirted with him."

"No, thank you. I have enough going on."

"With your sexy detective?"

She'd left her phone in her purse all night and hadn't checked it, after promising Minnie that she would be available. What if Sam had called with great news? One shooter found, right on schedule—she could only hope.

"Sam and I are friends, that's all. Amy, where are the other actors? Are they showing up tomorrow?"

"I didn't expect Danielle and Neville to come to the wake or her parents' house . . . did you? The funeral, however, is unavoidable," Amy pointed out.

Because of the affair. "True!" They reached the table and put the desserts in the center.

"And the only reason *we* are here at the house is because of Kass." Their friend and Logan were chair to chair, and the heat between them was visible in the air.

She'd hoped to find out more about Madison tonight, and she had, but nothing that would help Sam get her killer.

Madison was like her grandma. Living life on their own terms and to heck with anyone who got in the way.

"Logan," Charlene said once she sat down again, "were you close to your grandma?"

"Not really. Grandma Boswell passed away, as did Grandma Phipps."

"That was the one in Beverly Hills."

"Mom's mom. I messed up, but I was nothing compared to that woman—she was the black sheep that made other black sheep look white as snow."

Kass chuckled. "I like her already."

Logan reached for a piece of pineapple on a toothpick. "Madison screwed me over—I don't want to get into it, but she made sure that I was no threat to her when it came to the family inheritance."

So, Charlene thought, the rumors were true.

"Your mom mentioned something about your grandmother absconding with her inheritance? It disappeared or something?"

"Mom must've been drunk out of her mind to ever have let that slip, especially to a stranger."

Charlene lifted one shoulder and didn't mention the empty tumbler. "I can only imagine her suffering. My heart goes out to you all."

Logan waved the words away. "Madison destroyed my life—well, I made those choices, yeah, but she did her part to keep me under her heel. Not the point." He smacked the table. "Madison disrupted the family dynamic, keeping herself in good graces, and once I was out of the picture, she took off to Grandma Phipps in Beverly Hills."

"Why?" Charlene nibbled on a piece of strawberry.

"Mom and Dad didn't approve of her being an actress. They might have condoned Broadway, but she didn't have the talent, no matter how much money they tossed her way. Maybe they were embarrassed by her mediocrity and worried she'd taint the Boswell family name? I'd already dragged it through the mud—how dare she?"

He shrugged, but Charlene could see his hurt.

"Grandma Phipps was only too happy to welcome Madison—and rub her own daughter's nose in it."

Kass put her hand over Logan's. "How terrible for you."

"I knew that it would eat at my mother—Dad is strong. Mom acts strong, but when it came to her daughter, she was . . . vulnerable. Madison knew just how to get to them and make it hurt."

"Why?" Amy asked.

"Because she could. She gets off on it." He gulped as if the pineapple had caught in his throat. "Or she did."

"So why were you at the Common to see her play, Logan?" Charlene asked.

"She invited me—it was her birthday, and she wanted to make amends. Now, I'm not sure she was being honest. I went, keeping up my guard, worried that she was going to dupe me somehow. In fact, when she was shot"— he brought his knuckles to his mouth and closed his eyes for a second—"when she was shot and called my name, I thought it was a trick for her to frame me. I did not hang around."

"Oh no!" Kass said.

"Even when we were kids, she always had to beat me, whether it was tag or Monopoly. She'd buy up all the best properties and crush me. Our parents encouraged what they viewed as healthy competition—which to her meant going for the jugular every time."

Kass scrunched her nose. "It became about the win."

"No matter the cost." Amy pushed the desserts away. "I've seen that side of Madison. In California."

"You knew her well?" Logan asked.

"Not especially . . . Once I realized the kind of person she was, I backed off. But . . ."

Charlene peered at Amy to see if she was all right.

"Madison got to you, didn't she?" Logan shook his head, his eyes narrowed. "How? I've spilled my guts—your turn."

The butler came around with another bottle of champagne, and Logan gestured for him to pour them each a full flute.

Once the butler left, Amy drank deeply. "Madison befriended me at a theater we were both at. She can be very genuine and charming. I was totally fooled, and I think that's what got to me the most. I mean, I study people. I know people. And she slipped right under my radar."

Charlene took a drink of the effervescent liquid.

"Me too, Amy," Kass said. "I see"—she glanced at Logan—"auras. I didn't notice anything either. Until later."

"But that's just the thing," Logan said, unfazed by Kass's pronouncement. "Madison becomes whoever she needs to be in order to play her part—but she can't hold it together to keep it up in the long game. She always faltered. Did you see that in California?"

"Your sister was a very successful model specializing in eyes or lashes. But what she wanted to be was an actress. It didn't matter who I introduced her to. Who she met. She couldn't land a part. Even the successful agent Tyler Lawson couldn't find her a decent role."

"Exactly." Logan pounded the table once with his fist, and the flatware jumped.

"She couldn't even do full body modeling because she didn't know how to emote." Amy gestured with her dessert fork. "As an actor you have to feel with your entire being and give that to the viewer in a way that conveys intense emotion."

Kass nodded. "Modeling is even more difficult because you have to use your body language alone to give that meaning."

"It would've pissed her off that she didn't get her way." Logan's mouth curved upward, but not in joy.

"Madison blamed me for her not getting any roles." Amy shook her head at Logan. "Which isn't true."

"She would view that as a failure, even with the lash contract." Logan tilted his head back to view the sky. "I wouldn't be surprised if that's why she left LA. When was that?"

"Four months ago." Amy perched forward, her cerulean gown brushing the ground. "I'd mentioned to her that I was moving to Salem. That Neville Hampton had a theater that I'd been accepted to. Then . . ."

"I know about Madison and Neville." Logan scowled. "Mom and Dad found pictures in her apartment—they burned them before the cops could get their hands on them and drag their baby through the mud."

Charlene shivered and remembered her phone—had Sam or Minnie texted her? "Sheesh! I need to make sure that Minnie hasn't called."

"Who is Minnie?" Logan asked.

"My housekeeper."

He nodded like this was the normal answer.

"I own a bed and breakfast," Charlene explained. "In Salem." She wasn't born with a silver spoon in her mouth and wanted to make sure he understood that.

Nothing from Minnie. Her shoulders lowered in relief.

Sam had sent a message telling her that Hunter had finally shown up at the station. For Charlene to give Sam a call before the funeral tomorrow.

What could he want? It was almost midnight and too late to call or text him back.

Charlene yawned and covered her mouth. "Sorry! I was up early."

"No problem," Logan said. "This thing will go on for hours. With Mom in bed already, Dad's probably in his den with his buddies, smoking cigars and doing anything but talking about Madison."

Charlene sighed at her beautiful flute, half full and fizzy with bubbles. "I'll need to switch to coffee or risk falling asleep at the table."

"I think we should go," Amy said. Her upbeat mood had deflated.

"If you don't mind, I'm going to stay here." Kass didn't even glance at Logan, which meant they'd already discussed her sleeping over with him at the guest house.

"No problem." Amy rose and offered her hand to Logan. "Thank you for welcoming us to your home."

Charlene gathered her things. "Thank you, and I'm sorry." For the loss of his family member, for poking through his house, for questioning his mom. For wondering if he had killed his sister.

"See you tomorrow, Kass?" Amy asked. "Let us know if you need us to bring your things . . ."

Charlene bit her lip to keep from telling them to have a good time. From the way they were playing footsie under the table, fun was guaranteed.

CHAPTER SEVENTEEN

Wednesday morning, Charlene woke up before Amy, and rather than wake her friend, who'd she'd chatted with until after one, she dressed in her jeans and sleeveless blouse to get coffee in the downstairs restaurant.

"Morning," she told the hostess. "Is there a place that I can buy a paper?"

"I have one left by a customer," the woman said. "You're welcome to it. There's a beautiful tribute to Madison Boswell, the daughter of one of our local families. Her funeral is today."

"Thank you!" Charlene flipped her hair over her shoulder. "Did you know her?"

"No, not personally, but I was older than her by a few years." The waitress lowered her voice as if in church and not a busy café. "She sure was pretty, and a model, *and* an actress. Such a shame."

Charlene accepted the paper. "It is." She took it to her seat and opened it as the woman brought her coffee.

"Will you have breakfast?"

"Not just yet, thank you." Charlene strung the strap of her Kate Spade over the back of her chair.

"Take your time."

Charlene sipped from her cup and read the article. Madison had graduated from high school with honors and then moved away to pursue a successful modeling career. On the surface, she had it all.

Why hadn't it been enough to make her happy?

But it didn't matter—someone had shot this young woman, cutting her down the day before her twenty-ninth birthday. It was completely possible that she would have been able to grow and change as she got older.

Whoever had killed her had taken away that chance.

At eight o'clock, Charlene called Sam. "Hey there. I got your text about Hunter."

"Morning, Charlene." Sam chuckled, and she imagined him smoothing his mustache at her impatience. "How's Boston?"

She switched from coffee to water and calmed down. "I've seen Trinity Church—I can't wait to bring Dad—and Copley Place mall. Not bad so far. Oh, and the Boswell mansion. Today I'm going to—"

"You were at their home? How'd you manage that?"

"Logan and Kass hit it off, that's how," she said with a laugh. "Sam, I don't know if this will help at all, but Laura Boswell told me something I thought odd last night."

"Oh?"

"About her mom, Priscilla Phipps, and her daughter, both stealing from her. Is there a way you can check into their finances? If it matters . . . I don't know. Priscilla, according to Logan, was the black sheep of the family who left Boston for Beverly Hills to marry her plastic surgeon. Over the years, she left several husbands behind and a string of broken hearts."

Sam groaned, and she imagined his hand moving from his mustache to tug on the hair at the back of his head.

"Just see . . . Laura told me that Madison and Priscilla got along very well, and that her mother had accepted Madison into her home just to upset Laura. I have no idea why Priscilla seemed to dislike her own daughter so much." She sighed. "This family makes mine look like *The Waltons*." The TV family had been revered for their good old-fashioned values. "You need to thank your lucky stars for your sister, Sydney." She'd never met his other sister.

"I do!"

"Anyway, we're supposed to go to Fenway and the Cheers bar. The service is at three today, and we'll be home afterward."

"Did you see any of the actors last night?"

"No—it was family friends, mostly. Tyler was there, searching for his mom's emerald ring. The wake was full of gossipy ladies who didn't like their schoolgirl friend. Logan really got the shaft by Madison."

"Did you find out why he was ostracized from the family?"

"Yep." Good vibes warmed her from head to toe as she was able to help Sam. "Madison set Logan up for drugs and got him blacklisted by both parents. She was all about having to be the best."

"Ouch. That didn't come up in his background report. If Logan hadn't been doing the crime . . ."

"So logical, Sam." She glared at the phone, good vibes dimmed.

"Whoever had her shot, knew her, Charlene. Don't be getting chummy with the family. I'll be at the funeral service today. To observe from the back—I'm only telling you so you don't blow my cover."

"I won't." That sounded a little thrilling, and she kind of liked it. "Did the video thing ever work out?"

"I've had to scan so much data. We have a whole team dissecting it piece by piece. No big breakthrough yet, but I saw Hunter going into the tent to get his money."

"He was telling the truth."

"Yeah. The surveillance camera that was destroyed near the bandstand had the best angle of the stage and vendors. I can't get anything else in the area. If the shooter broke that camera, that means they knew exactly where to stand to be out of sight. We've done some tests on being able to shoot from that distance with accuracy . . . it was possible."

Tim, her guest with a friend on *Top Shot*, had told her the same. "What about the sound, though? Certainly someone would have heard something." There'd been ten rows of benches, and she'd been near the front—nothing had stood out as strange.

"When Hunter dropped the musket, it fired. If the handgun had a silencer on it, then maybe it would have been muffled enough to not cause alarm. There were fireworks all day because of the Fourth of July." Sam exhaled. "This was planned, the timing perfect."

"Right." She tapped her fingers on the table, feeling the weight of Madison's mesmerizing stare from the color photo in the paper. *I'm trying. But you had more en-emies than friends.*

"I talked to Neville Hampton. He said that the play was written for that day, one-time only. But they did re-hearsals at the theater for a week. His goal was to make it so memorable that he'd be asked by the town council to do it every year in Salem, just like the reading of the De-claration of Independence—guy thinks highly of him-self."

"Madison gave Neville kudos that day for writing and producing. He wanted his moment of glory and profes-sional acknowledgment." She smoothed a lock of hair be-tween her thumb and finger while trying to make sense of it. "Thing is, Danielle knew that killing Madison would not only take out her husband's lover, but ruin the success of the play. What'd she have to say?"

"She claims Madison really used hypnosis on Nev-ille."

"Did you believe her?" Charlene liked having this conversation over the phone because she could hear his inflections without being distracted by his eyes.

"If I was her, I'd want something to excuse his infi-delity. You were right about the prenup."

Charlene finished her water and had to go back to her cold coffee to wet her throat. "What time will you be in Boston?"

"Two thirty. Stay out of trouble until then, will you? No asking questions to possible suspects or members of the family." He ended the call.

"Huh!"

"More coffee?" The waitress appeared like a genie at her side.

"Yes, please. I'd also like a bowl of fruit and an English muffin. Also, if you have a pen and a piece of paper that I could have, I would appreciate it."

"Sure." The waitress returned with Charlene's requested items. "Anything else?"

"No, thanks."

The waitress left, and Charlene brushed her hand over the piece of composition notebook paper and tapped the pen to it. She wanted to help Sam find the shooter today, for the sake of the family.

Madison must've known her shooter, and that person needed to know her schedule. Had to be someone who knew the play, *Salem's Rebels*, down to the second. That cut Logan from the running, if he was telling the truth about Madison contacting him recently to make amends over her birthday.

He hadn't trusted her enough to talk to her and had even worried that her being shot and calling his name had been a trick.

Sam's presence meant that he expected the shooter to be at the funeral, so she'd keep her eye out too.

Charlene thought back to the playbill that she and Jack had studied. Neville needed his play to be a success in order to get the backing of Salem's town council. Now, he'd be lucky to get a crowd to his summer shows on the Common.

Madison's murder had ruined his plan of building his reputation and attracting better actors, if that was his goal. He wouldn't have done that to himself.

Danielle, on the other hand, just might have decided to teach her husband a lesson about playing around. Murder was a pretty big lesson—maybe she'd been trying to scare him. Charlene could see it, so she wrote Danielle's name with a star.

As much as it pained her to think of Logan being responsible, the truth was, Madison had called out his name. Was it her last regret, an apology that now could never be heard? She reluctantly re-added Logan to her list.

Madison's powerful need to be number one in their family had destroyed them all, and then she'd moved on to Grandma Phipps.

Grandma with all the husbands and a mansion in Beverly Hills. She must have had oodles of money. Upon her death, had she given money only to Madison, skipping her daughter and her grandson?

Logan might have been infuriated by such an unfair act, once again brought on by Madison. What about his mother? She'd been a disaster last night. Maybe driven by more than grief?

Charlene tucked her hair back over her shoulder. What about the ring? Where had it gone, and when? Amy and Jane had been there at Madison's side.

She jotted a note to herself to check the video to see if Madison had been wearing it in the second act.

"There you are!" Amy plunked into the chair across from her at the oval table.

Charlene's heart lodged in her throat. "You scared me!"

"You looked pretty intense—ew, what's this?" She tapped her forefinger on the newspaper image of Madison. "You're breakfasting with Madison? You could've woken me up—I'd be better company."

"For sure. I was in need of coffee and thought I'd let you sleep." She lifted her mug. "Have you heard from Kass?"

"We've been invited to lunch on Logan's yacht." Amy grinned and crossed her legs—she'd dressed in her jeans too. "La-di-dah!"

Sam's warning to not trust the family echoed in her head. "I don't know . . . won't we be short on time?" Any other day, Charlene would love the chance, but she was here to help Sam find Madison's killer.

"We have hours until the funeral." Amy nudged Madison aside.

She couldn't tell Amy about Sam, since he was going to be in the back watching, and so she couldn't explain his warning either. "I thought we were going to see the Cheers bar? And Fenway . . . That was the plan."

Amy waved to the waitress. "Plans can change—unless you don't like the water?"

She was a water baby through and through. "I don't want to intrude. I'm sure Logan would prefer having Kass to himself."

"I think she's trying to help us get to know the family." Amy unrolled silverware from a paper napkin.

That was the problem—Sam suspected them.

And the actors. He suspected *everybody*.

She exhaled and studied her list. "I would never make a good policeman."

"Of course you wouldn't. You're not cynical enough."

The waitress arrived with the coffeepot and a cup. "Can I get you anything else this morning?"

"This is good to start." Amy smiled at her. "Thank you." She turned her gaze on Charlene when the waitress left. "What should I tell Kass?"

"Tell her to go and have fun. We'll see her at the funeral."

Amy's brow arched, and she sent Kass a text.

Kass called before Amy had a chance to put the phone down, so Amy set her on speaker in the middle of the table, covering Madison's eyes. "Morning, friends!"

"Good morning." Charlene read her list. Logan was on it. How to cross him off for sure? "Kass—what color aura do you see around Logan?"

Kass's laugh was low and sultry. "Sexy reds and oranges."

Amy chuckled.

Charlene rolled her eyes. "I mean, is he a good person?"

"Madison screwed him over pretty bad, but he's been in therapy for years," Kass said in a more serious tone. "Logan's going to keep the door open with his parents, a forgive thing, not a forget. He feels they should have stood by him."

Therapy sounded healthy. Not something to launch a murder spree.

"I don't blame him for being cautious. Once bitten, twice shy," Amy said. "What Charlene is really asking is—do you think he killed his sister?"

Charlene glared at Amy, who shrugged and tapped Logan's name on Charlene's list.

"No, I don't," Kass said, end of subject. "So you don't want to join us on the yacht for a day of sun?"

"Sorry, Kass." Charlene was so tempted it hurt.

Kass muted the phone and then came back after a minute with a giggle in her voice. "All right. We'll see you at the funeral."

The dial tone sounded, and this time Charlene didn't bother trying to hide her laughter. "She's having an amazing time."

"So, which should we do now? Cheers or Fenway?" Amy looked disappointed in missing the boat trip.

"Whatever you like, Amy. I'm sorry. My only thought

is that we'll need fortification before the funeral, but your call. Oh—do we have time to get that massage you wanted?"

Amy perked up. "That, and lunch."

And there, Sam, I won't be having lunch with a family of murder suspects.

CHAPTER EIGHTEEN

Charlene decided after the morning of being pampered with a massage, mani, and pedi, that she wouldn't wait another lifetime to treat herself. She paid for her and Amy's lunch at Cheers as a thank-you. Margaritas and nachos piled a foot high with cheese, meat, olives, and salsa would be enough fortification to get through the funeral.

"Where should we sit?" Charlene asked Amy. This part of Trinity Church was grander even than the Rose Chapel.

Amy scanned the pews. "I don't see Kass—should we wait?" But Amy was already walking up the center aisle to a row four from the front. "Let's save seats for the other actors since we're here so early."

Charlene followed Amy to the left. To the right in the very front pew were Foster and Laura, dressed in formal black. Logan had not yet appeared. She hoped when Kass and Logan arrived, they'd be discreet and able to keep their hands off each other, but that kind of chemistry was hard to hide.

She touched her earrings, missing Jared. Charlene said a prayer for him, to him, then sat back to read an obituary leaflet with Madison's face. The biography was short, as had been her life. Amy waited at the end nearest the aisle to watch for her friends.

Two screens were set up at each corner with a continual slideshow of Madison as a young girl, her first birthday, tiny fists mashing a piece of cake. Photo by photo her life was revealed, the little princess with her parents and her brother, laughing, adorable, and loved. Pictures of her on the beach making sandcastles, riding a pony, her polished black boots perfectly placed in the stirrups, skiing in Aspen with her brother—every triumph in her life on display.

It was more than a normal childhood. They had sailboats and trips to Europe, a family picture at the Egyptian pyramids, the Eiffel Tower, and the Taj Mahal. Another photo op was in an open Jeep on an African safari. Not an average person's childhood but by the happy faces, a joyful one. Then it all changed.

Logan was missing from the later photos, and Madison had a bad case of acne in her early teens—she'd lost her glossy shine. Charlene wondered if this was the period in her life when she began to doubt herself. Her power, or lack of it.

This was the first time Charlene glimpsed a vulnerable girl.

Had that doubt been the catalyst for her to destroy her brother and secure her place in the family as the perfect daughter?

By her high school graduation, Madison's acne was long gone, and her beauty had emerged. Like a caterpillar to a butterfly.

Amy slid down the pew. "Wow, that's a lot of pictures. She did more in her twenty-eight years, and saw more of the world, than most people in ten lifetimes." She craned her neck to look around. "Uh-oh. Guess who just walked in?"

Charlene turned and her pulse sped. "Hunter. I'm amazed that he'd show up here. I mean, if it weren't for him, that gunshot might never have happened."

"Holy crap!" Amy put her hand over her mouth as Hunter strode up the aisle to the front pew and Laura and Foster. "I can't believe he'd have the courage to face them."

"Neither can I." Charlene made herself a little taller in the pew, angling for the best view to see him. His shoulders shook in his chocolate-brown suit. "Is he crying?" she asked in a low voice.

"As he should be," Amy said with some bitterness. "Taking money like that. He aided and abetted a murderer. Not sure why he's not in jail."

"According to Sam, er, Detective Holden, Hunter was only told to drop the musket. He needed the money and had no idea what was planned. Just stupidity, not a real crime."

"Hmm." Amy pursed her lips self-righteously. "I'd give him six months in a jail cell to smarten him up."

Charlene bit back a soft laugh. "If everyone got locked up for being a fool, think of all the politicians who'd be there."

Amy reached for a prayer sheet. "Guess you're right." A loud gasp sounded from the front row.

Laura Boswell had tossed back her veil and stood nose

to nose with Hunter, her hands on Hunter's face. "She's either forgiving him or, or, wait a minute!" Charlene's mouth dropped open, and she snapped it closed in shock as Laura grabbed on to Hunter's ears and tugged. Foster got between them as the priest clapped for order.

"Unbelievable," Amy said. "What a sideshow!"

Hunter barreled by them with a flushed face, his head down.

Charlene fanned her cheeks with the prayer sheet. "How awful. And embarrassing. For all of them."

"If I was the one being laid to rest, I'd want my dad to beat the pulp out of the guy who did it." Amy sat back down.

Hunter hadn't been the one to shoot Madison though. Madison had disgraced herself plenty. Hunter paused next to Amy and huffed, "What are you looking at? You know what a rotten person Madison was . . . but it's not my fault."

Amy narrowed her gaze at him, not agreeing. She shifted to a tall guy in the aisle behind Hunter. "Hey, Patrick."

He lifted his hand to Amy, then slung his arm around Hunter. "I'll be back. C'mon, Hunter. Let's get some fresh air. Maybe you should go home, bud."

Charlene turned at a commotion from the entrance and heard Danielle Hampton's loud voice. "I told you he'd show up, Neville."

"You got what was coming, Hunter. If I could fire you twice, I would. Get out of here," Neville ordered. Hunter left, flipping them all the bird. Neville, Danielle, Brooklyn, Jane, Lissa, and Patrick were in a group near the doorway. Amy waved to them, indicating that she'd saved them seats.

Jane was first down the aisle. Charlene kept her seat at

the end, saving room for Kass, but she smiled at Jane in welcome.

"Can I sit with you guys?"

"Of course," Amy answered. "And the rest of the gang."

Jane's eyes were bright with liner and mascara as she perched on the edge of the wooden pew, her black-and-white polka-dot dress to her knees. She'd curled her short hair and was very pretty. Who knew Plain Jane could be so cute?

"Danielle and Neville want to be in the back," Jane whispered to Amy. "You know why." She turned to Charlene. "Have you met the other actors? This is Brooklyn, Madison's understudy; Lissa, who plays Puck; and Patrick plays Egeus. I don't play anything."

"You keep us all together," Amy said.

Jane blushed with pleasure, the color in contrast to the blusher she'd applied to her cheeks with a semi-heavy hand.

Charlene glanced back to see if Hunter had actually left. She smiled at Danielle and Neville, who bristled next to each other. They hadn't brought the kids. She shifted her attention to the next row and locked eyes with Sam. His hair was slicked back, and he'd trimmed his mustache. His suit was black, as was his shirt. He gave her a nod, and she turned around and clasped her hands. Peace slid over her like a soft ocean breeze—he would find the shooter for the family.

More actors joined them, and Amy introduced the others: Mary, Naomi, Jasmine, and a man named Ken. Jane leaned over Charlene to ask Amy what had happened to Hunter. Amy explained, and Jane burst out laughing, causing several people to look their way. She swung her legs and bounced around as if excited to be part of the gang.

Charlene was just glad Jane hadn't gotten fired as she'd feared.

"Did you ever find out who broke into Madison's dressing room?" Charlene asked quietly.

Jane put her finger to her lips and darted a panicked expression back to Danielle and Neville, who were too far away to hear. She picked up a prayer sheet and whispered, "I didn't have the guts to say anything, but I was able to fix the cape and reupholster the vanity bench with velvet from my props room. Can you imagine?"

"I'm glad it worked out."

Her phone, on silent, buzzed with a message from Kass, saying to save her a seat, as she and Logan were just a few minutes away. Charlene, laughing, showed Amy.

"I turned my phone off." Amy flashed her and Jane the black screen. "I was at a rehearsal once where I thought I'd hit the silence button, and I was so embarrassed when it rang."

Jane reached into her roomy fabric purse for her cell and turned it off. "Good reminder." It spilled to the ground, and Charlene helped her with the contents. Jane, embarrassed, scooped it all in, then switched her seat to the other side of Amy to chat with Brooklyn.

The priest took his place at the lectern just as Logan and Kass rushed through the doors. Amy stood up, hand raised, and Kass quickly joined them in their row. Logan headed to his parents' side.

Thankfully, they weren't in beach attire. Logan had a button-down shirt over a pair of khakis, and Kass wore a sundress. Both of them looked a little sunburned and windblown, but it was better than not showing up at all.

After they were seated, the priest lifted his hands in prayer. The congregation repeated the Lord's Prayer with him. He spoke of Madison and brought most people to tears with his compassionate voice. Foster's younger brother Stephan climbed to the podium and lightened the mood by telling stories about some of the antics his niece would get up to, and how she loved to trick people. Every day was April Fools' Day to her.

Charlene and Kass exchanged a look. That was one way to describe her character.

Stephan continued by saying how Madison was high-spirited, full of life and adventure. Captivating and elusive. When he stepped down, organ music began to play.

Charlene crumpled a tissue. She hadn't known Madison, but any loss of life was so very sad.

A lovely friend of the family was next at the lectern and in the most beautiful voice sang the Latin prayer, "Ave Maria." Jane pursed her lips and giggled when the woman went for a high note. Charlene arched her brow at Jane, who immediately bowed her head.

Logan took the podium, and Charlene glanced backward at Sam. He gave her a wink, and she turned away with a blush. The room had silenced to hear the black sheep brother say his final words to his deceased sister.

"Madison was a bright light that faded all too soon. At times hilarious, there were others where she could be mean and cruel. She lived life on her own terms and made no apology. She was good, and she was evil. She used people and destroyed them on a whim. Nothing she did had any consequences. Yes, I loved her and hated her too. I'm not sure if Heaven will open the door for her, but if she's there, she'll be up to her old tricks and won't be there for long."

He descended from the dais and sat next to his father. Forest blustered and spluttered but then just bowed his head.

"God stole the wrong child from me," Laura Boswell cried into her handkerchief. "How could you say those things, Logan?"

Kass half stood, ready to join Logan if he needed her against his family.

People started talking, standing up, unsure what to do.

The priest cleared his throat and leaned over the lectern. "Ladies and gentlemen, if you could please go to your cars . . . the funeral procession will begin. The hearse will lead, followed by the family. May God bless you all."

Charlene was glad to leave and get out into the open air. She, Kass, and Amy stayed together as the rest of the actors gathered around Neville and Danielle.

Kass took several deep breaths and wiped away a few tears. "That was brave of Logan to say what he did. I know his sister tortured him, and he could never forgive her for it. But he loved her too. I heard him crying during the middle of the night."

Amy put her hand on Kass's back. "Their family is very complex. They all need a lot of therapy to sort things out."

Charlene looked around for Sam. Would he be at the grave site?

Amy drove and followed the procession. They arrived at the lush green cemetery with shade trees and old stone mausoleums.

The Boswells had a family plot going back two hundred years. The memorial site was large, with an office building in the middle. Headstones and flowers went on and on in every direction. Magnolias in full bloom were plentiful, as were oak trees and elms. Hedges separated one area from another. One was called The Garden of Tranquility; another The Garden of Peace, and Madison was laid to rest in The Garden of Love.

Charlene was sure her parents had chosen that spot for their beloved daughter.

As they waited for the priest, Charlene said another prayer for Madison. She hadn't been nice, but the person who'd killed her had cheated her of ever making amends.

Surveying the faces around the grave site, Charlene wondered if it was someone here who'd murdered this young woman about to be buried in the ground. A shiny walnut casket had been covered in a spray of roses and lilies.

Danielle was stone-faced as she linked her arm through her husband's. As handsome as he was, his cheeks had lost color, his eyes red-rimmed. He'd told Charlene that he hadn't loved Madison, but was this grief? If so, Danielle would likely make his suffering worse. Neville had been taken in by Madison's beauty and her cunning—he'd called her a witch.

Charlene caught a glimpse of Hunter hiding behind a tree as he watched them all. Was he here out of guilt? Torturing himself for his part in Madison's death? Did he know more than he was saying, or had he finally leveled with Sam?

Jane flitted around the gathering like a sparrow, speaking to anyone who would listen. She tried to be included, but somehow she was always just outside the circle.

Brooklyn and Lissa cried together. Patrick had his arms around Naomi and Jasmine.

"What's up with Jane?" Charlene asked Amy. "She seems really wired today."

"The girl lives off caffeine . . . but this is more." Amy clasped her hands as the priest arrived. "She's probably relieved that Madison is truly dead, and wants to make sure."

"What are you talking about?" Charlene whispered.

Amy hesitated. "Jane despised Madison for a very good reason. Remember how I told you that Madison had studied hypnotherapy and practiced hypnosis?"

"And you didn't look her in the eyes," Charlene said.

"Well, one day in May, Jane didn't believe that Madison could do it."

"Oh no."

"Yep." Amy bit her lip and studied the ground as the priest greeted people. "Madison had no trouble hypnotizing Jane. She made her pretend to be a chicken and had her running all over the place clucking. Madison thought it was hilarious, but most of us were embarrassed for poor Jane. She didn't remember it, but Brooklyn had recorded it, and at Madison's urging, she shared it with everybody."

"What a wicked thing for her to do."

"Madison clucked and squawked whenever she saw Jane after that."

"That's just cruel." Charlene put a hand to her heart. "What did Jane do?"

"She broke into tears and ran out of the building. Didn't come back to the theater for a whole week. Neville had to sweet-talk her into returning. Everyone else let it go, but not Madison."

No wonder Jane was bopping around and chatting with folks—this was her day to shine, now that Madison was in the ground.

Logan stood behind his parents, who sat by the grave in folding chairs. His expression was borderline bored. The priest prayed.

Tyler was a few feet from Logan and the family. If he and Madison had married, he'd have every right to be there with them, but Madison had broken his heart without explanation.

Danielle glared daggers at Neville and Logan and Tyler. She put her hand up to Jane when Jane spoke to her. Brooklyn studied what was happening as if there would be a quiz later.

Sam, hands folded before him, kept watch over the service. He didn't speak with anyone.

"I see Sam," Kass said.

"Me too." Charlene did her best to not keep looking his way. "But he's on duty."

She felt safer with him here. At the end of the service, folks crowded around the grave. Once again, Charlene wished the Boswells peace. Amy and Kass stayed to chat with Logan, and Charlene caught up with Tyler, who'd stepped aside.

He stuffed a handkerchief in his suit pocket when he saw her coming. "Are you stalking me?"

Charlene half smiled. "No. But I wanted to ask if you'd found your ring. I never did thank you for buying my frozen lemonade the other day."

"It was nothing. I'm sorry I spilled my Frap on you. As you can imagine, I was preoccupied. Why did Madison invite me to see the play? Did she want to reconcile?" He clenched his fists. "I'll never know now."

"I'm so sorry." So, Madison had wanted to make amends with her brother and her ex-fiancé? Maybe she'd been trying to grow up. Charlene scanned the grounds for Hunter.

Tyler hunched his shoulders. "I searched Madison's hands today at the funeral home, and she wasn't wearing my ring. My last chance to get it back is Friday at the reading of the will. I don't know what I'll do if it doesn't turn up."

"I'm so sorry, Tyler, but I know she was wearing it that day."

Tyler choked up and bowed his head. "Somebody must have stolen it right off of her cold finger." He searched the sky before looking at Charlene. "My father had guns while I was growing up. Mounted deer heads in his home office. Sick bastard. The fact that Madison was shot . . ." His blue eyes shimmered. "I'll always love her, even though she's gone."

"I understand how that feels." Charlene touched her earrings and glanced over her shoulder. "I have to go. Amy and Kass are waiting for me. Good luck."

"Take care, Charlene. Let me know if you're ever interested in coming to LA. You have this Jessica Biel thing about you."

She laughed, then walked away, her head down, her thoughts full. She ran into Sam and knew right away it was him. Hard chest, subtle cologne that he only wore occasionally. His arms righted her as she stumbled.

"Hey! I lost sight of you and got worried." Sam put a hand on her back. "Are you all right?"

She nodded. "I was talking to Tyler—Sam, he loved Madison so much. We have to find that ring. If you tell me that he's a suspect, I won't be able to believe it."

"Of course he's a suspect, and an angry one, for good reason. But just now during the service I got word that his alibi checked out."

"What about Logan? Or Neville? Or Danielle?"

"One at a time, Charlene, one at a time."

CHAPTER NINETEEN

As the priest returned to the church, Charlene said a prayer not only for Madison and the family but one of gratitude that the funeral was at last over. She'd be fine waiting a very long time for another one.

"Ready to go?" Amy asked.

"*So* ready," Charlene said. Maybe it would be different if the person laid to rest had been nicer in life?

Kass nudged Charlene. "I know what you mean. Where did we park? I'm all turned around."

"This way to the side street. The lot was full, and I believe you were texting Logan the whole drive." Amy turned to follow the others who were leaving.

"Yeah." Kass smiled cheekily—an unrepentant sinner.

Danielle's anger was palpable as she walked rigidly at Neville's side. When she twisted her heel on a rock, Neville reached for her elbow, and she yanked it away from him. "Don't touch me," she hissed, her eyes on the ground.

Jane trailed after them, next to Brooklyn and the other actors. Charlene, Kass, and Amy were just behind the group and could hear everything.

"It's over, Danielle." Neville glanced at his wife.

"Yes, it is." She strode ahead, and Neville clenched his jaw.

Was Charlene witnessing the end of their marriage?

Jane trotted forward in her low-heeled black pumps. "Neville, I'm sorry to bother you, but I was wondering if we could swing by the theater before you take us home?"

He shook out his fisted hands and flexed his fingers, scowling at Jane as if he'd forgotten why she was there. "What? Oh, yeah, I guess. Why?"

"I left the revised script for Brooklyn, and she wants to study it before Friday's rehearsal."

"Definitely a good idea." Neville peered over his shoulder at them all and must've realized that his and Danielle's actions had probably been witnessed. His body sagged.

Brooklyn joined Jane. "Thank you, Neville," she said. "I promise not to let you down again."

Neville waved the comment off. "Just do the best you can, Brooklyn. I realize you only had one day to practice, so I didn't expect perfection. Where are the others?"

"They cut across to the van. Thanks for driving us all." Jane peeked up at Neville with a cautious smile.

Charlene wondered if Jane had more to fear from Neville than just losing her job, though that could be a big deal. A woman with Jane's skills might have limited options for employment—how many theater costumers were there?

They reached the crowded street, lined with cars.

"Where's Logan?" Charlene murmured to Kass. "I'm sure you'll want to say goodbye."

"He's with his family—where he's supposed to be." Kass flipped her long hair back. "I doubt I'll hear from him again. Neither one of us is interested in more."

"Seriously? I thought you were into each other."

"It was a pleasurable night. What more can a girl ask for?"

"Your bag is in the trunk with ours if you need anything from it before we hit the road." Amy pulled her keys from her purse. The top was up on the red convertible.

Which had a flat rear tire.

"Oh no! How did that happen?" Amy said. "I'm not sure if I have a spare."

Charlene knelt to view the tire, searching for a nail or a screw. "I have Triple A."

"Can you use that on someone else's car?" Amy paced around the rear of the Camaro.

"Yes. One of the perks—I'm the one insured so it doesn't matter if I'm a passenger or if this is my vehicle."

"I don't own a car," Kass said. "But if I did, that insurance sounds smart."

Amy exhaled and unlocked the front driver's side, dropping her purse in. "I drove in LA for years without a problem. Got lucky, I suppose." She glanced at Charlene. "I appreciate your help."

"It's the least I can do. I was happy for the ride." Charlene opened her wallet for the card.

Neville drove by, then slowed and reversed. He rolled down his window. "You need a hand, Amy?"

Amy shook her head. "No, but thanks. My friend has Triple A."

Charlene lifted the card. How considerate of the producer to ask, even with a van full of people. When Neville drove off, she dialed, giving the address for assistance when an operator answered.

"Ten minutes, they said." She leaned against the side of the car, one foot crossed in front of the other. The street had cleared of mourners, leaving them alone. Her phone dinged with a text. A warm pleasure swept over her. It was Sam. Did he have some kind of sixth sense when it came to her and trouble?

What's wrong?

Flat tire. AAA is coming. Where are you?

In the church parking lot. Should I wait?

Don't be silly. We've got this.

The next thing she knew, Sam was striding toward them, the jacket off of his lightweight black suit.

"Hey, Sam!" Amy said. "Look, Charlene—our knight has arrived."

"We have Triple A," Charlene scolded when he knelt down by the tire, examining it for punctures. "You'll get your slacks dirty."

"Is that any way to greet someone here to help?" he asked in a dry tone.

"No, but I already called." Still, Charlene was glad he was there. "Guess we ran over a nail or something."

Sam stood and tugged his mustache. "This tire was sliced with a knife."

Her stomach knotted. "What?"

"Who would do that?" Kass asked. "And why?"

Amy frowned delicately. "That would take some nerve to do in a crowd of people."

Sam brushed his hands together and looked at the cemetery behind them.

Charlene rubbed the goose bumps on her arms. "Someone who would shoot a woman in broad daylight would have no problem slashing a tire."

"Excellent point. But what would anybody gain by inconveniencing us?" Kass glanced around her, but everyone was gone.

"It could have been anyone." Amy sighed. "Some teenage prank. You can't see the street from the graveside, so maybe they were just messing with us. Had something against red convertibles."

Gorgeous old oaks blocked the view of the cemetery—*blocked* being the operative word. "You're right. It probably was random," Charlene answered.

Sam's phone rang, and he pulled it from his slacks pocket. "This is Detective Holden."

He ambled away from them just out of earshot.

"What if we're wrong, and it wasn't a kid, but someone trying to scare me, or us?" Amy asked. "Could I be next?"

"We're getting carried away here. It's just a slashed tire. Isn't it?" Kass twisted a braid, her eyebrows pinched together.

Charlene didn't know how to answer. "How can we know for sure until the killer is caught? Everyone in your cast should be extra careful."

"I hope that the detective is getting good news now." Amy hugged her waist, her mouth taut.

"Do you have a spare tire?" Kass asked. "It should be in the trunk."

Amy unlocked the trunk and opened it. A piece of

paper fluttered free, and Sam stepped on it to stop it from flying away on the summer breeze.

"What's this?" Sam asked, picking up the paper and stepping toward them.

"Don't know. What does it say?" Amy held out her hand.

It was a prayer sheet with a picture of Trinity Church on the front. Sam studied it, turned it over, then glared at Charlene. "Why do I feel like this message is for you, Mrs. Morris?"

"What does it say?" Charlene leaned back against the open trunk.

"*Butt out*." He showed it to Amy. "Is this yours?"

"No." Amy nibbled her lower lip. "But the tire no longer seems like a prank."

"This was from today's service." Kass read the scrawled message over Charlene's shoulder. "How did anyone get it into the trunk? Must have happened after the church thing."

"Is that eyeliner?" Amy asked. She smudged it with her finger before Sam yanked it back.

"Can I have this?" He curled it toward him to keep it safe.

"I guess so," Amy said. "I definitely don't want it.'"

Charlene realized that he might try to lift fingerprints from it. "Do you need to put it in something?"

"I have an evidence bag in my car." He pointed to an understated, unmarked gray Buick in the lot.

The AAA truck arrived, sparing Sam from getting his hands dirty. The mechanic quickly changed the ruined tire for the spare that was in a recessed area of the trunk covered by gray felt. It was brand-new.

Sam glanced at Amy after perusing the lining of the trunk. "It's possible the note was slid inside . . . it's not sealed very tight."

"Older car," Amy said.

"Mind if I also take the tire?"

"Of course not. You think they're related?" A crease deepened between Amy's brows.

"Looks that way. If the note ties it to the case." Sam's eyes raked over Charlene. "You ladies need to be extra careful, understood?"

"Yes." Amy took a deep breath and released it, yoga style. "Thank you."

"Glad I was here. Charlene, can you walk with me to my car?"

The mechanic left, with effusive thanks from them all and a tip from Amy, so Charlene nodded to Sam.

Would this have anything to do with the phone call he'd taken, or did he know she'd been asking questions again?

Sam rolled the tire down the street to the parking lot. "*Butt out* in black eyeliner. That's a strange message to leave for one of you, or all three. What do you think?"

He wanted to know? She was over the moon. "Well, Neville was here with Danielle and a few of the actresses—to carpool, I guess. I imagine they would all have makeup kits, but not necessarily with them." She remembered the blush and eye shadow that Jane wore.

"Who all rode together?"

"Neville was driving; Danielle was in the passenger seat. It's so sad, but I think they're going to get a divorce." She explained what she'd seen. "Uh, Jane, Brooklyn, and the other actors who were fairies in the play were seated in the back."

"Did you see Logan?"

"Yes. He was with his parents. Kass doesn't think he's guilty."

When they reached his car, he popped the trunk and pulled out an evidence bag for the note, then put the tire in and the bag. He slammed the trunk closed.

His left brow lifted. "Is Kass a police officer?"

"No . . ." Charlene crossed her arms at his clipped tone. "Is that all you wanted to talk to me about?" She sighed. "Who called, or is that a question you can't answer?"

"Officer Bernard." Sam didn't say anything else. "Charlene, promise me that you're going to go straight home. I'd love it if you'd stay there until the killer is found, but I doubt you'd agree to do that."

She raised her chin and lowered her arms. "That isn't reasonable. I have guests to take care of. A business to run."

"I know, I know." His mouth pursed, and he smoothed his chin. "No more asking questions. I haven't ruled Logan out. Why was he in the audience that day?"

"He says that Madison invited him because it was her birthday and she wanted to make amends. He thought it might have even been a trick."

"So why did he go?" Sam stepped back. "He spoke very emotionally at the funeral, and he had a reason or two to want her out of his life. I did some research into his background, and there are pictures of him with his buddies shooting geese."

"Geese? What's the connection?" She imagined long rifles and rubber waders, not a nine millimeter handgun that had killed his sister.

"Any outdoorsman like that will have a knife—strong enough to slash a tire."

"Logan was with his parents in the town car—not running around ruining tires."

"He remains a person of interest."

"You think he wrote the note in black liner? Why? It makes no sense. Kass was wearing blue, and I doubt his poor mother bothered. It dark and thick." She nodded. "Theater makeup is my guess. Even the male actors would be able to get their hands on it. Like . . . Hunter. He was acting very strange today."

"We'll see. I wish it were that simple, but Hunter was seen by multiple people all morning long before the play. Four people saw him pick up the envelope in the tent. We've checked his phone, and the number used to send the instructions through the secret app was traced to a burner phone."

Charlene's shoulders dropped. "Neville?"

"He's been very cooperative." Sam glanced back at Amy and Kass, who'd gotten into the car and were now putting the top down.

"Neither one of them is responsible either. They're my friends."

"You protest because you like them; I get it. I agree with you. July Fourth at noon, Kass was at her shop selling teas. I've checked Amy's phone records. She's clear. Tyler was having a drink at the bar across the street. That leaves Logan, who both admittedly loved and hated his sister, and was in the audience."

Sam had tangible things to back up his feelings. Charlene swallowed and looked away.

Amy drove toward them and parked behind Sam. "Hey, lady, can I give you a ride?"

Charlene laughed. The radio was on; they had on their scarves and sunglasses, and they could have been in a music video. She turned her back to Sam and lightened the heavy mood. "I'm ready!"

She was anxious to get home, unwind, and talk over everything with Jack. How had a ghost become her best friend?

Sam pulled her back before she climbed in the back seat. "Charlene, remember what I said—be careful. I don't want anything to happen to you."

"I will." He stared into her eyes, and she was unable to move for a moment before Kass cleared her throat.

Charlene got in the back seat, somehow resisting Sam. Now was not their time.

Sam tapped the car as Amy drove off. Kass turned up the volume, and they sang about girls just wanting to have fun all the way back to Salem.

CHAPTER TWENTY

Charlene hauled her overnight bag from the trunk of the car. "Thanks, Kass and Amy. Drive safe the rest of the way. It was . . . an interesting time."

"We'll have to do massages without the funeral next," Amy said. She honked and backed out as Charlene ran up the white porch stairs, happy to be back where she belonged. Dorothy had it right—there's no place like home.

Especially after a funeral for a woman who caused mixed emotions from the mourners. Logan's tribute had been brutally honest, and Charlene feared it might be the next reason for his parents to kick him out. He was a complex man, but he couldn't let his sister destroy his life a second time. Besides, she didn't want to think that Kass had slept with a possible murderer.

She opened the door. "Hello!"

"That you, Charlene?" Minnie cried out.

"Yup, it's me." She dragged her bag into the kitchen to greet Minnie with a warm hug. "How did it go? Didn't hear from you, so I figured you had everything under control."

"Of course we did. I actually think my cranky husband enjoyed himself. We shared a bottle of wine from your splendid wine cellar. Will found it when I sent him down for a cognac for James. Hope you don't mind, dear?"

"Not at all! I'm so grateful that you let me have a night away—which I enjoyed very much. It was a relief to know that 'Charlene's' was in your competent hands."

"I can't wait to hear all about your adventure. Your text said the three of you had been invited to the Boswell mansion for a late dinner. My, my, that must have been something."

"I'll tell you everything, but not now. I've kept you late enough as it is—it's almost seven, and Will likes his dinner at six."

"Fine, but I'll want every detail." Minnie took off her apron and washed her hands. "Will said to say thank you, by the way. He hasn't slept in such a comfortable bed for years, and now he wants a new mattress." With a bright smile, she added, "So I'm thanking you too."

She walked Minnie to the door. "How were Penny and James?"

"What a wonderful couple."

"Really?"

"Yes, they joined us with some music in the living room. James had cognac and Penny shared the wine with Will and me over a game of canasta. The men played against the women, and of course Penny and I won."

"I didn't mean for you to have to entertain, Minnie . . ."

"It was our pleasure. Penny told me that James has a

heart condition and high blood pressure and probably shouldn't be drinking. But he won't listen to her." Minnie shrugged. "After his heart attack last year, she'd suggested he step away from his big government job, but he wouldn't hear of it."

"Oh, I didn't know he was having such health issues. I noticed she seemed a little stressed." Jack had thought the man looked overworked.

"Yes, well, who wouldn't be? He doesn't like to be told what he can and can't do, so that leads to a few heated moments. Penny said they're handling it as well as they can."

"That's all any of us can do," Charlene said. "Any other news?"

"They plan on leaving tomorrow at noon, so tonight is their last hurrah. They're on another sunset cruise, and then they intend to hit the Hawthorne Hotel for a drink and a late-night snack."

"Sounds like a perfect way to end their stay." Charlene was even more grateful to her housekeeper and Will for making sure the Stewarts had a good time. "Say hi to Will for me. And if he wants, I'll give him the brand of mattress and the best place to get it."

"I'll do that. Oh, and Avery left just a half hour ago. She was sorry she missed you." Minnie pulled her car keys from her purse as they stood on the porch in the evening twilight.

"Thanks. I'll see her this weekend though. I hope she doesn't go too far away after graduation this year." Charlene tucked her hair behind her ear. "I'd love to keep her on as long as possible."

"You've become attached to her," Minnie said.

"Yes. I hurt for the life she had, the mother that couldn't take care of her. Not having a dad."

"Sometimes even a prickly family is better than none."

They both thought of Charlene's mother. "You can say that again."

"See you tomorrow." Minnie laughed. "Get some rest. You look a bit tired."

"There was a lot of drama. Makes me appreciate my life here."

"Can't wait to hear all about it—oh, Avery bought Silva a red bell to match her collar."

"What a sweetheart! I've been meaning to get one. Wait—did something happen where Silva behaved badly?"

Minnie raced down the stairs to her Volvo. "She's a cat, that's all."

Once Minnie was gone, Charlene wheeled her overnight bag into her rooms, hoping Jack might be there. She was instantly disappointed when she didn't feel his presence.

"Jack! Jack? Come on. Are you punishing me for going away for a night? You do that all the time."

She hung up her new dress and laid the jeans and top on her bed to exchange it for the black funeral dress. She unzipped it, stepped out, then hung it up too. Once she was dressed comfortably, she finished unpacking her other items, closed the bag, and put it away in her closet. She sat down on the bed and used all her mental powers to will Jack to appear.

"Okay, Jack. I won't tell you about the wake, the party at the Boswells', or the funeral. You'll just have to guess what I did while I was away." She stood up and entered her suite, closing her bedroom door behind her. "You'll be sorry. I had a very interesting trip."

A chill crept over her. She shivered with anticipation and turned around.

"You called?" Jack appeared, looking his always handsome self—in his jeans and Henley top that fit his strong shoulders and defined his body. Not body exactly, but the amazing shape he manifested just for her. Exactly like the photos she'd seen of him before he died. Oh, how she wished she'd known him then.

"Hmm. Nope. Couldn't have been me." She ended her teasing and gave him a bright smile. "But I'm happy to see you."

"Me too. I missed you when you were gone."

"Now you know how I feel when you just fly off to no-man's-land."

He grinned, and she felt a lurch in her heart. Why, oh why, couldn't he be a real flesh-and-blood man, instead of a beautiful, charming, and wonderful ghost? A temporary fixture in her life, when she wanted a permanent one.

"I don't leave you willingly, you know that."

"Yes, I do, and I understand—it's just that I have so much to tell you, and it couldn't wait!"

Jack sat down on the love seat and indicated for her to sit next to him, then he snapped his fingers and the TV was turned on low.

Charlene grabbed the afghan from the chair to ward off the chill and draped it over her shoulders. "Okay. So what do you want to hear first?"

"Tell me in chronological order, that way I get the whole picture."

"Well, first of all Amy has this cool Camaro convertible, and she brought us all fancy scarves to wear over our hair, and with our big sunglasses and the top down, well, it was all very Hollywoodish."

He laughed. "Is there such a word?"

"There is now. I added it to our vocabulary."

"You checked into your hotel . . ."

"Then we walked to Trinity Church." She plumped a cushion. "I'm sure you've probably been in it like a dozen times, but it was the first for me and Amy, and Kass since the renovation. It was gorgeous. The stained-glass windows and the murals were just amazing. Like being at the Vatican, I would imagine."

"Yes, I know the history of the church and have been in it a few times, but the Vatican is a city unto itself."

"Fine, not that big. The wake was in the Rose Chapel, where a woman played the harp, which was beautiful. Lots of people sitting around on the pews, visiting. We joined the line to pay our respects to Madison. She could've been a beautiful doll in that coffin. So sad."

"Who all was there?"

"Logan sat next to his mom and dad, Laura and Foster. Amy chose a pew behind some gossipy women. One was a teacher who knew Madison and Logan—it seems Madison has always lied to get her way. She was driven by a great need to be number one. Logan told us she always had to win at what she did; she'd cheat if need be. I think that's what got her killed."

"She sounds unlikeable." He shifted to face her. "Did you meet her parents?"

"At the wake . . . the dinner too. They were stricken with grief. They loved her, they really did. Maybe at the cost of Logan, but it didn't used to be that way."

"What do you mean?"

"The women said that Logan, who was the golden

child, was set up by Madison during his sophomore year for selling drugs. They didn't stand by him, and he ended up on probation, then his dad cut him out of the family."

"We'd wondered at why they'd had a rift. Didn't expect it to be quite so one-sided." Jack nodded at Charlene encouragingly. "You have a unique gift, Charlene."

"What do you mean?"

"It's through conversations. You learn things by getting to know people. They open up to you. Did you meet her ex-fiancé?"

"Yes."

"This I want to hear." Jack crossed a leg, making himself comfortable. "Where were you?"

"The private dinner at the Boswells' following the wake. Tyler was upstairs on the second floor of their home, while the party was in full swing. I ran into him while I was doing my own investigating."

Jack laughed in disbelief. "You went in the house?"

"Yep. There I was upstairs, looking for signs of what Madison's life had been like, you know? And I ran smack-dab into Tyler having a drink in the game room, skimming a photo album and teary-eyed over Madison."

"Did he know the family?"

"Logan said he only met him the other day when he came to the house, asking about his mom's gold and emerald ring. Logan didn't know anything about their engagement and hadn't seen the ring. Tyler told me at the funeral that it wasn't worth much, but it was personal. He wants it back, and I don't blame him." She jumped up from the couch. "Jack, both he and Logan told me that Madison invited them to the play!"

Jack tilted his head. "Why did she?"

"To make amends. Her birthday was Saturday, the day

after she was shot, and supposedly she wanted to make things right before then."

"That doesn't match what we know of her cruelty, where she only looked out for number one." He frowned. "A little like my ex-wife, I'd say."

"I hope that she'd changed and seen the light before she passed."

"We'll never know now."

Charlene continued her loop around the love seat. "Kass spent the night with Logan. They were hot for each other from the first moment they met. I don't want him to be the killer. Kass sees auras and is very intuitive—she says he's not guilty."

"What does Sam say?"

"He hasn't crossed Logan off yet." She perched on the arm of the love seat. "The dinner was terrific. There was lobster, oysters on the half shell, prime rib, and racks of lamb. Plus all the salads and sides. The desserts were amazing as well. Logan poured us champagne all night. The good stuff."

"Hmm." Jack rubbed his chin. "Sounds like quite a do. I imagine the house was grand?"

"A mansion with incredible history, but I wouldn't trade 'Charlene's' for it. Ours is better. On my way out of the game room, I discovered Laura Boswell studying the Boswell family tree on the second floor."

"Charlene—were you caught snooping?" His voice rose.

"Technically, yes, twice. By Tyler and Laura. But she was so upset by her daughter's death that it didn't faze her having me there. She confided some things that I'm sure she regrets, if she remembers."

"Like?" Jack asked.

"Madison and her mother both stole from her—Priscilla Phipps, a.k.a. Grandma Phipps, was trustee of Laura's inheritance and ran off to LA with a plastic surgeon after emptying the account."

"Not a nice family. Her granddaughter found her match, didn't she?"

"Yes, I feel sorry for Laura. She really is heartbroken. Dad too."

"Anything else?"

"Logan spoke at the church—brutally frank, to be honest. Basically, he said she was a prankster, lived life on her own terms, hurt and destroyed people on a whim, and that he both loved and hated her. Sam was there and heard it, which is why Logan's not off his list."

"I'm glad you're home." Jack smiled at her from his side of the love seat. "Did you at least get your massage?"

"I did. But that's not all, Jack. As we were leaving the cemetery, we got to the car, and someone had slashed the back tire. I called Triple A, and they were there quickly. So was Sam. He found a note in the trunk of the car and took that for evidence as well as the tire."

"What did the note say?"

"Butt out! And it was written with black eyeliner. Thick, like theater makeup."

"Do you think the message was for you?"

"I don't know. All the actors would have access to theater makeup. It could be any one of them, but why would it be for me? Amy, most likely. Hunter was there, and he got kicked out of the church for disturbing Laura. She attacked him when he came up to them to pay his condolences."

"Why was he there? What a fool. Be careful, Charlene. Someone might not like you nosing around."

"I know. Sam basically said the same thing. And he doesn't know the half of it."

The two shared a look full of mutual affection, heavy with things left unsaid, until Jack blinked and cleared his throat, a very human habit. "I had a bit of fun with Avery this afternoon."

Charlene went along with the new topic. "Oh no. What did you do?"

"Well, she was going on and on about this *Ghost Light*, telling Minnie it was such a good movie—I saw it after she raved, and it was so-so. I liked the ending." Jack grinned. "That girl has a flare for the dramatic. You should have seen how she told Minnie that Salem Stage Right had one too, but before the performance for Madison that you went to, it had been broken."

"I can imagine it now." Charlene chuckled. "What did Minnie do?"

"Minnie asked what a ghost light was, and Avery, with a hushed voice and wide eyes, explained that it's an exposed bulb placed center stage of a darkened theater to catch ghosts and keep the actors from being *cursed*." Jack stood in front of the TV, the newscaster semivisible through him. She averted her gaze, as she hated the reminder that he wasn't human.

"I'm sure Minnie handled it just fine."

"She laughed and said her grandchildren had seen that movie too. They always want to leave a light on in their bedrooms at night to keep ghosts away." He rubbed his hands together. "I couldn't help myself, and just as Minnie said ghosts, I flickered the lights and tugged Silva's tail—not hard but it added to the scare factor—and they both squealed."

"Jack! You didn't play nice." She crossed her arms.

His turquoise-blue eyes twinkled. "I petted Silva, and she got on her hind legs, trying to catch my fingers, her paws in the air. Avery was wide-eyed for real. Minnie distracted Avery with a cookie, explaining that Silva has always been a high-strung cat."

At that, Charlene laughed so hard tears came to her eyes and she held her belly. Since her guests were out, she didn't need to keep quiet. "You're so amusing—I love that about you."

Jack stepped toward her, his tone low. "And Sam?"

"He's not nearly as funny." She stuck a hand in her jeans pocket to stop from reaching out to him, and tilted her head at the laptop. "Did you find anything when I was gone?"

"Yes—I wanted to show you something on the video you took."

She walked to the desk and her computer. "Poor Jack—you're probably tired of looking at that thing. It's bound to be burned into your mind by now."

"Which is why I want you to take a peek." He tapped his temple. "I might be seeing things."

Charlene hit the power button to wake up her machine. "This sounds intriguing."

He chuckled and joined her as she sat at the desk. "Go to the video. I stopped it where I think you should look."

"The bandstand?" The stairs leading up to the covered platform had been blocked off with a chain and a Do Not Enter sign. The right side that was being worked on had a thick, clear plastic sheet protecting the stone and the egress window that hinted to the basement below.

"Is there a way for you to enlarge this single image?"

Charlene had already broken the video down into separate frames so that she and Jack could slow it down. "Hang on." She went into the edit function and selected the single frame, copying it to create a new picture. Using the zoom, she clicked to enlarge it. "What am I looking for, Jack?"

"There—do you see that shape on the inside of the bandstand?"

She squinted it into focus. "This matches Michelle's picture. Nobody should be in there." Chills ran along her nape and down her back. "That's long hair." A woman's hair.

"You see it too," Jack said with relief. "I wasn't sure if my brain was playing tricks on me."

"It's blurry. It could be a shadow." Charlene turned back to Jack. "I'll check it out tomorrow in person."

"I wish I could go with you."

"I know." What a great thing that would be, for Jack to have more freedom. "Listen, I'll call Sam and maybe he can join me."

"That's a smart idea." Jack scowled at the image. "That could be a shoulder, bending toward the pillar."

Charlene tried to zoom it larger, but it just went out of focus completely. "I'll go after Penny and James check out." Apprehension knotted in her stomach.

"What are you thinking?" Jack asked.

"Well—this is the bandstand. Someone vandalized that camera, Jack. This could be the shooter. Our killer is a woman with long hair. First thing in the morning, I want to go over every pixelated image we have, with that in mind."

CHAPTER TWENTY-ONE

Charlene had a difficult time going to sleep that night, but Silva, who indeed had a red bell to go with her red blingy collar, purred at the crook of her knees and lulled her off to dreamland.

Memories jumbled together with impossible scenarios—like Kass, flying across the ceiling of the theater at Salem Stage Right. The ghost light behind Brandy and Evelyn the night of the show, flickering like one of Jack's tricks.

The eerie mirage of Madison in and out of focus—like what movie producers thought ghosts should look like—a shadow without substance.

Kind of like the shadow of the figure in the bandstand.

Charlene's brain was on overdrive, sorting, discarding, trying to make sense of all the bits and pieces.

Dawn crept in from her bedroom window, and her

heart hammered so hard she placed her palm to her chest. *Thud, thud, thud.*

"Jane!" she told Silva, who cocked an ear but otherwise remained sleeping.

Jane. Charlene's mind had zeroed in on when Jane had spilled her purse. A flash of gold and emerald . . . a long black object she'd assumed was a pen. What if it was black eyeliner? What if she'd written the note?

Charlene shoved the covers back and ran into her living area to fire up the laptop.

"You're awake early," Jack said from the cave of the armchair.

Charlene screamed, then slammed her hand over her mouth to glare at where the voice had come from. No body—just a voice.

Jack slowly materialized with a grin. "Sorry. Just watching TV." The television had been on low, as was their custom. "What's going on?"

"I'm not sure, but I think Jane has Tyler's ring."

Jack straightened and was immediately at her side as she shifted on her chair before the desk. "What? Our little mousy Jane?"

"I know, right? But Jane tipped her purse at the funeral service. I saw something—my subconscious did, anyway. Gold. Black. Emerald. I'm going to talk to her today. It's Friday. Maybe the theater will be open for rehearsals? I know that she planned to help Brooklyn practice for the show tonight."

"Everybody has gold, Charlene. Or a pen. Don't barge in there accusing her of theft, just in case your subconscious had too much excitement before bed. Do you have any other reason to suspect her?"

"No." She tapped the side of her head. Why would

Jane take something as valuable and as noticeable as that? Was this revenge against Madison? "I need to talk to her, that's all."

"Don't forget to call Sam and ask him to go to the bandstand with you."

"I don't know, Jack." She studied the blown-up image on the computer screen, scrutinizing the shadow and the plastic sheet on the bandstand, with critical eyes. Compared it to Michelle's print photo she'd left her. Truth was, that smudge could be anything. "I'm just not sure it's a woman. Or an actual person." Charlene didn't want to bother Sam unless she was certain.

Jack tilted his head and crossed his arms. "So now what? Scrap the idea?"

Charlene was no quitter. "Let's look at each shot of the crowd and the bandstand with the individual frame enlarged. Maybe we'll see something."

"You mean Jane."

Jack knew her so well. "Jane was the announcer and in charge of the costumes. She *should* be there, so it wouldn't raise any questions."

"Let's see if we can find her where she isn't supposed to be," Jack suggested.

Charlene liked that idea.

Jane, she noticed, was a very capable costume and backstage manager and unflappable when it came to dealing with stress.

They saw her pinning costumes, repairing a damaged hem, fixing someone's hair, dotting perspiration from an actor's brow. She straightened the curtain before the stage, signaled for actors to enter and exit, taking direction from Danielle all the while. She soothed Hunter and assisted Madison with her English officer's coat. She carried a clipboard, with things poking from the pockets of her denim-shorts coveralls. An easy place to hide a ring.

It took two hours and three cups of coffee to go through each image. Madison had her ring on during the entire play. "Jane deserves a raise." Charlene stretched her arms over her head. "And she has short hair. I wish I had a printer, to look at the pictures differently. I feel like I'm missing something."

Charlene saved a few pictures to a flash drive to take to the drugstore and print out.

"What do you expect to find with those?" Jack gestured to what she'd saved, especially frames of folks seated on the metal benches to watch the play.

She had Michelle's photos too. The one of her and Kevin also had some of the other spectators behind them, where the gunshot had to have come from. The frozen lemonade stand. The bandstand.

"A woman with long hair? There must be hundreds." She had to let the idea of Jane go.

Jack sighed. "Unfortunately, yes. Most of the women are in ponytails or with sunhats—including you. It will be hard to match a blurry shadow."

Charlene skimmed the rows of spectators with a feeling of defeat. "You're right." She rose and stepped back from the computer. "I'll dress, then get breakfast started. The Stewarts are checking out today."

"I heard Penny tell Minnie about James having health issues—so she was being protective, in her own snarky way."

"Yeah—you just can't tell what's going on in someone's marriage." She smiled at Jack. "I hope they make it."

"Softie," Jack said to Charlene as she hurried into the shower.

Forty-five minutes later, Charlene had opened a can of cat food for Silva and poured her fourth cup of coffee. It was going to be that kind of day.

Two online registrations had come in, both requesting the oak room from next Friday to Sunday, so she would have to sort that out right away. There was no more dark roast for her Keurig, though she had plenty for her twelve-cup coffeepot. She jotted DR on her grocery list on the counter.

"Hellloo?" Penny called from the bottom stair. James was right behind her, and they each had a wheeled suitcase.

"Morning!" Charlene answered. "Are you ready for coffee or tea? Minnie picked up a loaf of wheat bread, if you'd like me to put some toast in for you, Penny."

"I'm sorry about that the other day," Penny replied with a hint of pink to her cheeks. "Whatever you have out is fine."

"You'll find lemon loaf, pumpkin bread, and blueberry muffins. But it really is no bother if you'd prefer toast. I was going to make some for myself."

Penny's shoulders bowed. "Oh, then yes, thank you."

James took Penny's luggage and placed it with his by the front door. Silva stalked down the hall, stopping to scratch periodically at the red jingle bell at her throat.

"I don't think she likes it," James said, heading into the dining room with Penny. "Why the bell?"

"She's a hazard to the wildlife without it." Charlene shrugged, then put four slices of fresh whole wheat in the toaster and went to the dining room.

Penny had a cup of tea, and James had chosen one of each of Minnie's pastries and poured himself a mug of coffee from the carafe on the sideboard.

Silva glared at Charlene and then darted out of the dining room and up the stairs—which Charlene knew because she could hear the cat. This was going to be a good thing. No more cat sleeping on the guest beds!

"Is there anything else you plan on doing in Salem before returning to Ottawa?"

"We've relaxed." James broke off a corner of lemon loaf. "Which was the point. I'm so glad that we discovered your bed and breakfast. I'm sure some of our friends would enjoy it as well."

"We'd like to book again for next summer," Penny said.

Charlene blinked in pleasure. "Oh—of course." She changed her mind about Mrs. Stewart. Running her bed and breakfast had taught her that most people were decent, and everybody had a story. Charlene preferred hers with happy endings and hoped that they would find theirs.

She brought the toast into the dining room, and then excused herself since the couple was in quiet and content conversation with one another, occasionally touching hands.

Jack appeared at his chair in the kitchen, and he smiled at her when he saw her pleased expression.

"I think they'll be okay," he said.

Charlene didn't answer her tricky ghost, but lifted her coffee mug in agreement.

After breakfast, she brought her laptop to the kitchen table and offered the first guest who'd paid, their choice of the oak room, talking up the middle room as being a bit larger and cozier for the second customer. She must've done a good job, because they sent back their acceptance a moment later, along with a payment.

Next, she wished the Stewarts safe travels, and once

they were gone, she pocketed her flash drive and grabbed her purse. "I'll be back," she told Jack and Silva. Silva ignored Charlene in her feline way, sitting on the bottom step of the grand staircase.

"Be careful at the bandstand," Jack said. "That note might have been a warning . . . for you."

"I will—but honestly, it's probably just a weird shadow from the plastic sheet. Or maybe construction equipment. My luck it will be a mop head. Sam will never let me live it down."

Jack chuckled. "See you later, Charlene."

She got into her Pilot and made a quick stop at the drugstore to get the photos she wanted printed out. Charlene eyed them and almost dumped them in the trash—no sudden jolt of awareness. No immediate recognition of the shooter. Just rows and rows of hot but happy people waiting for the play to begin.

She recalled the family of four redheads at the very back row to the far right, and the older couple on the far left. In her center row was a trio of kids with a middle-aged woman. A man and woman in their twenties, each in hats. Another couple. The beach bag on the last row.

"It was a long shot," she said to nobody, stuffing the photos in her purse and going back to her car.

She called Sam and left a message for him, then dialed Amy to ask for Jane's phone number.

"Hey, miss me already?" Amy teased.

"Of course—and don't take this personally, but who I really want to talk to is Jane."

"Jane?"

"Yeah, I just wanted to have her clarify something I'd recorded on the Fourth of July."

"Oh, well, she's still at the theater with Brooklyn right

now, to help her rehearse for the show tonight. We're doing a six and a nine o'clock, then three shows Saturday and Sunday. Neville ranted all morning about how we need to bring in money or Salem Stage Right will close its doors. Danielle didn't even bother to show up to the work meeting, and she normally runs it."

Danielle had long hair. Danielle knew the play. Danielle had hated Madison. While she might have hired a shooter, she hadn't shot the actress. She'd been to the left of the stage for the whole performance and had run from that direction when Madison had fallen to the grass.

"I might just drop by then." Still in park, Charlene stared into the stand of trees between the drugstore and the street.

"Is everything okay?"

"Yes." She dragged up the memory of the spilled purse and the flash of gold and emerald. "Hey, did you notice Jane wearing any jewelry?"

"Ha! This is about the ring, isn't it? Well, Jane had no gold on; I'd remember. Since you told me it was stolen, I've been checking everyone for gold and emerald rings. She had silver."

A lot of folks wore silver. Charlene put the photos on the console. "Thanks, Amy."

"Sure—oh, Kevin wants to know if we can do dinner next week if you have a night without guests? Come to our place since you had us over last."

"That would be fun." Wednesdays were usually a good bet, but she had to check her calendar.

"We can invite Kass and Logan too."

Her heart skipped at the news. "I thought Logan was out of the picture?" Why would he have changed his mind?

"Nope," Amy said in a happy-for-her-friend tone. "Logan showed up at Kass's apartment last night. She left him sleeping there for the theater meeting this morning but rushed right back to him when it was over. Normally, we grab a coffee."

The hair on Charlene's arms rose. "I don't want to alarm you, but I found out that Logan's an outdoorsman. Hunts geese."

"Lots of guys do—oh, you're thinking he could shoot a gun. Well, it is the Second Amendment." Amy hesitated. "Can you get away for dinner soon?"

"Weekends are booked for me. Wednesday? You'll be able to watch out for Kass during the shows."

"I don't think Kass is in danger. But I suppose we could keep our eye out for her. Should we warn her? I don't think she'd be pleased."

"True, and she might not be," Charlene assured her. "I know Sam is close to solving this." She thought of the possible figure with long hair in the bandstand—she was also getting close. Could be her questions made the shooter nervous and would force a move. A mistake. Perhaps Logan had come to Salem to make sure that Charlene didn't discover his crime.

"Call me later," Amy said and hung up.

Charlene decided to still talk to Jane about the ring; if she was wrong, she could cross Jane off her list and move on to Logan. She started the Pilot and drove down the sunny streets of Salem.

Sam sent a text. **In a meeting—can I call at noon?**

Charlene checked the time on her dashboard. Eleven. When she was at a stop sign, she texted Sam a thumbs-up.

Turning into the mostly vacant theater parking lot, Charlene snagged a spot beneath an oak tree and went to the rear entrance of the brick building, smiling at the memory of her last time here with Avery.

The door was locked. Charlene peered inside the window to the right and saw movement. She knocked on the glass.

One of the *Midsummer Night's* fairies she'd met, and seen again at the funeral, recognized her after opening the door. "Hey! Show doesn't start for a few more hours."

"I was hoping to see Jane?"

"Oh, she's in Madison's old dressing room with Brooklyn—helping the girl with her timing and going over her lines. After the quick run-through this morning, it's obvious she's a little shaky after her first debacle. I'm on my way out. Do you remember how to reach the dressing rooms in back?"

"Yes, thanks. See you later."

The girl left, and Charlene went down the dim hall. She followed the eerie path flanked by mannequins in wigs and costumes, to Jane's world of wonders with a sewing machine and racks of fabric. She recognized the orange cape that had been shredded. It still was. Hadn't Jane said she'd fixed it? Since the door was open, Charlene stepped inside.

"Jane?"

A can of silver spray paint was on a workbench. A dark-brown wig similar to Madison's hair was on a Styrofoam head. She saw a pale figure shrouded in white gauze. Her pulse skipped. Was that a . . . no. Just a mannequin made to resemble a ghost.

"Jane . . ." Charlene called again, but she knew she was alone and took the opportunity to search the young woman's desk drawers. No ring—not that she expected to find it. Jane was smarter than people gave her credit for.

A giant makeup kit was to the right on a long vanity table. Pictures had been tucked into the frame of a picture of Jane in a Wild Wild West costume, blowing on the tip of a pistol. Did she know how to shoot? Or had she been an actress before?

All the colors of eyeliner were there except for black—the sticks very much the shape of a pen. Jane's fabric handbag wasn't in sight.

Charlene used her phone to take a picture of the ghostly mannequin with the wig and admired the spectral image. This might be what Charlene had seen that evening near the ghost light. Jane had been the one to claim that Madison's room had been broken into, but she could easily have done it herself. She'd started the rumors of Madison haunting the place, knowing how actors were very superstitious.

Inconspicuous Jane was behind the scenes stirring things up. For what reason? Getting rid of Madison made sense—the woman had tormented her enough—but why the damage to the room, the haunting, being disruptive?

Jane must have written the warning on the Trinity Church prayer sheet. But why slash Amy's tire? It didn't make sense. Amy had always been kind to her, which made Charlene consider that the warning had been for her—after they'd sat together and Charlene had witnessed the purse spill and admonished Jane's giggle.

Charlene surveyed the top of the vanity table and the workbench. She doubted scissors could be strong enough to penetrate a tire, even heavy-duty ones. She sent the pictures of the makeup kit, cape, and Wild West photo to Sam. She knew that her "meddling," as he liked to call it, infuriated him, but he'd be at her side in a heartbeat if she was in trouble.

Jane's laptop was on her desk, and Charlene was tempted to see if it was on, but she couldn't bring herself to do it. Rifling through a drawer was a bit less . . . illegal . . . than going through a closed laptop. It would also be an invasion of her privacy.

Charlene took one last look around the room. Jane could have easily orchestrated the "ghost" when setting up the laptop from the orchestra pit before the slideshow of Madison for the actors fund.

She'd been all over the place that day, and it would've been a simple sleight of hand for Jane to pay Hunter to drop the musket. She probably knew Hunter was short on cash and would jump at the chance, no questions asked.

"What are you doing here?" Jane demanded, not a single hint of a tremble in her tone as she stood in the doorway.

"Hi!" Charlene's heart jumped; her voice quavered, and to cover her nerves, she cleared her throat. "Jane! Just who I was hoping to see."

Jane barged into the room and slammed the door closed, locking it behind her. She stepped forward. "Why?"

"I had a few questions and figured you'd be the person to ask. Amy said you'd be here, and when you weren't, I decided to wait."

"What questions?" Jane crossed her arms belligerently. "You're not my boss, and I don't appreciate you acting like it."

Since Jane seemed to hold a grudge, Charlene realized that directly asking about the ring, or the note, might not go down well. She had a very bad feeling about what Jane had been up to in the theater. She'd need to walk on eggshells.

She gestured to the mannequin with the gauzy fabric. "Funny," she said, changing the subject, "when I first came in, I thought this was a ghost. Scared me."

"So?"

"Well, the day of the Madison show, I thought I saw a ghost. Above the box seats, where Danielle Hampton was sitting."

Jane lowered her arms slowly.

Charlene lifted her phone and showed Jane the image of the ghost she'd taken with Jane's props. "It's very clever." She smiled to defuse the situation she found herself in. "Still, I'm curious as to why you would want your acting friends to think the theater is haunted." She gave a careless shrug. "Whatever! You sure had me fooled." When Jane didn't answer, she continued speaking in a soothing voice. "I thought it might actually be a ghost since Madison had been murdered, but I was wrong."

Jane moved another half step closer to Charlene, her expression menacing. "Why are you asking me this, and where'd you get that picture?" The young woman glanced at her laptop and then back at Charlene.

"I'm not your enemy, Jane. I came as a friend. But it looks like yours, doesn't it? The photo you used to "haunt" the theater—but I took it, just now. I thought it was so good and found it interesting enough to send to Detective Holden."

"Why did you do that?" Jane's composure slipped further. "You shouldn't have involved the cops!" Her face grew pinched, and she fisted her hands.

Charlene pointed at the shredded cape and scissors on the worktable. "Did you vandalize Madison's dressing room and start the rumor about the theater being haunted?

Was that to get back at Neville? He wasn't very kind to you, was he? I've seen how hard you work, and I'm sure you aren't paid enough."

Jane quivered as if afraid, but Charlene no longer believed the woman lacked confidence. "You don't know anything. The money was only part of it."

"You're very smart, Jane, and I can't figure it out. You said you were scared to be fired, but you're still here."

At that, Jane tossed the remnants of the shy, timid, overworked young lady to raise her chin and straighten her posture, staring Charlene in the eye.

"You're wrong again, Charlene. Danielle fired me July fifth." Her expression switched between hurt and anger. "After that fiasco, Danielle paid me a personal visit, waiting until after I'd put together that stupid tribute to Madison, and then she made me sign a statement, giving me two weeks' notice—and she wouldn't let me just quit, either. No, she demanded I stay until the scheduled performances were done."

"That's not fair to you. Not right at all. Is that why you almost dropped the laptop? You must have been furious. I could see you were doing a great job and not getting credit for it."

"You're right about that! I'd love to close this place down. I heard Danielle and Neville at each other's throats. It wouldn't take much, a little ghost action here and there, to get everyone to quit. It sure worked on Brooklyn." She giggled. "Girl totally bombed."

"You had a plan all along—so clever."

"I did everything for the Boswells. They paid me minimum wage, which was crap. I orchestrated the program, maintained the website, and personally managed all of the whiny actors who thought their changing rooms weren't big enough, or they should have had this or that role! Madison was the worst."

"I noticed you trying to keep everyone calm. You did a good job. Everyone knows how high-strung actors can be."

She snorted. "I always had the lead in plays in high school. That picture of me was my starring role in *Annie Get Your Gun*. My parents were so proud of me. Then I went to a community college and hated it there. Everyone was so mean to me. I quit after the first year and started working for the great Neville Hampton. Hoped I could get a role here and there. He's got this ego that won't quit. He tried me out in bit parts, and I don't know what happened, but suddenly I couldn't act my way out of a tin box. I, who was such a success, suddenly had stage fright!"

"That happens to famous actors. Even singers. I think Barbra Streisand had a bout with it. So, you were in good company." Charlene pacified her with a smile. "Did Danielle give you a reason for letting you go? Perhaps you could fight it?"

"And go to who? She and Neville own this theater, and he's not going to stand up against his wife while she's already threatening him with divorce. Danielle wants this theater closed as much as I do." She raised her gaze to Charlene. "They blame me for everything! How could I possibly have killed Madison when I was running around like a chicken with my head cut off?"

Charlene winced.

Her cheeks flamed. "Oh God, you've heard the story too. Madison was despicable. She deserves to be dead."

"She was extremely cruel." Charlene looked toward

the door. It sounded like Jane hadn't been the shooter. So why write the note or steal the ring? Dare she ask, and risk pushing Jane over the edge? The more she thought about it, the more she knew Jane had to have stolen it when Madison had fallen from the stage and she'd put the cape under her head.

Charlene decided that she should leave and discuss it with Jack or Sam when Sam called at noon. "You had a very good reason for disliking Madison, but so did others. I hope they find the guilty party."

Jane's mouth thinned suspiciously as Charlene took a small step toward the door. "Do you have any knowledge that might assist the police?" *Keep her talking and distracted.*

"No! I've already spoken with them. Madison got what she had coming, and I told them so. Doing that to me!" A large silver ring slid off her finger when she jabbed at her own chest.

The ring didn't fit her. Tyler's ring? No, wrong color. But wait!

Charlene darted for it and picked it up—the metal tacky with paint. "What is this?" She spoke in a quiet tone, her mind processing this new information. If this was the ring and Jane had stolen it, was it possible she'd murdered Madison too? Had she put herself in danger coming here? *I'm sorry, Sam.*

"It's mine. Give it to me!"

The girl was borderline hysterical. Charlene had ended up by the dressing table when capturing the ring, and now Jane stood between Charlene and escape.

"You need to give this to the police, Jane. Say you found Madison's ring. You could be the hero of this story."

Jane's eyes flashed. "I . . . said . . . give . . . it . . . to . . . me."

Charlene shivered—her brain deciding that yeah, she really should leave. Just not yet. "I will, once I know." With her fingernail, Charlene scraped some of the silver away to reveal the gold band and emerald stone. Tyler would be so relieved.

"I can take it to the police for you," Charlene said quickly. "I'm a friend of the detective. You might even get recognition or a commendation or something."

"For what? Taking a ring from a dead woman? It's mine! Madison owes me." Jane clamped her lips closed, then lifted her head and gave a chilling smile "She used it to hypnotize people. To get them to do what she wanted. Now I will have that power."

Charlene knew that Madison used her gorgeous eyes and didn't need a ring. "You don't need a prop, Jane. You have your own strength inside you." She tucked the ring in her purse. "This belongs to someone else."

"Charlene, no. It's mine," Jane snarled.

"Did you take it for safekeeping?" She inched away from the dressing room table. "I've been through the video, and Madison was wearing it during the entire show. It was gone after you went to 'help' her on the lawn, before Michelle arrived."

"You can't prove that!" Jane put up both hands as if she could physically stop Charlene with just a thought.

"It's all on tape." Charlene felt sorry for the woman. "Return the ring, apologize . . . prove you had no responsibility in harming Madison so you can put this all behind you and start over."

"Sure. Give me the ring, and I'll do just that." Jane gave her a mocking smile. "You think I'm stupid, don't you! I know what they'll do to me. And even if the police do believe me, it won't get me my job back, or respect either."

"You'll get respect when you do the right thing." Charlene patted the ring in her purse pocket. "Come with me to the station, Jane, and let's explain to my friend Detective Holden what happened."

"No, thanks." Jane pulled a folded knife from her shorts pocket. She flipped it out to reveal a thick, shining blade. "I'm done talking."

Plenty strong enough to cause a flat tire with that.

Charlene pressed 9-1-1 on her phone, telling the operator that she was in danger and to call Detective Holden as Jane stalked her around the desk. Charlene, needing both hands, stuck her phone in her pocket.

Maybe coming here alone had not been her smartest move. *Come on, Sam!*

Charlene scanned the room for something to defend herself with and jumped for the can of silver spray paint, the only weapon available, and aimed it at Jane. "That's a nasty knife you're carrying. Put it away, please, and we can talk."

"I'm done with talking. You should have left when you had the chance."

"I'll walk away right now. But I need to know one thing. Why did you kill Madison?"

CHAPTER TWENTY-TWO

"I didn't kill anybody!" Jane lunged for Charlene, an expression of fury on her plain face.

Charlene leaped back, her hip hitting the dressing table, but she avoided Jane's knife by a hair. "Don't make me do this!"

Jane stabbed forward again.

Charlene pressed down on the nozzle, sending a hard stream of paint toward Jane's face. The woman blinked, silver in her lashes.

"Put that down!" Jane stared at Charlene, the knife out in front of her, silver paint dripping from her forehead and chin. "Give me the ring and go."

"The police will be here any minute." She kept her tone of voice soothing so as not to escalate the situation any worse than it already was.

"This freaking stings—give me the ring, Charlene.

Don't make me hurt you." Jane blinked more rapidly. "Last chance!"

Charlene had her finger on the button of the can of silver spray paint, ready to douse Jane a second time, when the door was flung open—Neville at the knob with the master key to the theater rooms. "What's going on? The police are here! Jane, put down that knife! Have you lost your mind, girl?"

Officer Bernard and Officer Jimenez raced past Neville. Charlene dropped the spray can when Officer Bernard knocked the knife from Jane's hand.

"What's going on?" he asked. Pools of silver paint gathered on Jane's face as the paint dried. Clumps stuck to her lashes, the orbs veined with red.

Charlene explained what had happened and ended with, "I sent the pictures to Sam. I sprayed her in self-defense."

"We were already en route when we received the 9-1-1 call," Officer Jimenez said, pulling Jane's arms behind her back and cuffing her. The female officer had a stern jaw, pulled-back hair, and stony-gray eyes. She was a no-nonsense beat cop who didn't take crap from anybody.

"I'm innocent!" Jane yelled.

"You have the right to remain silent. Anything you say can and will be used against you in a court of law." She recited the Miranda rights as Jane struggled against her.

"Is that really necessary?" Neville asked. "I hardly think she's dangerous—she's been under a lot of pressure, that's all."

The officer shot him a look that warned him to shut his mouth.

"This is such BS," Jane shouted. "I didn't do anything! She doesn't even have a nick on her finger." She glared at

Charlene and told the police officer, "When I entered the room, Charlene was already in here, nosing around. She stole a ring from me! It's her you should cuff."

"That right?" Officer Bernard glanced at Charlene. "Aren't you a friend of Detective Holden's?"

"Yes, we're acquaintances. I didn't steal the ring, like I told you. It's part of the Boswell homicide investigation." Charlene could just imagine what Sam would have to say about this mess. "Jane took it from the dead woman's finger."

Officer Jimenez seemed to grow even colder as she told Officer Bernard, "Friends don't get special treatment." She turned to Charlene, her hand still on Jane's shoulder to keep the woman in place. "I want you both to come in for questioning."

"Me?" Charlene squeaked. "I run a bed and breakfast and have houseguests arriving."

"And that affects me how?" the female officer snapped. "Do you have the ring in your possession?"

"I do." She nodded to her bag. "It's in my purse. Side pocket."

Officer Jimenez passed Jane to Officer Bernard. "Do I have permission to search?"

What could Charlene say, no? Anything but cooperation with this officer would not go down well. "Yes, go ahead—on the side there."

The officer put on a glove from her black vest pocket to reach in and lift the ring out. "This is what you were arguing over? It looks like costume jewelry." She wrapped it in the glove. "Who does it belong to?"

"Me!" Jane insisted and smirked at Charlene. "You better arrest her, too, for stealing."

"Tyler Lawson," Charlene answered firmly.

Neville stayed on the edge of the room but watched with uncertainty and, yes, concern in his expression. Maybe it was just Danielle who wanted Jane gone. "Who is that?"

"Madison's ex-fiancé," Charlene said. "He was at the funeral. Did you know him?"

"No." Neville rubbed his chin. "I was a little preoccupied."

"Charlene attacked me," Jane said, sensing she was losing the crowd. "I need to wash my face. What if she blinded me?"

"You came at me with a knife—you slashed my friend's tire and threatened me."

"You're a liar." Jane sneered.

"I say we take you both down to the station to answer questions," Office Jimenez decided. "You have the knife?"

Officer Bernard lifted an evidence bag, glancing toward Charlene. "Are you sure . . ."

Sam entered the prop room and cut off what Officer Bernard might have said. Husky, broad-shouldered, unsmiling Sam. He was a worthy sight for sore eyes.

"What's going on?" he asked Officer Jimenez, who had removed a second pair of handcuffs from an inside pocket.

"Charlene Morris sprayed Jane Wallace in the face with silver paint after stealing a ring from Ms. Wallace. Ms. Wallace had a knife on Ms. Morris—they each claim to have been attacked. I plan on questioning them both in the interrogation room. Is that a problem, sir?"

Officer Bernard bristled, his jaw tight, but he didn't contradict Officer Jimenez.

Neville broke in. "I told the officer this wasn't necessary. I can handle Jane."

Ignoring Neville, Sam gave Charlene a long look, his eyes dark and mysterious.

She swallowed hard. "Sam?"

He turned to Officer Jimenez. "No problem, Officer. Do your job. Are handcuffs necessary to restrain Ms. Morris?"

Jane snickered. "And this was the 'friend' you wanted me to talk to at the station. You're screwed."

Charlene bit the inside of her cheek to keep from arguing. She'd done everything the officer had asked. Officer Jimenez put the cuffs away, her mouth pursed as she glared at Charlene.

Sam's expression remained inscrutable as he wandered the room, taking note of the gauze-wrapped mannequin, the picture of Jane with a gun, the wig to match Madison's hair. He returned to Officer Jimenez. "May I see the ring?"

Officer Jimenez handed him the plastic glove with the ring inside.

He flipped it around, studying it closely. "I don't understand why this would be worth stabbing someone for." He nodded at his officer and stepped aside. "Take them in. I'll meet you there."

Charlene's face flamed with anger, hurt, disbelief. "You can't do this! I . . . I . . ."

"I could charge you with interfering in an active investigation, Ms. Morris. So, if I were you, I'd keep quiet." Sam crossed his arms.

She lowered her head, hating that he had a right, if flimsy, to act as he was. She'd answer their questions, but no more. They only had the ring tying Jane to Madison because of her.

Charlene had never been in the back of a police car before, and riding next to Jane did not sit well. She drew on her pride. One day she'd have a lot to say to her previous pal, Detective Sam Holden, but for now, the silent treatment would prevail.

When they arrived at Salem Police Station, Officer Jimenez ushered Jane, in cuffs, and Charlene, who walked with her head high, to an interrogation room Charlene had never seen before. There was even a window-mirror thing, like on television.

Sam waited for them inside and gestured them both to take a seat. He and Officer Jimenez were on the other side of the rectangular table.

She opened her mouth to explain or protest, then slammed it shut. Jane giggled, and Charlene shook her head.

"Who wants to go first?" Sam asked, leaning back in his chair, stroking his mustache.

"I shouldn't be here," Charlene said, trying to stay cool and calm. "I have guests to check in."

Officer Jimenez tapped the table. "This is serious."

"She's the guilty one; it's me who should be free. My face really itches. Can I wash it yet?" Jane bounced around in her chair like she had at the church. Excited, as if this was a great new game for her.

"Ms. Morris. What do you have to say for yourself?"

"I plead the Fifth." She gave him a steely look that could frost all outdoors even in the dead of summer.

His mustache twitched. If Sam laughed at her, she'd . . . she'd lose it completely. She was so angry and afraid, and worse—ashamed. What had she been thinking, to march into the theater to ask Jane questions about the ring? She should have relayed her suspicions to Sam and let him handle it. Her job was the bed and breakfast she adored.

What would Jack say if she left him now for a stint in jail? What about Avery and Silva? Who would take care of them?

She swallowed down tears, which she wouldn't shed no matter how hot they burned behind her eyes.

Sam drank from his chipped Red Sox mug. She would have bought him a new one, but not now. They could never be friends after this.

"Ms. Morris. Why were you at the theater and in Jane's workshop?"

She cleared her throat. "Still not talking."

Officer Jimenez rose, with the handcuffs outstretched toward Charlene. "Would you like to reconsider?"

Charlene shifted on the hard plastic seat. Jane laughed nervously.

Sam put an arm on the table. She couldn't read his expression and didn't want to.

"I won't ask again." He was done teasing her, and she straightened. She would never be able to forgive him for this.

She folded her arms and leaned as far back in the chair as she could go. "As you know, I called to talk about this, and you were in a meeting."

His jaw clenched, but he nodded.

"I remembered seeing something at the funeral when Jane's bag tipped over. It was a flash of emerald and gold, which could have been anything. And something black, too, long and skinny. I assumed a pen."

"And why would you care what was in her bag?"

Oh, he had her there. How many years of jail would that be? Should she call a lawyer?

"I can't believe you went through my purse!" Jane said.

"I helped you put things back in, after you spilled it." Charlene turned to Sam. "Jane had acted strangely during the service, giggling, bouncing around. I figured she was nervous or something. She hated Madison, with good reason." She scooched forward a little. "I didn't think at the time that she'd murdered Madison. I wondered if she'd stolen the ring out of spite. As it turns out, Jane said she took it from Madison because she thought it had hypnotizing power."

Jane wriggled on her chair.

"I see," Sam said, still focused on Charlene. "You went to the theater to confront Jane about the ring?"

"Not just that—I think the pen I glimpsed was really eyeliner. I figured Jane wrote the note and slashed Amy's tire as a warning to me."

"You are crazy," Jane said. The silver paint had dried completely and now flaked free like clumpy glitter on her lap.

Sam turned to Jane and Officer Jimenez. "You have the knife from Jane?"

"Yes. Well, Officer Bernard took it to the evidence room."

"Match it to the tire I brought in yesterday."

"What are you talking about?" Jane asked. For the first time, fear laced her tone.

"Jane was the first person besides Amy to reach Madison from the stage." Charlene had to make Sam see the truth. She had found the killer for him. He should be thanking her, not putting the guilt trip on her. "Madison wore the ring during the performance, but it wasn't there after she was killed. I know Amy didn't steal it."

"Yes." He steepled his hands. "Because you're friends."

"Right." She glanced around the room, refusing to

meet his eyes. "Anyway, I was waiting for Jane in her prop room to ask about the note, and she grew hostile immediately. Danielle fired her, and she only has two weeks left at the theater. She was using those ghostly images to feed rumors that Madison was haunting the place, in order to close it down in revenge."

"I hate you," Jane sobbed.

"How did you come by the ring?" Sam asked.

"It slid off her finger, and I grabbed it from the ground. I didn't steal it." Charlene stared at Officer Jimenez, then Sam. "I told her that I would come with her to talk to you about the ring, to return it. It's not worth much according to Tyler Lawson, but he wants it for sentimental value. It doesn't have hypnosis powers," she told Jane.

"Is this true?" Sam asked Jane.

Jane slumped to the side of her chair. "Yes."

"Why did you want to stab Char . . . Ms. Morris? Did you slash her tire?"

Jane broke into fake sobs. Officer Jimenez offered a tissue then took it back, remembering Jane's hands were cuffed.

"You tried to stab me in the prop room," Charlene said to Jane. "Twice."

"Yeah," Jane muttered. "So what? You deserved it. You trespassed and took pictures of my things. You found my ghost."

"How did Ms. Morris defend herself?"

"She grabbed a can of spray paint and aimed it right in my face. Good thing that nasty officer of yours burst in when she did, or I'da been blind for sure."

Sam and Officer Jimenez both rose from the table and conferred. Jane hummed under her breath.

Charlene interlaced her fingers over her lap and considered how to get out of this station. Should she call Minnie and warn her she might be late? Or worse, might end up behind bars?

Sam sighed, his dark brown eyes locked on Charlene. She was frightened beyond words, more so by the sadness in his expression.

"Ms. Morris, you may go directly home and stay there until I call you. It's that or I can hold you in a jail cell for twenty-four hours. Take your pick." Sam put his hands on the interrogation table, leaning in her direction. "One more thing. You don't take spray paint to a knife fight, unless you're prepared to die."

"I didn't expect to be in a fight, Detective." Charlene stood, her knees shaky. "Much less die." She grabbed her purse.

"Why does she get to go home, and not me? I'm the victim here," Jane cried. "I didn't kill anybody."

"Officer Jimenez and I have a few more questions that need answers," Sam told the hysterical young woman. "The more honest you can be, the sooner we can move forward. Now, what did you mean by hypnotism?"

"I'm not sorry Madison's dead. She turned me into a chicken!"

A police officer escorted Charlene from the station. She was relieved to walk away from the disappointment on Sam's face. She'd blown their friendship for certain this time, and she was to blame. Even so, she wouldn't forgive him anytime soon for his treatment of her, as if she were a common criminal.

CHAPTER TWENTY-THREE

Charlene hailed a cab to take her to the theater, where her car was parked. She knew Amy and Kass were inside, rehearsing for tonight's play, and she longed to spill her guts and tell them that it was Jane who'd killed Madison, that the police had her in custody right now. Jane who'd slashed their tire and stolen the ring and threatened Charlene with that warning note in the trunk of Amy's car.

But she talked too much; that was half the problem. Her asking questions always ended up putting her in harm's way. Sam was right about that. She should leave it to the police to conduct the investigation, but every time she'd been involved, it was because the crime had happened with her on the scene.

That was hardly her fault. It played out in her mind over and over as she went about making tea for her guests or cleaning the bed and breakfast. She and Jack happened to be a valuable resource, if only Sam would let them help. However, the detective didn't believe in ghosts, nor did he believe in civilians crime-solving.

Truth was, if she continued down this current path, one day she might end up dead.

Charlene drove home, not feeling as happy as she'd hoped to be with the shooter caught. Jane would pay for her crime. Madison had pushed the woman too far with her hypnotism tricks. Jane was a little whacky, but until an hour ago, she hadn't thought her crazy . . . or cruel. And yet, Jane would have used that knife on her if Neville hadn't unlocked the prop room for the police in the nick of time.

She burst inside her home, silently calling for Jack. She had guests showing up any minute, and Minnie was busy in the kitchen, putting the ingredients together for tacos. Jalapeño and cumin scented the air. Charlene had suggested it in case the couple were tired from traveling and didn't want to dine out. They also had an excellent list of available takeout places within a two-mile radius that delivered.

"Hi, Minnie!" For the first time ever, Charlene didn't stop to chat but went directly to her suite. She needed a shower to wash away her nervous sweat. Jail. She hated feeling guilty when she hadn't done anything technically wrong. And the episode with Jane trying to stab her? Her adrenaline pumped, and she turned on the water in her bathroom. Being treated like a person of interest at the jail had been the final straw, and now her stomach churned.

After a long, cool shower and a change of clothes—no Jack—she went to the kitchen and apologized to Minnie.

"Sorry I ran past you like that, but I've had an upsetting day. Nothing that I can discuss right now, but it's good to be home."

"Oh?" Minnie put her hands on Charlene's upper arms to study her. "You're all right now?"

"Yes." Charlene's nose stung, so she looked away before she fell apart.

"That's fine," Minnie said, releasing her. "I'm glad you're feeling better. Can I get you some iced tea or fresh-squeezed lemonade?"

"Yes, thanks. Lemonade and a few of your oatmeal cookies will put me right as rain." While Minnie poured her drink, Charlene found the cookies and put them on a small plate. "I'm going to sit outside on the back deck for a while."

"All right, Charlene. I'm heading out. You have an hour before your guests arrive—they're driving and running late, said around fiveish. I told them the front door would be unlocked."

"Thanks, Minnie. And for making the taco fixings. Have a nice evening—I'll see you tomorrow."

"You rest if you can, sweetie. You're a little pale under your tan." Minnie peered closer, and Charlene ducked to hide the tears that blurred her vision. She desperately needed a few minutes to relax and regroup.

This would not be a story she'd be sharing with her parents. "See you later!"

Balancing her drink on her plate, Charlene passed through her suite to the door leading to the back porch and went outside. She breathed deeply, filling her lungs with healthy fresh air, enjoying the smell of the recently mowed grass. Will had trimmed the hedges, and around the wooden barrels filled with gorgeous geraniums that bordered the yard. Smaller pots overflowed with impatiens—pink, white, and red flowers bursting with color.

Hanging baskets hung on either side of the door on her porch, creating a riot of color in her yard. A hummingbird flitted from petal to petal on a low pot. Silva pounced but missed, thanks to the bell.

Charlene walked down the wooden stairs, her cares easing with each step. She'd put a lounge chair on the lawn for when she wanted to relax and read in the sunshine. She set her cookies and lemonade on the small table next to it.

Birds chirped, and a squirrel chittered hello from a leafy branch of the oak tree. The blue sky was dotted with cumulus clouds. This was her oasis.

The horror of the police station receded and freedom tasted as sweet as the oatmeal cookie. Unfortunately, lowering her guard allowed a riot of thoughts to bombard her mind.

What was happening to Jane right now? Would she be fingerprinted and officially charged with murder? Did she even have an attorney? Would Neville help with her defense? What had driven a young, shy, nonviolent person like her to do something so brazen, so outlandish it was more theatrical than Neville's production of *Salem's Rebels*?

She bit into the cookie and chewed. The timing had to have been perfect. Hunter had said he'd been instructed to drop his musket when Madison shouted *yield*. Jane had been there all along, fixing the stage curtains. Announcing the play. Mending costumes. Visible but invisible by her quiet nature. She would know about the camera with the view of the bandstand, and how to break it before the show.

How had Jane managed to shoot Madison? She wished Sam had gotten her to give a full confession while Charlene had been there.

"Jack? Where are you?" she whispered. "I really need to talk to you."

The air chilled, and a swoosh of breeze ruffled her hair, and then there he was. Blue eyes flashing, a grin on his strong, handsome face.

"What's the matter, Charlene?" Jack sat down on the porch steps. They each faced the swing under the broad oak. "I could feel your tension when you returned home. Are you all right?" His face showed concern—not disappointment, like a certain detective.

She sipped from the frosty glass of tart lemonade and was brought back to the day Madison had been shot. She'd had a frozen drink and shared a laugh with that poor clerk. Leo/Tyler had paid for her beverage after bumping into her. She hoped he got his heirloom back from Sam. Today had been the reading of the will, and Tyler had planned to fly home to LA.

Sam. How could he have been so mean? Charlene sighed. "Yes, I'm fine. But I think I may have learned my lesson."

Jack folded his hands over his bare knees, leaning toward her. "Oh?"

Charlene poured out the entire disastrous event to an empathetic Jack, not leaving one embarrassing thing out. And there were plenty.

"You could have been killed!" Jack jumped up and paced the lawn. "Jane could have stabbed you with her knife over that ring."

"I know. It was so humiliating . . . I really thought that Sam was going to let the officer cuff me and read me my

rights. I had to ride in the back of a police car with a murderer. I can't believe Sam allowed that to happen to me.
But he did." Tears welled in her eyes. "I don't think I'll
ever forgive him for that."

Jack stopped pacing to stand before her. "I would normally be on your side with this, but Sam got the message
across, didn't he? Instead of letting you go, he made you
see what could have been the consequences of your actions."

"Really?" As if she didn't hurt enough, Jack was piling
the guilt on.

Jack knelt by her chair, peered into her eyes, and ruffled her hair with a caress of his fingers. "I'm to blame as
well, for encouraging you to help with these dangerous
homicides. I don't want anything to happen to you. I
couldn't bear to be that lonely again. You've made eter-
nity something worthwhile."

Charlene set her plate and glass aside. "I was thinking
about you during the drive to the station, in the back of
the police car. How you'd be alone, and I'd lose you, my
house, my cat, Avery, and my liberty, all because I didn't
stop asking questions. And that's if I just went to jail, and
wasn't . . . hurt, or worse."

She dabbed her nose with a red, white, and blue paper
napkin and reclined slightly in the lounge chair. Silva lay
on Jack's previous spot on the porch stair, lazing in the
summer afternoon. The sun warmed her face and Charlene let her eyes drift to half-mast, then closed. She was
sorry.

"Just rest, Charlene. I'll be around."

"Only for a minute," she murmured. "We have guests
coming."

She drowsed to the light wind in the leaves of the oak,

the slow rhythm of the ropes on the swing, the soothing sounds of crickets—Charlene got so relaxed, she considered apologizing to Sam. She would mind her own business before it killed her.

Limbs heavy, she thought of the bandstand and the blurred figure on the video. Not Jane. How could it have been? The girl had been all over the place but always in sight.

So, who?

The shooter. Logan? He'd also been in full view the whole time. He'd been worried that his own sister was trying to trick him with her death. Tyler had been there, too, and then he'd gone across the street for a drink rather than watch Madison on stage. Sam had checked Tyler's alibi.

Their situation didn't make sense to her . . . if Tyler loved Madison so much, and she had really invited him to see her show, why hadn't he been there in the front row to cheer her on? He knew how much she wanted to be the star. Even he hadn't been able to pull it off. Was vengeance why she'd left him and taken his ring?

Charlene made out the jingle of Silva's collar as the cat darted across the porch to the bushes. Heart hammering, she widened her eyes from her doze and prepared a smile for her guests.

"Hi, I'm . . ." She swallowed her words on a hard gulp.

Tyler Lawson, agent to the stars, was on her porch—had been in her house. Minnie was gone. Where was Jack? Her pulse sped erratically.

"I know who you are, Charlene. We're practically best friends after all this."

He smiled, charming, practiced, and fake. Tyler's eyes

were hidden by dark designer sunglasses. His arms were tan in a Ralph Lauren short-sleeved shirt, his frame trim but strong, like a runner's.

She sat up and rubbed her lids with the back of her hand to wake fully.

"I hope you don't mind that I let myself in. I knocked, but no answer. You were out here resting on this perfect summer day."

His casual words and tone caused sparks of alarm rather than set her at ease.

She started to get up from her chair, but he waved her back, showing something matte black at his waist.

He tapped the handle of a gun tucked into his belt.

A gun. Her brain spun, the pieces coming together to form a whole. The height of the shadow inside the bandstand was the same as Tyler's—but he wasn't female by a long shot, and Sam said he had a solid alibi.

"I gave you a clue, Charlene, the day of the funeral. Figured you were smart enough to figure it out." His stance on her porch was relaxed. "I enjoy a challenge."

"I don't understand."

"Your confusion is quite entertaining." Tyler patted the weapon again. "I liked you from the moment I bumped into you on my way to the bandstand basement."

She thought back to the billowy linen shirt he'd worn, untucked and cool in the summer heat. Large and roomy.

"Bet you didn't know that I'm captain of the Beverly Hills Gun Club—fastest draw on the team."

Her tummy churned, the hair on her arms stood on end. "You acted like you hated guns. Your father?"

"All part of the game."

She gulped, mouth dry. "They found your ring—it's at the station."

"*You* found my ring." Tyler caressed the handle of his gun but kept it in his belt. "Clever. And now the game is over."

"Just leave, Tyler, before Detective Holden arrives. Should be here any minute." Jack! Where was he? Silva watched from behind the whiskey barrel of flowers. Charlene scrambled to her feet, keeping the long lounger between them. The swing was at her back.

"I doubt that, Charlene. Jane just called from her house. Neville sprung her out on bail—chump feels responsible for her. Your detective is going after Danielle Hampton for the murder of Madison Boswell, thanks to Jane's misdirection."

"Why would Jane lie for you?" Charlene tried not to look at the gun but the weapon drew her focus.

Tyler removed his sunglasses, his blue eyes flat. "We've been 'friends' on social media for months. Ever since I tracked down Madison at Salem Stage Right. I gave Jane a sob story about how Madison ensnared me with her hypnotic ways, and Jane was putty in my hands. Seems Madison had made her cluck like a chicken? You just have to know how people tick. Easy."

His voice gave her a chill all the way to her bones.

"If you're working together, why did she steal your ring?"

"I didn't tell her about its importance beforehand." Tyler shrugged. "My mistake. I don't usually make mistakes." His gold watch glinted. "I'll pick it up at the station on my way out of town, after tidying a few loose ends."

Charlene thought back to the footage she'd gotten of the people in the crowd. What had she missed? The woman in a long dress, her hair down to her shoulders, in the center back aisle. Not with the man, or kids, but by herself. The gold watch.

Tyler had worn it when he'd spilled Frappuccino, and so had the woman with the beach bag on the bench. It would be the perfect shot down the center aisle. Tyler was part of a gun club. She imagined him in a long wig and sucked in a breath, nauseated. "You were there. In disguise. Across from the redheaded family. You said you weren't an actor but . . ."

"I said I was *the* agent to the stars . . . I do plenty of acting, believe me." Tyler's smile didn't reach his pale blue eyes. "I was a million times more talented than Madison. I knew it was only a matter of time before you realized that it was me, I even tried to nudge you along."

Charlene swallowed over the lump in her throat. "You should go!"

"You're the first of my two loose ends." He grinned, only his mouth moving.

"You don't have to shoot me."

"Charlene," he chuckled, "I *want* to shoot you, and then set up Jane to take the fall."

She tried to step around the lounge chair toward the porch, but he pushed her backward.

"Jane will crack and can't be trusted. You didn't heed my warning so it's your own fault I'm here. Two birds, one stone and I'm a free man. I win."

The gun was out of his belt and pointed at her. At a foot apart, he couldn't miss. "Please go before my guests arrive." She scanned the yard in a panic. Where was Jack? *Jack*.

"Charlene, Charlene." Tyler rubbed his chin, his cool gaze fixed on her.

Silva prowled behind Tyler and twined between his

legs, pawing at him. Tyler kicked at the feline. Silva hissed and darted behind the barrel. "I hate cats."

Charlene used the distraction to push the chair into his shins. If she could jump up onto the porch to her suite she could get inside and lock him out before he shot her.

He leveled the gun toward her before she reached the steps. "I know how to shoot you so that you don't make a bloody mess. Don't move."

She froze in place. To keep him talking was her only plan. "Being a star was all Madison wanted. She was an heiress. Fame was the only thing she didn't have—and you couldn't give it to her. You're the loser."

He grabbed her upper arm and squeezed. "I arrived in Salem to get Madison back . . . but I saw her screwing around with Neville and had a change of heart." His face remained without expression. "I chose to kill her that day during the play so that her name would be forgotten along with this backwoods theater. That slut didn't deserve to be Hollywood famous." His controlled justification made her blood run cold.

Charlene tried another step, but he dug his fingers into her muscle and she cried out.

"I wanted to marry her. Me. I could have anybody in LA; do you understand that? In Hollywood, I am the man to know. And Madison played me for a fool. Unforgiveable." He shoved her back, and her calves hit the chair. "Who's dead now?"

"You're just like her, don't you see? Having to be the best . . ."

He fired a shot near her as she tried to run, taking out a divot of grass at her toes. She felt light-headed and he pinched her wrist as she stayed in place. Her property was too large for anyone to have heard the sound. This time of year people would dismiss the noise as fireworks.

Jack arrived in a blurry whirl of cold. "What's going on? Charlene, watch out." He created a tornado with his anger, trees blowing, the hanging flowers swaying madly, the swing ropes twisting.

Tyler glanced around with alarm as the wind howled. "What the . . ."

Charlene stomped on his foot. He yelled, then snapped her back, his arm around her neck, her body against his. The tip of the cold gun hurt her temple. "Time to die. Say hi to Madison for me. Jane will be joining you shortly."

Silva bolted from behind the whiskey barrel, this time jumping up on Tyler's legs to knock him off-balance. Tyler shot out his arm to stay upright. Jack made the wind hurricane-force, pushing him backward, and trapped Tyler in the twisting ropes of the swing.

Charlene kicked the gun from Tyler's hand and used a planter to pop him on the back of the head, where he collapsed over the wood of the seat like a forgotten marionette.

"Is he . . ." She glanced at Jack, then the unconscious man.

"He's alive. Go call Sam," Jack said, his gaze raking over her to make sure she wasn't hurt. "Charlene. The folks from Connecticut are here."

She looked from Tyler to the back porch and her suite, drawing in quick breaths. "Make sure he doesn't go anywhere, Jack. I'll try to send them out to dinner."

They made a great team.

Chapter Twenty-four

Saturday afternoon, Charlene was sweeping the front porch when Sam arrived. He got out of his SUV, holding a planter of bright blooms.

"Are you still mad at me?" Sam didn't sound sorry. He was in summer gear, a polo shirt and jeans with boots.

Last night had been chaos, with the police officers showing up as the Connecticut couple had gone to their room, wanting a shower and a rest before going out again, even though Charlene had offered a gift certificate to Bambolina's. It had worked out somehow by the skin of her teeth.

The couple had come down just as Sam was leaving . . . Tyler already on his way to jail in the back of the patrol car. Luckily, they hadn't realized that anything was wrong. Jack had turned the volume up on her television to try to cover the noise of the police arresting Tyler in her backyard.

"Maybe." Charlene leaned on the broom handle and gestured for him to put the planter on the step.

"I hope you got my point." Sam set it on the edge of the second stair, then crossed his arms, the move defensive.

Which brought up her defenses. "I would have to be completely dense not to understand that you don't want me to put myself in danger."

He rubbed his palm against his thigh as if brushing off dirt from the planter. "Exactly. And do you know why I allowed my officers to make such a strong case?"

Charlene blew out a breath as she recalled Officer Jimenez pulling out the handcuffs at the theater. "Because you could?"

"No, Charlene." Sam stared at her. "Because I care."

Her eyes stung, and she blamed the dust on her porch.

Sam leaped up her stairs so that he could see her face and smoothed back hair that had come loose from her ponytail.

Charlene wondered if he would kiss her. That would complicate things even more than they already were.

"Do you understand?" he asked softly.

"I do. You're a detective, and I'm just a civilian with extremely bad luck. I don't go looking for dead people, Sam."

Sam blinked in surprise, then chuckled. "Charlene . . . what am I going to do with you?"

Jack arrived from nowhere and tipped the planter over, drawing Sam's attention from Charlene.

"Oops. Must've put it too close to the edge. Sorry about that." Sam hopped down and righted the planter on the step. "I just thought you'd want to know that our profilers got it right. Tyler is a classic sociopathic personality. All about him. When Madison dumped him and stole his mom's ring, he had to make her pay."

She'd realized that for herself yesterday. "Madison blamed him for not making her a star in LA and he couldn't stand not being her hero. He also wants to be the best. What a couple! Her theft of the ring was salt in an open wound."

Sam scuffed his boot on the driveway and shook his head. "He was bragging about his shooting skills to one of the officers. Tried out for some show."

"What a fool!" Charlene sighed. "Was he really hiding out in the basement of the bandstand?"

"Yep. He'd used that disguise to go in and out of the theater all week, to study the exact timing to shoot Madison. Jane helped him—her acting skills aren't so bad. She conned everyone."

"She had me completely tricked."

"Tyler said he never would have been caught if it wasn't for you, tracking down his ring. That's why he wanted you dead." Sam hung his thumb in his pocket. "You had him in his dress on video, in a sunhat. His print matched the partial print we took from the hundred-dollar bill, and we found the burner phone in his rental car."

"And Jane?"

"He was going to kill her, too, and have her confess to everything before committing 'suicide.'"

She swallowed, her throat dry.

"Don't worry, Charlene. We're gonna put him away for a long time."

Did he mean that "we"? Or had that been a figure of speech? Charlene didn't press her luck.

Sam walked to the door of his SUV. "I have to finish up some paperwork. See you later."

"Bye, Sam." She fluttered her fingers at him.

"I thought you were going to hate him forever?" Jack asked, holding the dustpan for Charlene. Silva snoozed on the porch railing that had the best shade.

"I can't. Did you hear that? We helped catch another bad guy." She swept up a pile of leaves, trying not to watch Sam's taillights go.

"He will never give you credit for the assist." Jack created a funnel with the leaves and she laughed—all was right once more in her world. At least Jack was on her side.

"I don't need credit."

Avery opened the door carrying the house phone, her hand over the receiver. The leaves dropped to the porch. "It's your mom—on mute."

"Take a message?"

"She said that she really needs you to call her back about their trip in a few weeks." Avery offered the phone.

"Ten minutes," Charlene promised. "Let me finish up here."

"Okay." Avery clicked the mute button to speaker on the phone and told Mrs. Woodbridge that Charlene would call her in ten minutes, then hung up before Brenda could argue.

Jack chuckled. "Kid's a fast learner."

As Avery turned to go in the house, she noticed the planter. "Oh, who brought the flowers?"

"Sam." The gesture had warmed her . . . but she wasn't completely over his allowing her to be taken downtown like that.

Avery walked back out to the porch and searched the driveway. "Where did he go?"

"He just stopped by." Charlene joined the teen on the top step. A part of her wished he'd stayed longer too.

"Darn it. I wanted to ask him about being a police officer. That could be a cool career, right?"

Charlene almost swallowed her tongue. Avery could not be serious. It was dangerous. As an officer of the law, you went *looking* for the bad guys.

"I wonder if he'd let me do one of those things where you get to drive around in a patrol car for a few hours? See how to nab crooks and killers."

Her pulse pounded at her temples.

Jack laughed heartily, and Silva lifted her head to see what was going on.

"I think you'd give the good detective a heart attack if you asked him that." It was certainly making Charlene's heart thud ominously. Charlene studied Avery for any sign of a practical joke. "Are you serious?"

"Yeah."

Charlene bowed her head over the broom handle. Jack said, "You can't say no, or she'll want to do it even more."

She set the broom against the side of the house. "Tell you what—if you really want to, then we can ask Sam about what you'd need to do to be a police officer. Although"—Charlene thought hard and fast—"I think if you go to college, you can be a detective."